TH
WORLD

Abraxas spread his wings further, slowing as he approached the summit.

A great roaring sound welled up from behind him.

The world groaned beneath him—and fell.

A great finger of land dropped downward below him. The waters of the Inner Sea rushed forward into the sudden absence of land, an enormous wave crashing downward and burying for all time the images of Hesirus and the basin of the reflecting pool that would never again shine with the light of the stars.

The upward rush of the heated air from the firestorms vanished, pulled downward as the land fell away.

Abraxas felt himself being dragged downward with it...down with the fire and water at the end of all things.

*****

The turbulence jostled him awake.

Ethan Gallows shivered then sat up suddenly, gasping for air.

"Excuse me, sir, are you all right?"

A

FIREBORN™

NOVEL

EMBERS OF ATLANTIS

BY TRACY HICKMAN

Fantasy Flight Publishing, Inc.

To Dave "Zeb" Cook, Jeff Grubb, Douglas Niles, Mark Acres,
Al Hammack, and all the gamers of games past...
And to Christian Peterson for all the games yet to come.

Cover illustration by Mathias Kollros.

This is a work of fiction. The characters, incidents, and dialogue are
drawn from the author's imagination and are not to be construed as real.
Any resemblance to actual events or persons, living or dead, is entirely coincidental.

ISBN: 978-1-61661-100-2

Fantasy Flight Publishing, Inc.
1975 West County Road B2
Roseville, MN 55113
USA

Find out more about Fantasy Flight Games
and our many exciting worlds at

www.FantasyFlightGames.com

EMBERS OF ATLANTIS

CHAPTER 1
DREAMS OF FIRE

Abraxas, dragon of ancient Trocea, bared his long, yellowed teeth with strain and fear. His wings pulled hard against the currents of the air, rising and tumbling around him in unpredictable gales. Dense smoke mixed with the clouds, the glowing embers caught in the heat of their updraft whirling and vanishing, then falling again as leaden ash that made the dragon's flight even more difficult. The dull orange glow beneath the obscuring clouds and smoke was often the only reference he had to whether he was flying upright or inverted.

It had been this way in Trocea, Abraxas remembered. He had smelled the burning of wood and flesh and could taste the end of joy at the edges of his lips. His eyes there, too, had stung as much from his own despair as from the ash. Dragon tears are magical and their powers are great, but they are hard won *and not easily elicited from any of the dragonkind.*

Abraxas had wept easily that day for the senseless loss of the noble city, whose streets were lined with trees and filled with the sound of children playing between the statues of the Gardens of the Air. All that had ended in 4891 when the Kurgan tribes descended on the city and lay siege to it. Its walls withstood the assault, but by subterfuge and betrayal the tribes gained access to the city and opened its gates from within. In the end, they left nothing and no one behind. Abraxas had arrived too late and had only his own tears to console him as he made his way back to Atlantis with the news of what had befallen the colony they had called the Jewel of the Northern Shores.

Now the world itself was ending, its life writhing beneath him in fire and agony.

Abraxas craned his long neck around, his eyes desperately searching the roiling billows. Where were his broodmates—his brother dragons born of the same clutch? They were bound to him as he was to them—the powers of their inherited karma woven tightly into the fabric of their common life-force. They were his strength and his might, just as he was theirs. He could feel the threads unraveling in the karma itself and knew in his heart that there was little time remaining in which to act. That he could not see them worried Abraxas, for the world was collapsing beneath them and he would need them if there were to be any hope for a dawn.

A sudden explosion of fire shook Abraxas's right wing, flipping the dragon nearly on his side. He roared with indignation and frustration, beating his right wing furiously in compensation. He had barely righted himself in the air when the clouds and smoke suddenly parted.

Atlantis lay dying beneath him.

The city was on fire. The heat in many places had grown so intense that firestorms had erupted in several areas—impossible cyclones of flame twisting into the sky. Each pulled air into its base to feed its voracious appetite, mostly from the cooler atmosphere above the waters of the sea and the bay of the city, resulting in hurricane force winds that whipped the waters off the Atlantis coasts into angry whitecaps of terrifying size. The still waters of the fabled reflecting pool running from the bay to the base of Temple Peak had been drawn completely dry. Nearly half of the 365 great stone statues—each representing a different attribute of Hesirus, the Sun-King—had fallen over, and many lay broken in the empty pool.

Abraxas cursed the keenness of his eyes. He could see the Atlantean humans clearly as they ran in panic in the streets below. Great fissures were opening everywhere, buildings collapsing into their maws. Throngs of people fleeing were suddenly cut off in their retreat, piling up on the verge of the crevasses, some tumbling with horrific cries into the molten depths below. Despite the obstacles, thousands had reached the shores of the bay, the cacophony of their *cries rising up to fill the dragon's ears. The bay had offered no better hope for them, as they confronted the waters of an angry sea that was already laying claim to the ships foundering at their moorings.*

A trumpeting caused Abraxas to glance behind him. Fafnir and Apalala—his two broodmates—were with him still, their leathery wings illuminated by the conflagration below. They beat fiercely against the turbulent air around them, desperate to gain more altitude. They called him higher, for there was safety in distance from the calamitous ground beneath them.

Ground, Abraxas knew, on which he must land one last time.

The ancient dragon of Trocea banked suddenly, pulling up hard and soaring around a whirling column of the firestorm. The concentric canals of Atlantis were broken, their waters rushing down the remaining streets and crashing into the fires and molten fissures. Explosions of steam now obscured many parts of the city. The towering obelisks that had once watched over the walls of the city were no more.

The dragon watched the desolation as yet another earthquake rolled through the city, felling more buildings and opening even further the cracks in the face of the dying world.

Abraxas fixed his enormous head forward. There was nothing he could do for them today. He had to remember that his task dealt with what lay beyond the end.

Before him rose Temple Peak. At its pinnacle, rising to a height of over twelve hundred feet, stood the remains of the greatest achievement and glory of Atlantis. But the marble façade of the pyramid was crumbling, sliding down its sides with each successive quake. The statue of the dragon which had once graced its peak was nowhere to be seen; even from this distance, Abraxas could see that the carefully and closely fitted stones were beginning to separate in places.

But the pyramid was not his objective. Several hundred yards down the ridge of Temple Peak stood the Temple of the Sun, for which the mountain had its name. Abraxas fixed his gaze upon it. One of its towering spires had fallen completely. Two others swayed precariously while a third stood at an odd angle. The dome over the central courtyard had collapsed, but even from this distance he could see the Master Priests moving at the edge of the great gardens.

They were looking for him. They had called him.

Abraxas spread his wings further, slowing as he approached the summit.

A great roaring sound welled up from behind him.

The world groaned beneath him—and fell.

A great finger of land dropped downward below him. The waters of the Inner Sea rushed forward into the sudden absence of land, an enormous wave crashing downward and burying for all time the images of Hesirus and the basin of the reflecting pool that would never again shine with the light of the stars.

The upward rush of the heated air from the firestorms vanished, pulled downward as the land fell away.

Abraxas felt himself being dragged downward with it...down with the fire and water at the end of all things.

*****

The turbulence jostled him awake.

Ethan Gallows shivered then sat up suddenly, gasping for air.

"Excuse me, sir, are you all right?"

Ethan looked up into the face of the stewardess. He took her in all at once, noting details and framing her face instinctively as he would have captured it with his camera. She was in her late twenties, he guessed, caucasian, with short-cut hair dyed blond, showing mouse-brown roots. She was unhealthily thin; her British Airways uniform, threadbare and stained, sagged slightly on her frame. Her tarnished name tag proclaimed her to be Alicia Murdock. She wore no makeup and her eyes were sunken with dark circles under them.

He also noticed that she had her right hand held behind her back—no doubt fingering the Glock 27 subcompact automatic that all the British Airways stewardesses kept tucked under their jackets. They were light, relatively small, and packed nine rounds of .45-caliber stopping power.

Ethan guessed someone at British Airways had figured that nine rounds would be sufficient to fire inside an aircraft cabin at pressure altitude. Contrary to popular belief, airframes of commercial aircraft were designed to prevent any kind of explosive—or even rapid—decompression from bullets fired inside a cabin. No one would get sucked out or blow up from the infamous "sudden loss of cabin pressure." The best you could hope to achieve was a bad leak.

There were far worse things in the world than a hole in an airplane in flight—which was why stewardesses now answered every call from a passenger with one hand on a gun.

"I'm fine," Ethan answered through a slow yawn. It was best not to make sudden movements on an aircraft these days. "Just a nightmare."

Could have been worse, Ethan thought with a shudder. At least she hadn't touched him. He hated being touched, and their combined skittishness might have ended very badly for him.

The stewardess breathed in through her nose and nodded without interest. "We will be landing at Heathrow in approximately forty minutes. Please have your passport and documents in order before we land. Have you been to the lavatory?"

"Uh, no—not yet…"

"There is a vial in the seat pocket in front of you," she said. "You need to deposit your urine into it and secure the stopper before we land. There's the devil to pay if you don't have that in hand once you reach

Immigration. New regulations, you know."

"Thank you, Alicia," Ethan said. "I'll do that right now."

The stewardess nodded without a smile and stepped wearily toward the back of the economy cabin. Ethan undid his seatbelt and turned to watch her go down the aisle.

He eyed the bulge at the small of her back. *That's definitely a Glock 27.*

He was turning back forward when his eye caught sight of a young boy lying across three seats several rows back opposite him on the aisle. The boy could not have been more than eight years old. He was curled up tightly across the chairs with an "unaccompanied minor" slip pinned to his jacket.

Ethan stood up in the aisle and stepped back toward the boy. The 767-300ER was nearly empty; if it were full there might have been as many as three hundred and seventy passengers aboard, but he had counted fewer than fifty in the waiting area when they had boarded in Atlanta.

The boy had kicked off his blankets.

Ethan glanced at the stewardess. She was standing back by the aft galley, and her gaze was fixed on Ethan. She looked casual, but Ethan noted that she was standing sideways and had spread her legs slightly in her stance. It was a firing position. *That Glock must have quite a kick for someone as slight as she.*

Move slowly, Ethan told himself, *and whatever*

you do, be obvious.

Ethan carefully reached down and picked up the blankets. He stood up so that the stewardess could see them as he spread them back over the child.

Why would anyone risk sending their child unaccompanied on an airline these days, especially to London? He figured it was best to let him keep sleeping for now—any nightmares he was having couldn't be worse than the waking world.

"Hey, Gallows!" came an entirely-too-chipper voice behind him. "I'm glad to see you're up and ready to go."

No good deed goes unpunished, Ethan thought as he turned.

"Morning, Collette," he said flatly.

Ethan already knew more than he needed to know about Collette Montrose. He had not had much time at CNN to get intel on his latest babysitting job but what he had learned, he did not like. Collette was twenty-four years old, and kept her brown hair short because it looked better on camera and would key out better in front of a weather map. Her eyes were a bright, striking green—which as far as Ethan was concerned was her most interesting feature—set in a pleasant olive complexion. She was officially a meteorologist at the CNN Weather Center, although her degree was in Art History. Someone thought she was bright enough, clever enough on camera, and eager enough to work weekends, holidays, and the 3 a.m. shifts most weekdays. She was too eager, too chatty, and too focused on her non-existent career. She was the kind of woman that Ethan rarely met on field assignments.

Which, he reminded himself, was just another of the several million reasons he preferred to be in the field.

"Come on and sit down, you!" Collette said, patting the seat cushion next to her. "I've got a need to talk."

"Collette, I've got to go take care of a little 'business,'" he said, waving the small sealed box with the plastic vial inside.

"Oh, that can wait a few minutes," she said with a flash of her smile. Her mouth was wide and seemed to have too many teeth. She patted the seat cushion again. "We need to discuss the assignment. Just for a few minutes. I promise I won't bite."

Ethan eased his large frame down into the narrow seat.

"My, you *are* in good shape," Collette smiled. "Do you work out, like, all the time?"

"I'm a field cameraman, Collette," Ethan said, his tone making it clear he was stating the obvious. "Equipment is heavy and sometimes you have to move pretty fast. The job's a workout on its own."

"Yeah," she said, her voice falling into concern. "I was so sorry to hear that you were called back. It's so unfair. Do you think it was…racially motivated?"

Ethan closed his eyes. He could hear his father saying those same words. It seemed to be part of the roots of his African-American experience. His skin was a deep chocolate color and, according to his mother as well as a few other opinions he valued in other ways, a lovely texture. He kept his black hair short because it was easier in the field. He preferred several days' worth of growth on his beard before he shaved because a razor was sometimes hard to come by in the places his job required him to go. It was his dark brown eyes, however, that were his special gift—the perfect windows, he thought, through which he could look out on the world through a lens.

He'd experienced the effects of discrimination and racism growing up, but it had been mitigated by the closed circle of the academic community in which his parents both orbited as teachers in Spokane, Washington. When he'd left Spokane to find a larger world, his parents had sent him on his way with a tough hide and a proper grounding in his African heritage and roots.

"No, Collette," Ethan said. "I do not think it was racially motivated."

"But you're the most honored field cameraman in this business—no, it's true and you know it," Collette said. "You were *the* most sought after cameraman in all of CNN. There wasn't a field reporter that wouldn't give a month's pay to get you assigned to them. And now here you are working *features*. I mean, what Jonas Farben did to you may have been well intentioned, but—"

"Could we please not talk about this?" Ethan said. After the public pummeling he had received from Farben, he was surprised that his assignment editor would let him out of Atlanta—let alone cover an art exhibition in London. However, a series of recent disappearances from the CNN Bureau in London had left them short-staffed—and the British government wanted the exhibition prominently featured around the world as a symbol of the stability of London and the government's efforts to "normalize" the situation there. Ethan knew there was nothing normal about London any longer—or anywhere else in the world for that matter.

"I guess your luck can't work every time," Collette said.

"What luck?" Ethan asked, almost as if he cared.

"Everyone says that you've got a special luck," Collette said. "You know…always in the right spot to get the money shot, even in the most horrible of circumstances. Wherever the worst of things is going down, you seem to be there with tape already rolling."

Ethan sighed. "Some people would call that bad luck."

"Not in our profession," Collette said with what seemed like genuine admiration.

Ethan wanted to change the subject. "You said you wanted to talk about the assignment—and I've still got to go pee for Queen and Country."

"Oh, right," Collette said, pulling out her notepad.

Ethan drew in a deep breath. *Ace cub reporter on the job.*

"We're scheduled to meet Dr. Rene Benoit at the National Gallery—that's in Trafalgar Square—"

"I know where the National Gallery is."

"—at 1:00 p.m. local time. There won't be time for us to go by the hotel and drop off our things, so we should go straight there. Dr. Benoit has arranged for us to be admitted to the exhibit ahead of time… You know, they say that this is the first time he has agreed to show his private collection. It is supposed to be amazingly controversial. 'A bizarre and frightening juxtaposition of the common and the occult…'"

Ethan chuckled.

"What?"

"I've seen a lot of things lately," Ethan said. "It's hard to imagine what people might think of as 'bizarre and frightening' in art any more—especially in London."

The plane jostled suddenly.

The seatbelt light came on immediately.

"Well, if you'll excuse me, I had better get back and prepare this little souvenir," Ethan said, rising into the aisle. "Tighten that belt, Miss Montrose. There's no such thing as a smooth landing anymore."

Ethan held the seat backs as he made his way aft. The plane lurched again under his feet. As he reached the lavatory he saw the stewardess already strapped tightly into her jumpseat, the harness tight across her uniform. She did not look up or acknowledge him in any way, her eyes fixed forward as she shook in abject terror.

The plane shuddered again, violently.

We must be getting close to London, Ethan thought as he closed the lavatory door behind him, sliding the lock to "occupied."

CHAPTER 2
LONDON CALLING

British Airways Flight 357D bounced twice before the pilots managed to stick its wheels to the pavement of runway 09R. It was not the best of landings, Ethan thought, as he unconsciously gripped the armrests of his seat tighter than necessary, but any landing you could walk away from—especially in these times—was a good one. The engines reversed thrust moments after the aircraft was firmly pressed to the ground, shoving everyone in the cabin precipitously forward against their seatbelts, eliciting a handful of cries from the passengers. Then, nearly as quickly, the pressure was released at the same time as the brakes, and the wide-bodied aircraft was trundling down the runway. It veered to the left onto the taxiway in short order.

"Ladies and gentlemen, let me be the first to welcome you to London." It was the stewardess's voice, but its tone and cheerfulness expressed a profound relief. Ethan had been told by the travel editor at CNN that all flights into Heathrow were now being diverted from their normal routes to a more western approach up the Bristol Channel and then eastward over Bath. There apparently had been some incidents with aircraft flying over the Salisbury Plain. Ethan was glad the flight paths had been altered; he did not relish the prospect of flying over Stonehenge.

Ethan looked out the window as they continued to taxi. His seat was on the right-hand side of the aircraft and, given that they had landed from west to east and that the international Terminal 5 was on the western side of the airport, he had a good view of the Heathrow terminals as they taxied the long way back. The perpetual storm centered over London extended over the airport—a slowly swirling, ominous mass that cast an unrelenting pall over the city and its surroundings.

The terminal—what was left of it—appeared nearly deserted. Terminal 3 remained a burnt-out hulk after what the government had called "the Siege of Heathrow," when a determined group of youths attacked the building in a bid to force their way onto aircraft and leave the country. The British government had spun that one nicely, Ethan thought, calling it a terrorist act. His information was more accurate and disturbing regarding who—or what—had originally made the assault. In any case, the building was just a shell now, with no apparent effort being made to even remove the debris. They probably couldn't find a contractor willing to go in and do it.

The bustle of ground-support trucks, equipment, and crews was clearly absent. Only a smattering of ground personnel could be seen moving between the empty gates now devoid of all but a handful of aircraft. More conspicuous were the armored vehicles and heavily armed British troops stationed in carefully positioned redoubts set at intervals along the perimeter of the terminal building. The concrete bunkers were painted in cheerful themes to look inconspicuous, but the bristling armament about their walls belied the deception.

They taxied by a large, open space with aircraft parking facilities. Ethan watched as they slowly rolled past an enormous Singapore Airlines A380. There were panels on the wings that had been pried upward and peeled back from the airframe all down the main spar of the wing, and several cowling panels were missing from the port engine. He had heard about that flight. The aircraft had barely made it. Wing sections had torn free, falling all around Isleworth and Hounslow before the pilot managed to get the craft onto the runway. The CNN Bureau had dutifully reported it as a case of metal fatigue, but that did not stop the port-side passengers from talking about creatures crawling along the wing in flight and trying to take the wing apart by hand.

"Next stop...the Twilight Zone," Ethan muttered.

*****

"This is so exciting!" Collette gushed, her natural ebullience in stark contrast to the studied cynicism that her superiors at CNN encouraged her to cultivate whenever she was on camera. "I've never been to England before."

Ethan grimaced as he adjusted his grip on his hard-shell camera case in one hand and the backpack he had slung over his shoulder with the other. "Have you ever been *any*where before, Collette?"

"Well, to be perfectly truthful, never anywhere outside the country—I mean, America," Collette said, trying to take in everything around her with her large green eyes.

There was a lot to see, Ethan agreed, but little of it was terribly comforting. He had passed through Heathrow more times than he cared to think about, but there were changes here, too, since the last time he had passed through Customs and Immigration. Baggage claim was now half the size it once had been, with a concrete partition separating the sides. They retrieved all their baggage from the carousel first and then followed the queue through the partition to Border Control in what had once been the other half of the baggage area. Now the tall room was a cement vault on all sides overlooked by pillbox emplacements in each corner. By the tint color, Ethan could tell that each of the pillboxes had been fitted with heavily armored glass. There were gunports in each of the emplacements, the heavy automatic weapon muzzles obvious as they slowly swung their field of fire across the room. He thought one of them might even be a Heckler & Koch 40mm Grenade Machine Gun, which was a serious weapons upgrade for the London Customs Bureau. There were also a number of soldiers armed with lighter automatic weapons stationed along the walls. It was as perfectly engineered a killing zone as Ethan could imagine…and the passengers were being herded into it.

Not that there were that many of them. Ethan counted forty-seven passengers, plus eight members of the flight crew who were being ushered into Border Patrol as well.

A line of new model luggage scanners bisected the room, each flanked by a full body scanner linked to a short pedestal device. Even a few months ago such precautions would have been found at the beginning of anyone's journey before boarding a plane, but that was before everything had started to unravel. Now it was no longer just the in-flight safety that was the preoccupation of airport security, but the survival of every nation on earth.

At least, that was what Ethan had filmed and the story he'd tried to tell. It had landed him behind a desk with his lens pointed deliberately anywhere but where the problem could be seen.

"You know, I've always been a big fan of Vermeer," Collette said, her low heels clicking against the tile floor as she pulled her two small, wheeled cases behind her. "I understand that *A Young Woman standing at a Virginal* is still on display at the National Gallery. I hope I have time enough to see it."

"'*A Young Woman standing at a Virginal*'?" Ethan repeated, raising his eyebrows.

"Oh, yes! It's a wonderful piece!" Collette said, coming to stand in line and lifting her first case up onto the conveyer for the luggage scanner. She tossed the jacket of her pants suit into a plastic bin along with her shoes. "It dates from about 1670—the date is undocumented of course, but then so many of Vermeer's works are. I just love the way the soft light comes in through the window and casts a slightly obscuring shadow across the woman's face. Much more subtle, in my opinion, than his *A Young Woman seated at a Virginal*."

"I've no doubt," Ethan said without any idea what she was talking about. He was trying to make room for the camera case and his backpack, but Collette grabbed another bin, slipped her laptop out of the second of her bags and placed it inside. "Listen," he continued, "I don't know what you may have read about London in books or seen on the Travel Channel, but things have changed here. This isn't Atlanta, and things are a good deal more dangerous here than you probably know."

"Do you think so?" Collette had a habit of answering questions with questions.

"All I'm saying, Collette, is that you need to develop a little better…concern…about your surroundings, is all," Ethan said, slipping off his own shoes.

"Miss? Please step forward!" The inspection agent's voice made it clear it was a command. Ethan framed the man in his mind's eye: forties, but looking older; two days' growth of grey beard with matching grey eyes and parchment-thin skin; bald under his cap; and though only slightly overweight, the man was sweating profusely in the chill air of the hall. His name tag announced him as Felix Boothroyd. His hand was outstretched toward Collette from where he stood next to the scanner and its attached pedestal.

"Oh, sorry," Collette said as she handed the man her ticket and passport.

The agent gave a sigh deeper than oceans. He handed her back her documents.

"Your vial, miss. You were instructed before you landed."

"Oh!" Collette flushed slightly. She reached into the pocket of her pants and handed over the vial with the amber liquid. "Sorry—my mistake."

The agent set the vial into the pedestal and closed the lid. Ethan could see the needle arm puncture the top of the vial, plunging downward into the liquid.

The light over the scanner turned green.

"Step inside, miss," he commanded. "Both arms over your head."

Collette stepped into the scanner. As she did, the clear enclosure panels swung closed with a whoosh and locked with a decisive *thunk*. Collette held her arms over her head as the scanner arms swung around her.

Light suddenly flashed down from the ceiling panel of the scanner, startling her.

"What was that light?" Ethan asked the inspection agent, who eyed him warily. "I've just never seen that before," Ethan said in his most conversational tone.

"It's new," was all that the man offered.

The locks clanged open again and the clear panels slid open once more.

"That's all, miss," the agent said, already looking at Ethan as he spoke. "You may carry on now."

Collette gathered her items from the end of the luggage scanner conveyer, reassembling them and herself in a ritual that had become entirely too familiar to anyone who traveled by air. Ethan, in turn, was scanned, and the strange light flashed down around him. He stepped out of the scanner, having passed the agent and his inspection, and quickly checked his camera case and backpack to make sure nothing was out of place or missing.

"Satisfied?" Collette asked.

"Yes," Ethan replied. "Let's get through Customs and Immigration. All these guns are making me nervous."

Collette laughed. "You've been in the field too long. It's like my brothers used to say, 'Fear is just false evidence appearing real.'"

"That was Veer Sharma who said that," Ethan said, lugging the hard-shell case and his backpack across the wide space between the scanners and the Customs booths near the end of the hall.

"Well, my brothers said it, too," Collette said with a frown, "and no matter who said it, it's still true."

"I've got another saying for you," Ethan said as they stood between the ribbon-defined stanchions, awaiting their turn with a passport official in their enclosed booth. "'Just because you're paranoid doesn't mean they're not out to get you.'"

"Oh, you!" Collette laughed as they stepped up toward the booth with the beckoning official inside. "We're here covering an art exhibit, not some bizarre occurrence in Laos! What could possibly go wrong—"

In that moment, peace was shattered as shouts and a spurt of automatic gunfire resounded through the hall. Screams erupted as the passengers and crews reacted. Some fell to the floor, trying to cover themselves with whatever was at hand. More still were simply running in the enclosed space, filled with blind panic.

Ethan looked behind them and saw a handsome, clean-cut, middle-aged man in an impeccably tailored grey suit running directly toward the passport booths. Ethan recognized the man from their flight—someone in first class, he figured, given his look of an ideal proper gentleman.

As he watched, though, the man began to transform. His body became strangely contorted inside his own clothing; coarse fur erupted from under his starched cuffs and his hands elongated, his fingernails extending into lengthy claws. His chest expanded even as his waist narrowed, the buttons on his shirt exploding away as the seams of his coat tore apart from the strain. His nose and jaw were pushing out from his face with every step, his groomed hair growing wildly into a hoary mane.

Another spurt of automatic fire echoed in the hall. A screaming woman—Ethan remembered her from six rows behind him—ran in her mindless flight into the path of the bullets, falling at once onto the floor, her momentum sliding her across tiles and leaving a horrific, long bloodstain.

Soldiers were shouting and enormous metal doors at both exits from the hall began to fall closed. The sound of gunfire was becoming more pronounced as the weapons in the pillboxes swung toward the disturbance.

The grey-suited creature had become more animal than man. It heard the gunfire and dropped down on all fours without missing a stride, rushing purposefully directly toward Collette—its blood-red eyes fixed on her. It needed a hostage. It needed *prey*.

Ethan dropped his case and his backpack, his mind racing as he turned to confront the horror charging in their direction. He steeled himself as the creature leaped, reaching out with its erupting claws.

A sudden impact threw the creature sideways, splitting a long gash along its right jowl. It flipped over in the air, howling in outrage. It rolled once across the tile before righting itself on all four feet, crouching and baring its now-fanged long teeth as it coiled its muscles to pounce.

Gunfire exploded against the creature's side. It was thrown sideways from the impact of the bullets, clawing in mindless anger at the air as it barked furiously. It once more regained its feet, its ears pinned back against its head, the tatters of its suit hanging in shreds about its grotesque frame.

The soldiers were converging. They had it cornered now.

Another burst from their guns, and the creature lay shaking on the ground.

A customs officer in heavy boots stepped up to the quaking monster and drew his 9mm pistol. He jammed his boot against the furry neck and, looking dispassionately down, fired a single bullet through the monster's head.

Ethan spun around to face Collette. The young woman was standing with both hands gripping the handle of Ethan's hard-shell camera case, its polyethylene shell pushed in, cracked, and bloodied on one corner.

"Your brothers taught you that?" Ethan asked in surprise.

"They always said, 'If the boar's a chargin', sometimes all that's left is to charge back.'" Collette stared at the growing pool of dark blood flowing out across the tiles from under the torn grey cloth and misshapen body that had moments before been a businessman from her flight. She suddenly turned, dropping the bloodied equipment case, and vomited into the trash can next to her.

Ethan simply picked up the case and his pack and stepped over to look down on the creature.

"That's new, isn't it?" Ethan said to the customs officer.

"Aye," the officer said, pushing his cap back on his head. "Werewolf—or near to it, we figure. Been seein' a few of 'em these last few. Had them lunar spectrum lamps put in the scanners last week. Triggers 'em, like. Bloody hard to stop 'em. That gal of yours packs a wallop there, gov."

"She'd surprise you," Ethan replied. "Mind if I take some pictures?"

"Sorry, gov…regulations, you know."

Ethan nodded and turned back toward Collette, who was shakily straightening up, wiping flecks of vomit from her mouth onto a handkerchief from the pocket of her business jacket. He took her passport and her declaration from her hand and pushed it into the tray beneath the Customs window.

"Miss?" said the agent behind the window.

Ethan turned Collette around so that she was facing the Border Control agent.

"Miss?" the agent asked again.

She looked up as though returning from a distant place. "Oh, yes?"

The agent picked up her crisp, new passport and examined it.

"Welcome to London, miss," he said with a tired smile. "First time here?"

CHAPTER 3
CABBIE

Ethan pushed with his back through the glass doors, exiting Terminal 5 and entering the courtyard. He managed to just catch the door with his foot as Collette rushed through after him, the wheels of one of her roller bags bumping over his toes.

"Did CNN send a car for us?" Collette asked. The cheery lightness had evaporated from her tone. London was becoming entirely too real.

"There's nothing about one in the travel itinerary, which always means that we're on our own to get into the city," Ethan said.

The courtyard between the great glass face of the building and the parking garage was almost completely deserted, and there was a distinct and unnerving lack of traffic sounds. Occasional individual motors, of course, but not the overwhelming and constant cascade of noise that Ethan was accustomed to when leaving the airport terminal in search of a cab. The queues were there at the taxi stands, but there was no one in them and only a handful of cabs were to be seen.

Ethan moved directly to the taxi stand with Collette in tow. The first of the traditional black cabs pulled up, with the driver seeming to extract himself from the driver's position before the vehicle had completely stopped.

"Hallo! Hallo! Velcome to London!" said the wide-shouldered and broad-faced giant who emerged from the cabbie's seat as though it were a black clown car. He was enormous. He wore a plaid flat-hat that perched atop his head as though attached by Velcro. He wore a dark windbreaker over his black t-shirt, and his wide smile showed perfectly spaced gaps between his gleaming teeth. "No need to vorry, Valja vill take care of bags."

"'Valja'?" Ethan asked. "*You're* a London cabbie?"

"Absolutely," Valja replied, his blue eyes gleaming. He yanked the camera case away from Ethan, who wisely chose not to contest the cabbie for its possession. Valja gathered up Collette's bags as well, scooping both of them up and lodging them under his arm. "Fortunate to get such prestigious job. It vas much vork and perseverance but, by Jove, now I am London cabbie."

Valja pulled open the boot of the cab and tumbled their luggage into the back, slamming it shut. He snatched his flat-hat from the top of his head. His hair, Ethan noted at once, was a military crew-cut, the bristles all standing at strict attention. The large man bent down slightly as he reached for the left rear door of the vehicle which, as with all traditional London black cabs, were rear-opening coach doors—what Americans called "suicide doors."

"Please. I vill make your journey comfortable and safe."

Collette stepped toward the cab but Ethan grabbed her shoulder and held her back. "You're not exactly from Bristol, are you, Valja?"

The large man's smile dimmed only briefly.

"Ukraine, I think," Ethan said, his dark eyes studying the man. "Kyiv, perhaps?"

The cabbie's dark eyebrows arched. "You are unusually perceptive, sir. *Da*, I vas from Kyiv originally, but are ve not all immigrants?"

"We certainly have all become wanderers," Ethan answered.

Valja's smile had returned. He gestured toward the car door with his free hand. "Then let us vander for a time together."

Ethan nodded, releasing Collette's shoulder. She shot him an irritated look and then ducked into the back of the cab. Ethan followed, dropping onto the seat next to her and putting his backpack at his feet. He automatically reached for his seatbelt, nudging Collette to do the same.

"Are you my mother?" Collette said.

"No, I'm your nanny," Ethan said, snapping the

belt into place. He turned away from Collette as he settled into his seat, gazing absently out the window over the deserted courtyard between the road and the glass façade of the terminal—

—and found that it was not entirely deserted.

A lithe woman stood next to one of the towers supporting the elevated roadways overhead. Her skin was a creamy pale complexion, smooth and unblemished. Her pencil-thin eyebrows arched over eyes that, even at this distance, Ethan could see were a vibrant violet color. Her jawline extended down smoothly to a pointed chin beneath distinctive, pronounced cheekbones. She wore a long jacket into which she had thrust her hands, her collar turned up at the neck against a cold wind apparently she alone felt. Her hair was a shocking white color, a carefully cropped and coifed exploding nimbus around her face.

A cold chill congealed in Ethan's stomach.

She was so familiar to him—yet he was certain that he had never seen the woman before.

"Ve are off on our vanderings!" Valja shouted from the front of the cab. He put the cab in gear.

They pulled quickly from the curb, leaving the white-haired woman with the unblinking violet eyes behind.

*****

They were traveling eastward down the M4 motorway. The traffic was much lighter than Ethan had

ever seen it before on his previous visits. He couldn't
be certain if it was gas rationing or just that people
were more inclined these days to stay close to familiar territory. There certainly were a good deal more
bikes being used on the regular streets. CNN's London Bureau had uplinked a number of stories lately
about the London Underground and the recent efforts of the Metropolitan Police Force and the City
of London Police to make subway transportation safe
for commuters. It had been a good effort and was actually garnering an increase in riders—all of whom
were ignoring the rumors of three vanished trains
and the fact that the tube between Aldgate East and
Temple had been closed for nearly six months, along
with truncating the Circle Line. Apparently anything
underground near Tower Hill was not to be traveled.

Nor, by the look of things, was much above
ground faring any better. They were still a full five
miles from the center of the city, and the ominous
black cloud, whose vortex was centered over the
Tower of London, spun over their heads as an ever-
present and terrifying reminder that the old world
had passed away.

Ethan was shaken from his thoughts as Valja ex-
ited the elevated section of motorway on the left for
the surface streets—along with nearly every other
vehicle traveling in their direction.

"Valja?" Ethan asked, leaning forward toward
the opening in the plexiglass that divided the cabbie
from the passengers.

"Yes, my friend?" Valja responded as they passed an old church on their right. The road curved to the north, and they began flowing with the traffic around a large bus station.

"This is Hammersmith," Ethan said.

"*Da*! So it is," Valja said cheerfully as he continued circumnavigating the block.

"And you know we're trying to get to Trafalgar Square," Ethan said.

"What's wrong?" Collette asked, leaning forward to join the conversation.

"Nothing yet," Ethan said, then turned his attention back to the giant cabbie crammed into the driver's seat. "We just crossed under the London motorway. Valja, that sign says we're headed toward Castelnau."

"You are most correct," Valja responded. "That green iron bridge is Hammersmith Bridge. First bridge here vas built in 1824 by act of Parliament—"

"I'm not interested in the bridge history," Ethan snapped. "You're taking us the wrong way."

There was a long and thoughtful pause. The green iron bridge slipped beneath their wheels and, below that, the River Thames.

"I am driver sanctioned by PCO," Valja said. "I have the knowledge of London, sir."

"What's he saying?" Collette asked anxiously. "What knowledge of London?"

Ethan leaned back. "Well, he knows nearly everything about London. That's what 'the knowledge of

London' means to a cab driver. They have to pass an extensive test of the streets. It is the most thorough and demanding training course for any cab driver in the world. It usually takes more than three years training and failing the test before an applicant passes it."

"I passed in just more than one year," Valja said with pride.

"So why the detour?" Ethan asked.

"The knowledge is now more than just about streets," Valja responded. "No more it is enough to know only vhere to go in London—now ve must also know vhere *not* to go. Further down A3 motorway not so good right now. Brompton Cemetery is there. It started to move."

"Move?" Collette said. "You mean they were moving the cemetery?"

"No," Valja corrected. "Cemetery began moving self. Everyone thought screams vere coming from soccer game in Stamford Bridge Stadium—but no game vas in play that night. Army now occupies most of Fulham, trying to put dead back to rest. Better ve come into London from south. Vestminster Bridge get you close enough to—you are headed to Trafalgar, yes?"

"Yes," Collette replied, leaning back in the seat again. "To the National Gallery."

"Say, my friends, you are from the States, are you not?" Valja said suddenly. "Just arrived, no?"

"Yes," Ethan smiled. "We are from the States."

"Tell me, friend," Valja asked, licking his lips.

"Are your Indians of the plains still in revolt?"

Ethan drew in a deep breath. "They have taken back territory in the northern plains—the Dakotas and parts of Minnesota and Wisconsin. Right now there is a truce and the government is considering a settlement.

"Texas seceded from the Union—no one is quite sure whether they will support the Native American Nations or the United States now. The 7th Armored Cavalry has taken a lot of casualties, but no one knows for certain where the power that the Native shamans are wielding comes from. They find it hard to fight what they don't understand."

"It's magic. Changed it all," Valja asserted. "Started right here, you know. Ground Zero for return of madness, monsters, and sorcery. Not that rest of vorld has been spared—it most assuredly has not. Did you see pictures of uprising of spirits outside of Hanoi—far side of vorld mind you—vith spirits tearing down city? Of course, all pictures vere discredit afterward but I've heard from traveler just last veek that—"

"You shouldn't believe everything you hear." Ethan turned to look out the window at the swirling black mass over the city.

"You are, of course, right as ever, my friend," Valja nodded. "You shall not vorry. Valja has the knowledge of London. I vill keep you safe and only on roads that you should travel."

"Tell you what," Ethan said. "If you don't mind

keeping us on the meter, we would be grateful if you would just work for us for the rest of the day."

The big man's face broke into another wide grin. "I had no other idea in mind."

*****

They motored across the Westminster Bridge through a grey rain. The Houses of Parliament and the tower of Big Ben slid past them on their left. Collette leaned across Ethan, pressing her face against the glass so that she might catch a glimpse of the icons of the British Empire.

Ethan did his best to keep out of her way. She would never know the difference; he had memories of the city before the change, and the comparisons were painful to him.

He remembered London as a city filled with life, exuberance, and more than a touch of madness. It was, in its own right, a city of contrasts—at once both staunchly traditional and wildly exploratory. It was a place where stiff upper lips and counterculture walked the same streets in oddly the same measured steps, both dealing with the ubiquitous pickpockets maintaining their own London traditions. Everyone, it seemed, was happily engaged in the business of determining the furthest edge of just far enough.

Now there was a subtle and terrible turn to London, as though something in its foundations had shifted out of line.

The London Eye was still standing, though it had fallen into disuse after the day when enthusiastic tourists went up on one side of the enormous wheel and vanished into the circling cloud above. Workmen who had scaled the Eye never reached the top, reporting that they could hear the voices of those who had disappeared calling out above them but could not see them.

The Tower of London and its environs were abandoned by nearly all normal people, the magical emanations spinning in the cyclonic cloud overhead radiating its own fearsome aura. Several expeditions to the Tower by British Special Forces had each failed to retrieve the Crown Jewels of the Monarchy. The new emergence of magic was said to have its center beneath the White Tower, and while it still attracted thrill seekers and unwary tourists, no one entering the gates of the Tower since that day had been known to emerge again.

Even the clock tower of Big Ben—one of the most iconic London landmarks—had not gone unscathed. It was missing an entire corner, rumored to have been disassembled by a swarm of gargoyles who had built a nest around the enormous bell from which the tower and its clock borrowed the name. A scaffold had been erected to repair the damage, but Ethan could see that no one had worked on it for some time.

Tourism, once part of the lifeblood of the city, had largely devolved into a trickle of half-mad thrill seekers who came to London mostly on the dare of survival. The bustling streets were now nearly deserted. British citizens had never been much for distance travel even in their own country, but now it seemed as though all of London was boarded up in their individual flats, trying not to venture any further than necessary from those places where familiarity might give them the illusion of normalcy.

The double-decker buses still ran the streets, but there were far fewer of them than Ethan remembered in the past, and those that were running were largely empty.

The only exception that he knew to the rule of "lock your door" was just ahead of them—Trafalgar Square.

Valja turned north up the narrow canyon of Parliament Street, past the Foreign Office and Ministry of Defense buildings. Collette was moving about the back of the cab excitedly, catching glimpses of Nelson's Column and the ever-closer façade of the National Gallery beyond.

At last Valja deposited them at the edge of the square. Ethan shouldered his pack and managed to retrieve his camera case from the boot of the taxi.

"You'll be here when we are finished, right," Ethan said as more of a statement than a question.

"Of course, friend," Valja grinned. "I have not been paid yet…of course I vill remain!"

"All right," Ethan nodded. "The name's Ethan, by the way."

"Yes, Mr. Ethan," Valja said with a short wink.

Ethan turned and started making his way to the main entrance of the National Gallery, but suddenly slowed his steps.

There was a van parked to the side of the Gallery entrance with a bright and all-too-familiar sign fixed to it.

Myth-takes with Jonas Farben!

"Oh, please," Ethan muttered a vain prayer. "Not him!"

CHAPTER 4
SCIENTIFIC

Camera case in hand, Ethan charged up the wide stairs of the National Gallery and onto the black-and-white checkered tiles of the entrance portico. He allowed himself a glance from the portico over Trafalgar Square. This seemed to be one of the few places in London still teaming with life. People were gathered in small groups here and there in a spirit of joy and brotherhood despite the leaden clouds drifting overhead. It was getting toward afternoon, however, and Ethan was anxious about getting this shoot wrapped up. Trafalgar Square was a pleasant enough visit during the daylight, a stringer had told him while visiting the Atlanta headquarters, but not a place one wanted to be when night fell.

He remembered the man's coffee sloshing around as he held it with a hand that would not stop shaking.

Ethan followed Collette through the glass doors

being held open by one of the Gallery's security officers and into the marble vestibule. The officer—a paunchy middle-aged man with a shaved head wearing a blazer with a name tag labeled "Cardiff" attached to his lapel—pulled the door shut just behind Ethan, who continued in Collette's excited footsteps. Another officer, this one a British matron in a security blazer matching Cardiff's, hurried up the stairs ahead of Collette, leading them where they needed to go without any nonsense.

Ethan took in the old world beauty of the vestibule as he crossed the mosaic of Roman gods set in the floor of the main landing. Three staircases rose from this platform in the center of the vestibule, flanked by towering, warm-colored, marble columns. Angled glass roofs were fixed as skylights above each of the three richly carved doors at the top of the stairs. Ornate Victorian detail work abounded, giving everything the slightest hint of Jules Verne to his eye. Directly above him was a magnificent glass dome. There was a rich warmth to the room and its colors that appealed to Ethan—a pleasing juxtaposition of warm rust colors in the marble with cool mint of the walls. He could only hope that the location of their shoot would be as stunning.

The matron opened the door at the top of the stairs and preceded both he and Collette into the next chamber. It was another magnificent room, appropriately labeled "Central Hall." Here the walls were crimson-salmon color and accented with grey wainscot and crenellations. The ceiling was arched and coffered with an ornate Victorian greenhouse skylight set down the length of the room.

"This is the Northern Italian Collection!" Collette gushed, her steps slowing so precipitously that Ethan nearly ran into her in his haste. She started walking toward one of the paintings on the wall. "That's Melone's *The Road to Emmaus*! Did you know he was a pupil of Romanino…"

Ethan switched the camera case to his left hand, then firmly grasped Collette's upper arm and pulled her along with him. He was grateful that the sleeve of her jacket spared him the discomfort of touching her skin. "Come along, Miss Montrose. Let's not keep the job waiting."

A stanchion in the center of the hall held a sign proclaiming *The Unique Perspective of Benoit* with an arrow pointing to the left. The frowning matron was standing at the door exiting the west side of the hall, holding it open expectantly.

They passed through a smaller, short hall past an elevator and stairs and through a second set of doors into the exhibit.

Ethan instantly agreed—the Benoit perspective was most certainly unique.

The collection was being presented by cadavers.

"Aren't they stunning?" Collette purred next to him.

Hideous was more the word that came to Ethan's mind.

"They're plastinates, you know," Collette said. "Human bodies that have gone through that process that Gunther von Hagens made so popular a couple of decades back or so. Dr. Benoit made special arrangements to include these as part of the display of his collection."

"They're repulsive," Ethan muttered.

"Nonsense," Collette said, slapping her cameraman's arm. "The skin and certain tissues are removed in places so that you can get a better perspective of the interior of the human body. Dr. Benoit is using them in this exhibit as a platform for presenting the artifacts in his collection—a juxtaposition of the solidity of the human past against the fragility of our own existence. It's a rather dramatic statement in art."

That's not art, Ethan thought, *it's a freak show.*

A full set of Roman armor adorned one body, his mouth gaping open as his gladius was frozen in a slice down through the plasticized body of a woman holding a javelin, who was wearing a Zulu warrior skirt and an expression of surprise from the sword through her abdomen.

Another plastinate sat in a separate display in a suit of ancient samurai armor while most graphically demonstrating the midpoint of *seppuku* before the *kaishakunin*—in this case wearing a golf hat—could perform *kaishaku* with a nine iron.

Beside them, a skinless woman wore a gas mask while affectionately cradling an M1 Garand in her arms. Another female, wearing an Elizabethan dress, stood with her head split down the center, looking both ways at once. Behind her stood a male cadaver balancing a headsman's axe by its handle on one extended hand.

Ethan looked down the hall and into the small rotunda.

"Well, there's one cadaver I'd like to avoid," he said—though he had to admit, he was almost happy for the distraction from the grotesque "art."

Jonas Farben stood beneath the dome of the rotunda, gloriously basking in the bright glow of production lights. Ethan could have recognized him in his sleep, or at least in his nightmares. Farben was a celebrity commentator, the "get" when it came to answering any questions of science. His star had begun to rise when the rumors of magic and turmoil had first been reported in London. In those first weeks, his long and always perfectly coifed honey-blond hair and his firm, dimpled chin were a comforting and stabilizing influence seen on nearly every television screen around the world.

His was the voice of reason—the kind of reason that had explained the world for four millennia. Science was his religion and Reason the gospel that he proclaimed. He had parlayed his bankable onscreen personality and shameless ridicule of anything or anyone that disagreed with his view of the world into regular appearances on Fox News. For weeks, humanity turned to him—the turtlenecked and sport-coated savior of the status quo—to reassure the world that there were no such things as magic or monsters, there were only things that science had not yet fully explained. All that humanity needed was to shine the light of Farben's keen intellect and razor wit on the unexplained, and the world could sleep at night once more.

But the real turning point for the handsome, personable, and thoroughly unscrupulous Farben had been Ethan.

It had cost Ethan his career and credibility, elevated Farben to stardom, and it was all a lie.

Standing with his face to Farben and presumably basking in his glorious presence was a bookish-looking man with round, wire-rimmed glasses and grey-flecked brown hair with a receding hairline. He wore a herringbone sports jacket, an Oxford shirt open at the collar, khaki slacks, and comfortable shoes.

The Lowell portable lights switched off just as Ethan and Collette approached. Farben, however, continued to chat with the man in the herringbone jacket.

"Hey, Curtis," Ethan called over to Farben's cameraman.

The young man with a goatee beard looked up from the viewfinder of his camera. His smile fell at once when he saw who had addressed him. "Oh… hey, Ethan."

"Ethan? Ethan *Gallows*?"

Ethan turned toward the voice.

"Why, if it isn't Mr. Farben."

"That's *Dr.* Farben now," the man returned through his brilliant, capped teeth.

"Really?" Ethan responded. "Tell me, just what esteemed institution of higher learning accredited you *that* title?"

"Oh, you are still as quick as ever," Farben said, still smiling. "It is, strictly speaking, honorary, but I like to think it is a reflection of the academic community's appreciation for my work on their behalf."

Ethan smiled back with matching sincerity. "I'm sure that you do."

There was an increasingly insistent poking at Ethan's back.

"Ah, yes," Ethan continued. "*Dr.* Jonas Farben, may I present Miss Collette Montrose, Duchess of Art Antiquities."

Collette reached forward at once, pushing past Ethan as she gushed, "I can't tell you what an honor this is to meet you! I find your work fascinating… just fascinating."

Farben's ego rose at once to the occasion. "Why, thank you. So you're the talent on this shoot, eh? Please, allow me to apologize for taking up some of your time with Dr. Benoit—but I assure you it is all in the name of science."

"So, did you find something *funny* here?" Collette asked in a rush.

Ethan groaned. *Funny* was the word that Farben always used in his program to describe something unexplained or mysterious that defied logic. He would then set about tearing apart the mystery, explaining away its components and generally debunking such events as shams, scams, or frauds. Thanks to his highly overrated series *Myth-takes*, the word *funny* had come to mean, in general usage, anything un-usual that would eventually be exposed as a fraud.

"Well, there are a number of items in the Benoit collection that look *funny* to me," Farben chuckled. "But, as I so often say, 'We turn on the lights…'"

"'And find nothing in the dark but our own fears.'" They both finished Farben's tag line together.

Ethan turned back to Curtis, who was leaning on his camera with a bored expression on his face. "Nice location here under the dome. Mind if we use the setup?"

Curtis held his hands up in a shrug. "Sorry, man… company policy not to loan the equipment. Besides, it's gonna take twenty minutes for the lights to cool as it is."

"Right," Ethan said. He turned back to Collette still chatting with Farben. Dr. Benoit stood uncom-fortably silent just beyond them.

"Listen," Farben was saying, "we have a few more reactions to shoot and a couple pick-ups; it shouldn't take but a few minutes. I could give you a few on-screen bites for your piece if you like when I'm fin-ished here."

"Thanks, Jonas," Collette beamed. "That would be really nice of you."

"Excuse me, but we need to find another place to set up," Ethan cut into the conversation between them. "If you're finished with the guest, perhaps

Miss Montrose could do her pre-interview with Dr. Benoit now?"

"Where am I going?" Dr. Benoit asked.

"With me, Doctor," Collette said, taking him by the arm.

"Doctor, do you mind if I look around the collection for a few minutes?" Ethan asked. "I need to find a good place to film our interview."

"But of course, Ethan Gallows," the doctor replied, blinking his eyes. "Find something you like."

Ethan frowned but nodded. He took his case and moved down the southern hall. The pleasant crimson color of the walls now looked more like blood to him, especially set against the plastinate cadavers posed in the hall. The hall that had once held masterpieces of the Renaissance now housed a mortuary of the absurd.

Ethan stopped in front of a stone table whose label indicated it was from Pompeii at the time of the eruption. Atop the table lay an Egyptian mummy, its wrappings cut down the center, while a plastinate corpse—skinless and itself splayed down the chest and gut as though it had been autopsied—leaned over the mummy holding an 18th century surgical knife.

Everywhere he looked as he walked down the hall were tableaus of increasing bizarreness. It was, indeed, a most eclectic collection: the rarest of antiquities mingled together with what looked like common garage sale trash, all being pored over by the partially dissected and carefully posed plastic dead.

One female cadaver was holding a common stove iron, hovering it over a Greek necklace that predated Rome. Another female figure had her arms crossed over her filleted breasts, her head—emptied of its brain—turned away, all while wearing a Victorian-era dress. The figure of a young man, also devoid of brain, held up a 1940s egg carton in which was a Fabergé egg. Ethan guessed there must have been over a hundred of these tableaus set throughout the four halls intersecting with the rotunda.

Unexpectedly, one figure arrested his attention.

It was a young woman. The skin had been left intact on her face, though it had been removed everywhere else. She was posed as though in flight, a set of Da Vinci mechanical wings strapped to her back, a black support post holding her aloft. Her hands, the muscles rendered in exquisite detail, were reaching out toward him and offering a small object.

There was something actually beautiful about it. It framed well in his mind's eye. This would do.

Ethan judged the angles and distances, setting up the shot in his mind. He set down the camera case and his backpack, knelt down, and flicked open the latches of the case. It was a new field kit using the latest in high-capacity, high-yield built-in batteries to power the quartz halogen bulbs. They would not last long—only long enough to get an interview recorded—but they cut down on setup headaches tremendously. He checked the power levels and was pleased to see that all three had kept their charge.

He then turned his attention to the new Sony HDR-VP5500 camera in the case—a professional hand-held HD video camera. It had extraordinary image stabilization built into both the lens and the parallel CMOS processors; these worked in tandem to both oversample the image and reduce it to rock-solid imaging in real-time. It was light, and with Ethan's practiced, already steady hand, further lightened his load by eliminating the need for a tripod. He slipped the camera from the case, initiated the power, and looked through the lens.

Quite suddenly, Ethan stopped.

It was perfectly framed in his viewfinder. The hands of the Da Vinci winged woman held a thumb-sized bronze figurine of a winged man.

Ethan carefully set the camera back in the case and stood up. He could not take his eyes from the figure. It looked so familiar to him, as though it were something that he had once lost but could barely remember.

Despite the placards everywhere warning him against it, Ethan reached forward with his hand and touched the figure.

In that instant, Ethan's mind was filled completely with the memory of another place and time.

CHAPTER 5
LONG, LONG AGO

Abraxas desperately scooped at the rushing air, his leathery wing membranes billowing with every frantic downward thrust. The waves below him exploded in steam, roiling the air around him with violent and unpredictable eddies. The great dragon craned his neck upward, yearning for altitude as the northern face of the mountain loomed before him.

It was the northern wind that saved him. Rushing off the violent ocean to feed the firestorms in the city, the sudden extinguishing of the flames pushed the momentum of the hurricane suddenly toward the mountain. Abraxas felt the cataclysm slide suddenly beneath him as the gale drove him faster toward the mountainside. But Abraxas was an old dragon and knew the ways of sky and land. He dropped his right wing, turning parallel to the mountainside, and angled slightly into the wind.

The onrushing air collided with the immovable mountainside and, having nowhere else to go, swept upward. Abraxas felt the upward rush of air lifting him with it, shooting him toward the clouds with the face of the mountain barely a claw's length from the tip of his left wing. The membranes of his wings filled with the upward-rushing air piling up against the mountain. He could see the end of the ridge approaching, so he dropped his right wing once again, pivoted in the air, and reversed along the face of the mountain—rising further with every moment toward the temple at the other end of the ridge. It would be difficult—in fact he would have to almost land backwards—but there was no time for anything else.

Abraxas slowed as much as he dared. The great pyramid was collapsing off to his right, its stones cascading down the slope toward the angry sea. The temple was ahead, and he had gained enough altitude to look down into the garden. He could see in the dim light that Fafnir and Apalala had both managed to land in the lawn, at one time carefully manicured, now ripped apart by fissures. Abraxas rode the winds, turning into them and facing away from the temple.

The sight before him tore at his heart.

The great city was in utter ruin, its horrific devastation being swallowed forever by the Inner Sea. It was not just the lives of the citizens that were being buried, but the very memory of their existence.

All that they were would be hidden from history and vanish with the fall of the world.

Abraxas craned his head downward, fixing his gaze on the edge of the garden, as he dropped slowly to the ground. His talons dug deep, gripping the soil, and he folded his wings against his long body.

So Abraxas has come to Atlantis, *the old dragon thought sadly to himself,* for the last time.

"*Apalala! Fafnir!*" the old dragon called to the two other dragons swaying near him on the uncertain ground.

"*We are here, brother,*" Fafnir acknowledged. The grey dragon turned his good eye toward Abraxas. Fafnir's right eye was dead, a long scar running across it from an unfortunate encounter with a Titan. He was a fierce warrior and a creature whose honorable heart was unquestioned.

"*This will be a story to tell, if there is anyone left to hear it,*" said Apalala, a smaller, bronze-and-turquoise-plated dragon.

Abraxas shook his great horned head. Loyal Fafnir and cheerful Apalala. The end of the world could come—had come—and they would never change. Both were Abraxas's broodmates, born of the same clutch and raised together. The bond between them went beyond companionship; their souls were knitted together by the power of karma. It was that same power that bound their eternal souls to the mortal realms and gave them the mystical powers they wielded on behalf of creation. Their bond as brood-

mates was, therefore, bound to their very existence in the world.

And it was that same power that was draining from them with every passing moment. Each of them could feel the bonds unraveling—not just between them as broodmates, but with the world itself. The karmic shell of their physical manifestation was failing with the world.

The time of dragons in the mortal world was slowly coming to an end.

"You are certain we were summoned?" Abraxas asked. Fafnir had heard the call first, and convinced Abraxas and Apalala to answer with him. Abraxas was the elder of the three, and by the custom of dragonkind, spoke for and assumed leadership of all younger dragons present.

"With certainty," Fafnir answered.

"The Grand Master may be dead," Apalala said. "The summons may be in vain."

Abraxas swung his head around, searching the gardens. There had been so many here before, but now they seemed to have all vanished. "Not Apogean—he wouldn't dare die without having the last word on me!"

"We should go," Apalala said. "Atlantis will fall."

"We should go," Fafnir growled, "but where could we go? Is there any place safe from this—"

"Abraxas! Abraxas!"

The dragon twisted his head, desperate to find the

source of the called name, then smiled. "Apogean!"

The Grand Master Priest of the temple was filthy. Abraxas always remembered him as immaculately clean whenever they met, regardless of circumstance. He was a keeper of the karmic fire, the heart of Atlantis, and had always said it was his duty to present himself as an example of the purity and trust of his position. Yet now he came limping toward them, his robes smudged with soot and his long, flowing hair in tangles. Three days' growth of grey beard softened the lines of his angular jaw. There was a bad bruise across his large, hooked nose, but his eyes were still as bright as ever.

"Thank the sun and stars you have come!" Apogean cried, tears welling up in his eyes. "We feared you would not!"

"We are here, Apogean," Abraxas said quickly. "The karma is failing and with it goes the world. Has the taint had its victory at last?"

"No, although perhaps the taint had more to do with this calamity than not," Apogean said.

"What has happened?" Apalala asked impatiently.

"We do not know," Apogean answered as his tears flowed once more. "Something terrible has upset the foundations of creation—a wound is draining the lifeblood out of our world. We have tried in vain to discover the source of this wound, but we cannot. Some of our brothers think it happened in Midgard, others think perhaps further west among the Fomodorians of the Western Sea."

"It is the taint!" Abraxas rumbled. *"Its darkness has had its victory over the light of karma at last!"*

"No, Abraxas, we think not," Apogean said, shaking his head. *"It is true that for too long the taint has been growing. As the very corruption of karma, it stood in opposition to the order of the world. We had hoped to achieve a balance between the two of them but now...now* both *karma and taint are bleeding from creation, to the death of our world—and there is nothing we can do to stop it!"*

"But you called us," Fafnir said. *"What is there that we can do?"*

"For us...there is nothing." The priest's words came through choking sobs.

"Then why have you called?" Abraxas demanded.

"It is for your sake that we have called you here," Apogean said, drawing in a great breath.

"Our sake?" Abraxas asked.

"We did not call you here to save us," Apogean said. *"We called you here so that we might save you."*

Abraxas shook his head. *"We are creatures of karma. Our physical existence in mortal realms depends upon it. If the karma is gone—"*

"But your souls are eternal," the priest interrupted.

"Then we will be terrible ghosts upon a dead world," Abraxas said.

"No! There is a dawn after this long night," Apogean shouted. *"We have seen it. The foundations of*

*the world have been twisted and the warring powers
of taint's darkness and karma's light are fleeing. The
well of our life has been reversed and sucked dry.
The war between the sun and the night will sleep in
the foundations, their battles bubbling up into the
world down the ages like half-remembered dreams
and nightmares to afflict mankind. But, but, my old
friend, there will come a day when the foundations
will be turned again, karma and taint will return to
the world. In that day, those foundations will still
be twisted, but you, you must be there to set them
right!"*

*"Me?" Abraxas asked. "My kind is in our last
day. How could we rise from the dead bones of the
world to—"*

*Abraxas, dragon of Trocea, took in a great
breath.*

*Gathering from the shadows behind the Grand
Master Priest Apogean, several lithe, hooded figures appeared. Abraxas had been younger when the
Summer Courts were known on the maps of men in
the western lands, known then as Elysium. He knew
well the unique appearance of the Seelie—the faeries who had long since fled to Avalon.*

*The garden shook suddenly beneath their feet. A
new fissure opened up in the lawn, a jagged chasm
that ran from the edge of the collapsing garden
wall all the way to the temple stairs, splitting the
marble and toppling one of the columns on the portico. Abraxas's head snapped to his right toward a*

terrible roaring sound. The great pyramid was, to his astonishment, moving away from him and sinking slowly out of sight.

"You must make a strange journey, my friend— you and all your kind," Apogean told Abraxas. "You must surrender to a sleep that will last down through the Ages of the World. One day, in a time beyond our sight, you will awaken again and make right what has gone so terribly wrong."

A Seelie woman then stepped out from among her kin to stand next to Apogean. She pulled back her hood. The faery's smooth jawlines came to a dimpled chin. Her hair was jet black and her eyes a brilliant green. As with all of her race, her ears came to a point, though they were not overly large. Humans would have considered her strikingly beautiful.

Abraxas reared back at the sight of her. He did not trust her. The Seelie had abandoned the world once before. His associations with them had shown, so far as the dragon was concerned, that they were changeable and untrustworthy.

Abraxas's left arm lifted from the ground, its talons curling into an open grip. Sparks flew between the talons and a ball of fire erupted between them, rolling and roaring menacingly between the tips of his claws. Then his sharp eyes caught something...

Suspended around the Seelie's neck by a silver chain was a small bronze figurine of a winged man.

*****

"You really shouldn't touch that," Dr. Benoit said, pulling Ethan's arm away from the artifact. "Didn't you see the signs?"

Ethan snapped his head to look at the doctor. Rene Benoit was looking at Ethan with a curious smile. The doctor was still gripping the cameraman's sleeve. "I'm…sorry…I don't know why I…"

"Excuse me," Dr. Benoit said in a soft, kindly voice, releasing his grip and pointing across Ethan's chest. "But would you mind putting that out?"

"What do you mean? Put *what* out?" Ethan gave a puzzled look, turning his head to look where the doctor had indicated.

Ethan had curled the fingers of his left hand into a claw-like shape.

A single, tiny ball of flame was floating between them.

Ethan jerked his hand back at once.

The flame vanished with a quiet pop.

CHAPTER 6
DREAMS OF FIRE

"Are you about ready to shoot?"

Ethan shivered. He closed his left hand into a tight grip, trying unsuccessfully to stop it from shaking. "Excuse me?"

"If you're about set up," Collette said, "I think I'm ready to do this."

She didn't see it. Ethan's mind raced again over the details of the experience—the strange bridge from his nightmares that had been instantly realized in his hand. He questioned whether he had actually seen it, but at the same time knew that it had been all too real—just as the shadowy dead that tore down Hanoi handful by handful had been all too real.

This wasn't right; he was an observer of the world—detached and removed from its experience by hiding behind the lens of his camera, recording what happened around him. He was not supposed to get involved—a mantra he often repeated—and somehow felt that the world should at least reciprocate and not affect him either. There were fundamental powers shifting in the world and he had figured he would simply shift with them, recording the events as they unfolded and dispassionately documenting the world as it unraveled in front of his glass, electronic eye.

But somehow in that moment, those same unexplained powers had reached through the lens, slipped past his professional detachment, and shaken who he knew he was.

For the first time in a very long time, Ethan knew fear.

"Ethan?" Collette asked again, concern edging her voice.

"Sorry…I'm fine. I just…I was just considering the sight lines," Ethan said, forcing himself to concentrate on the task at hand. "If we place Dr. Benoit on the right of this winged—uh—display here and you on the left, it will give us the cross-shot we need and keep the display figure in thirds in-frame. I'll adjust the aperture and lighting so that we can get a little fuzz in the background depth of field so both of you will pop a little in the shot. That sound OK to you?"

Collette smiled slightly. "You're actually asking my opinion?"

"Hey, you're the talent," Ethan said. "I'm just the guy behind the camera."

"Since when?" Collette chirped.

Ethan shrugged, knelt down, pulled a set of portable light stands for the halogen lights out of the case, and rapidly set them up.

"Well, *thank* you," Collette finished to Ethan's back, and then turned to Dr. Benoit, extending her hand. "Dr. Benoit, I'm Collette Montrose of CNN and I'll be conducting our interview today."

"A pleasure, Miss Montrose," the doctor said, bowing slightly as he took her hand. His circular-rimmed glasses slipped slightly down his nose. Benoit released her hand at once, and as he straightened up, pushed the glasses back up on his nose with his index finger. He ran his hand back through his grey-flecked brown hair and adjusted his herringbone jacket as he continued, "But please—call me Rene. I am only too glad to discuss this marvelous exhibit with you…and your most able cameraman."

Ethan, still kneeling at the case, pulled a pair of white cotton gloves out of the light kit section of his case and slipped them on. With practiced ease, he pulled his small quartz production Lowell lights out of the case and began mounting them atop the light stands. He appeared the picture of apathetic indifference but was, in fact, listening to every word. This strange man was all too interested in him for Ethan's liking—trying too hard to include him.

Ethan removed his gloves and pulled a pair of lavalier transmitting microphones out of the case. He tossed one to Collette and then stepped up to the doctor. The new model of Sennheiser EW400 wireless microphones were a great improvement. The microphone body contained both the transmitter and battery; earlier models required that a separate transmitter case and antenna be suspended from the subject's belt, or some other inconvenient place, as well as a wire run through their clothing in such a way that it was hidden from the camera and yet still reached the microphone clipped to the lapel or blouse in order to pick up the sound. Getting everything in the right place had led to more than one awkward moment between crew and the subjects of the interview as both tried to navigate the wire through places that in other circumstances would have required a more intimate acquaintance. The new lavaliers were slightly larger than the older lav microphones, but replacing the wire was a little "rat tail" antenna requiring no external transmitter or wire to be run under clothing. Ethan reached up to the doctor's jacket collar and lifted it up, clipping the microphone beneath it and adjusting its position to get the best sound.

"Don't you have to plug those in?" Dr. Benoit asked, addressing Ethan.

"Huh? Oh, I'm sorry—what was your question?" Ethan said, turning to face the doctor.

"Those lights," Dr. Benoit said, pointing to the housings perched atop the stands. "Don't you need an electrical outlet to make those work?"

"No," Ethan replied quickly. "They can run on

their own long enough for the interview, Doctor."

"Speaking of which," said Collette crisply, "can we get this started?"

Ethan nodded, moving between the three lights and flicking them on. Dr. Benoit, he noticed, seemed to come alive with the lights, straightening slightly, his smile brightening. Ethan stepped back and picked up the camera from the case. He adjusted his distance and the angle in order to frame the shot, widening his stance on the marble floor. He flicked the camera on and swung it up to his face.

"Whenever you're ready," Collette said through a tight smile.

"Just checking levels," Ethan said from behind the camera, adjusting the lighting of the view through the camera lens. "Looks good. You're on."

Collette nodded and turned to face Dr. Benoit. "Dr. Benoit…"

"Rene," the doctor interjected with a pleasant smile. "Please, call me Rene."

"Of course and thank you," Collette responded. "Rene, for the last twenty years, you've been an associate curator of the Louvre Museum and have dealt with many of the greatest works of art throughout antiquity. Yet your personal collection has been characterized, quoting *The New York Times*, as 'an eclectic and lunatic chaos that runs from the stunningly rare to the insignificant and mundane.' How do you respond to such criticisms?"

Dr. Benoit smiled pleasantly. "One of the central

features of my collection is that I challenge the pre-conceived notions of value in art. Is it rarity alone that makes a piece of antiquity worthwhile, or is it our associations with it? Many of us cling to broken and useless objects from our childhood and trea-sure them above the Hope Diamond. Is the thing valuable in and of itself, or is there another quality that increases its worth? Especially in our chang-ing world today, discovering the true value of our material possessions—whether in our closet or in our museums—is being challenged. What makes an object truly valuable? The point of the collection is to pose that question in as challenging of terms as possible."

"Why, then, present your collection framed by plastinate cadavers," Collette asked, "which are clearly on their own one of the most controversial displays in the world?"

"We chose to frame the exhibit with plastinate cadavers—"

Ethan smiled. By rephrasing the question back to Collette, the doctor had given them video foot-age that was more usable. Dr. Benoit knew his way around an interview.

"—because the purpose here is to make people think—even if those thoughts are uncomfortable and challenge them to—"

A crashing sound reverberated through the exhibit hall.

Collette grimaced. Farben's cameraman had

knocked over a light stand and was kneeling down to pick it up—but he and Farben both were transfixed by something down the length of the side exhibit hall that led back toward the entrance.

"A little courtesy, please," Collette called to them. "We're conducting an *interview*!"

Neither Farben nor his cameraman acknowledged her.

"Do you want to start over?" Ethan asked, the camera still recording.

"No, let's pick it up with that last question," Collette said. "Dr. Benoit—Rene—please tell me again, why you chose to frame your exhibit with…Rene?"

Dr. Benoit had turned away, looking back toward the rotunda.

The woman was tall—perhaps just over six feet—with a slight, willowy build. Her hair was a cool, stark white, cut short with fringes and layered sides sweeping upward. Her long black leather coat draped down over a white knit blouse and a short black skirt. She had creamy skin, almost pale, and high, prominent cheekbones above a small, bowed mouth. Her eyes were hidden behind a pair of large, black sunglasses, despite the dimness of the room. The stiletto heels of her knee-high boots resounded sharply through the hall as she approached.

Ethan gaped. It was the woman he had seen in the courtyard at Heathrow just as they were leaving in the cab.

Dr. Benoit turned to the cameraman, urgency in his

eyes and sweat breaking out on his forehead. "Help me get out of here, Ethan, and I can protect you."

"What?"

"You need me, Ethan!" Benoit said. "And I need you. Help me and you'll be safe!"

The tall woman stepped up to them, turning to the doctor. Her voice, when she spoke, was smoky—a suggestive deep alto that was cool and controlled. "Dr. Benoit, I presume."

Benoit looked over his spectacles at the woman. "An unexpected pleasure."

The woman turned her face toward the cameraman, the lights from the halogens glinting off of her black sunglasses. "And I believe you are Ethan Gallows, am I right?"

Ethan's eyes narrowed. "Excuse me—have we met?"

The woman's hand flicked open, a business card appearing between her index and middle fingers.

Ethan reached for the card, but before he could take it, Collette, increasingly annoyed, stepped between them, snatching the card from the woman's hand and stuffing it in her jacket pocket. She was a full head shorter than the white-haired woman but seemed undaunted by her.

"Collette Montrose, CNN. We are *trying* to conduct an interview here, so if you wouldn't mind waiting over *there*," Collette pointed forcibly back toward the rotunda at the hall's intersection, "we'll just get back to our work."

The woman ignored Collette's existence and turned back to face Benoit.

"I've come to collect you, Rene."

Dr. Benoit shook his head slowly with a smile at the edges of his lips. "I'm not going with you, Sojourner. Not ever."

"I'm not asking, Rene," the woman said evenly. She took off her glasses. Her eyes were a radiant violet color unlike anything Ethan had ever seen before.

"This exhibit is closed to the public," Collette said, her balled fists now pressing firmly against her hips. "Just who do you think you are, barging in here like this?"

Ethan groaned inwardly.

Dr. Benoit glanced at Collette, his voice calm and quiet as he spoke. "Oh, please forgive my poor manners. Miss Montrose, may I present Sojourner Lee. May her carcass rot in the depths of the seas and her name be forgotten for all time."

"Charming, as always," Sojourner replied, placing her sunglasses in the pocket of her coat, then flexing the long, elegant fingers of her hands. "But it is getting late, and we have far to go."

"No, Sojourner," Benoit replied, flexing his wide hands. "If you were serious, you wouldn't have come alone."

"But I *didn't* come alone," the towering woman responded.

The face of the winged cadaver shifted. The plastinate woman, her musculature and bones exposed, reached

down with both her skinless arms, gripped the supporting post, and with a sickening sucking sound, pushed
herself upward. Free of the post, she stood in horrific
aspect, the Da Vinci wings still fixed to her back, now
looking like the rendered corpse of a gargoyle.

She turned toward Dr. Benoit.

The doctor stepped back, his right hand reaching
quickly inside his jacket. Ethan expected in that moment for Benoit to pull an automatic pistol from a
shoulder holster, but to his surprise, the man pulled
his hand free to brandish an elegant-looking, chrome-
plated pen. The shining implement flashed through
the air in tightly controlled arcs, a piercingly brilliant light appearing at its tip. The rapid arcs traced
light in front of him, forming a picture, a shape of
something.

The plastinate woman leaped from her pedestal
toward Dr. Benoit, the Da Vinci wings billowing on
her back.

The shape became more solid at the whirling command of Dr. Benoit's pen; the head and neck of a
fierce dragon rose suddenly up, colliding with the
winged cadaver, and knocking her back against the
warrior plastinate whose bowels were spilling out
from his samurai armor.

The glowing dragon's head shifted at once toward
the woman known as Sojourner. Dr. Benoit took a
quick, single step backward as a brilliant gout of
flame shot from the dragon's head with such force
that Dr. Benoit staggered back again.

The tall woman, however, had already raised her long, ivory hands, creating a disk of frost and ice spinning between her and the flames rocketing from the conjured dragon's head. The column of flame slammed into the frost disk, flaring around it.

Ethan clenched his teeth as he quickly looked about, movement catching his eye.

The samurai was rising up from his platform, his hands gathering up his own plasticized intestines and swinging them menacingly as he stepped toward them. Dr. Benoit saw the movement behind him, his pen flashing vigorously through the air as the dragon's head maintained the flame toward the woman. A second dragon's head formed in the glowing lines, roaring as it charged into the body of the advancing samurai. The plastinate jumped to one side, wrapping its intestine around the first dragon's head, trying to hold its muzzle closed while he reached for his sword. The samurai corpse lost its grip as the dragon's second head lifted it upward, slamming it against the curved ceiling overhead.

Every plastinate in the hall was beginning to move now, each wrenching itself away from the bolts fixing it to its exhibit platform. The split-headed woman snatched the axe from the executioner behind her, spinning its massive blade as she approached. She was in turn held by a third conjured dragon's head from Benoit's mystic pen, this one's jaws clamping down on one half of the female's head and holding her at bay while she tried to see with her one remaining eye, swinging her axe uselessly through the air.

The plastinate woman in the gas mask had fixed a bayonet at the end of her rifle and was charging.

Benoit countered each in turn, sprouting new heads of his magically summoned hydra with each threat, while the original dragon's head continued to spew a column of fire at Sojourner Lee as she tried to move closer to him with her protective disk of ice.

Ethan pulled Collette down low, shifting to stay away from the raging dragon heads and the approaching cadavers. Each animated monstrosity, partially dissected and skinned, reached out with its arms or crouched as though preparing to spring, quickly closing a circle around Sojourner, Dr. Benoit, Ethan, and Collette.

Ethan looked up at Dr. Benoit. Sweat was pouring down his face; whatever power he was wielding, the man was straining with the effort and could not handle much more.

Ethan looked intently about the hall. The plastinates from all three halls were still converging on them at the command of the mysterious white-haired woman. Beyond the dreadful images of the dissected faces, he caught a glimpse of Jonas Farben and Curtis. Both were pressed against the far corner of the rotunda, completely ignored by the animated dead.

Ethan had to do something. He glanced at the camera in his right hand and then reached out suddenly with his left, swinging one of the quartz lamps to shine directly into the eyes of Sojourner Lee.

The tall woman turned her head aside with a cry, tilting the frost disk formed in front of her. The rushing gout of fire was turned by its shifted surface, shooting upward and roiling across the ceiling of the hall.

The dead in the hall hesitated, but the sorceress was quick to recover. She righted the frost shield, but it was too late. The fire suppression system had read the heat from Rene's column of flame across the ceiling. Water suddenly erupted from the ceiling spouts, spraying down on the hall. Fire alarms resounded and the emergency lighting engaged even though the main lights in the hall remained on.

"Get ready to run!" Ethan shouted at Collette.

"Run?" Collette yelled back, looking at the wall of dead encircling them. "Run where?"

The water hit the quartz lamps. Each of the bulbs exploded in a brilliant flash, followed by an electrical overload. The batteries shorted out and exploded as well, their sparks flying across the hall.

The unexpected discharge distracted both Benoit and Sojourner Lee from their concentrations. The strange powers of the woman collapsed. Dr. Benoit, startled, dropped his pen, the dragon heads and the column of flame suddenly extinguishing while the plastinates in the hall fell to the ground.

"*Now!*" Ethan yelled, shoving Collette down the hall.

She needed no further encouragement. Collette dashed down the length of the hall, turning at the rotunda toward the right hall and the exit beyond.

Ethan grabbed the arm of Dr. Benoit with his left hand just as the curator was bending down. The cameraman started running down the hall with the doctor stumbling next to him over the corpses littering the floor.

"My pen!" Benoit wailed.

"Not now!" Ethan growled.

As they reached the rotunda, the plastinate corpses began standing again.

Sojourner Lee was raising the plastic dead once more.

"See anything *funny*?" Ethan shouted at Farben, cowering in the corner of the rotunda. "Maybe you should be filming *this*?"

Both Ethan and Dr. Benoit were running as fast as they could toward the exit at the far end of the hall.

The animated corpses—over a hundred of them—were running at their heels after them.

CHAPTER 7
THE VELVET UNDERGROUND

Ethan burst through the doors back into the Central Hall, his hiking shoes squealing across the wet marble as he tried to turn at a full run. He was soaked head to toe from the burst of fire sprinklers in the hall behind him. For a moment he thought about the camera still gripped in his hand, wondering if it had held up under the deluge and what he might need to do to keep it functioning. It was an insane thought, he realized at once.

He had far more pressing concerns at his heels.

Dr. Benoit's coat sleeve—and consequently Dr. Benoit—was still firmly in his grip as he skidded slightly over the floor. The doctor was thin but not as light as Ethan had anticipated. Benoit struggled to keep his feet under him as he swung around Ethan's side.

The partially dissected cadavers erupted through

the doors of their former gallery home. Those who still had throat tissue emitted horrible, unearthly screams from their plastic-saturated mouths. Water droplets glistened on their exposed muscles and skin, their plastinate feet slipping on the wet floor. One lost her balance, fell, and slid under the legs of two others holding rusty javelins. They slid against the far wall in a tangle, but it did little to stop the rising tide of the dead flooding into the hall.

"Come on, Doctor!" Ethan yelled, shoving the doctor ahead of him as they ran down the hall. "They're right on top of us!"

At the southern end of the hall, Collette was running with remarkable speed toward the double doors. The officious, uniformed matron must have been blind to what was happening behind them. She stood blocking the exit, the microphone from her security radio in her hand. She was holding up her free hand, urging Collette to stop.

The water from the sprinkler system suddenly turned to a heavy snowfall as the temperature in the hall dropped. Ice was forming on the marble beneath his feet. His own shoes were faring well, but Ethan could see Dr. Benoit's hard-soled dress shoes were starting to slide out from under him.

Sojourner. She's coming.

Ethan did not look back—told himself not to look back—toward the chattering, squealing sound of the dead at his heels. *Look back and you'll join them.* He kept running.

Collette dropped her shoulder and without slacking her pace, threw herself into the midriff of the security matron. The woman let out an audible gasp as she was thrown completely off her feet with full force against the crash bar of the exit door. Both the matron and Collette tumbled onto the stone landing beyond. To Ethan's astonishment, Collette rolled across the matron, who was sliding onto the stairs of the vestibule, pushed off, and leaped down to the landing with both feet firmly under her.

Ethan and Dr. Benoit reached the doors before they could close again, banging them wide. Both rushed down the stairs, following Collette over the mosaic just as a crash of glass exploded behind them.

Collette uttered a single enraged scream.

The cadavers had somehow gained access to the roof—probably through the skylights. Now they were not only pouring out of the doors of the Central Hall but down through the shattering glass and snow overhead.

"Out!" Ethan urged. "Get out!"

They rushed down the stairs, through the triple arches, and veered to the left through the two glass doors of the breezeway and onto the south portico.

Trafalgar Square lay spread before them under a deepening afternoon. The crowds were still there, however; the good spirit in the square still remained. A number of people stood on the portico, taking in the pleasant late afternoon. All that would change soon enough.

Ethan started down the eastern stairs leading off the portico, pushing his way through a group of young neo-goths who jeered at him.

"Follow me!" he shouted.

"Where are you taking us?" Dr. Benoit said.

"We have a cab waiting for us over by St. Martin-in-the-Fields," Ethan said, taking the stairs two at a time and catching up with Collette. "If we can outrun these—"

The safety glass in both entrance doors blew outward across the portico, the shining, pebble-sized pieces glistening as they showered the crowd. The animated dead burst into the screaming, panicked crowd, their own shrill cries becoming a counterpoint chorus.

The panic on the portico entrance ran like a tidal wave across the square, fueled by the appearance of the partially dissected cadavers pouring out into the square from the Gallery entrance.

"Come *on*, Collette!" Ethan urged as he ran eastward along the face of the National Gallery. The towering steeple of St. Martin-in-the-Fields stabbed the darkening sky, calling him onward to Charring Cross Road. Through the terror-filled throng desperately and mindlessly trying to find safety in any place but where they stood, Ethan caught a glimpse of the familiar black London cab and its imposing driver, Valja, standing next to it and urging them toward him.

The horde of animated dead seemed momentarily

confused by the enormous crowd in the square, but then a single shriek was followed in chorus by others, and Ethan knew they had been spotted.

Valja was just a few more steps away, leaving the door open as he climbed, ashen-faced, back into the driver's seat.

"Get in!" Ethan shouted, knowing as he spoke that the words were ludicrously obvious. "Doctor, don't wait for…"

Something flew past his head. A dark object.

He turned. "What the…"

It was a female cadaver—the closest of the horde. She was missing her epidermis, the musculature of her arms and legs exposed as well as the fatty membranes of her breasts. Her chest cavity, however, had been opened to expose her heart and lungs in the display—the heart swaying back and forth between the flapping lungs by its plasticized aorta. Her blank eyes were fixed on Ethan. He could not take his eyes away as she reached in with her exposed left arm, plucked a piece of her liver from her abdominal cavity, and hurled it at him.

Ethan ducked just as the plastinate liver flew over his head. He lunged forward toward the door of the cab.

His feet were suddenly tangled, pulled out from under him. He fell forward, instinctively rolling on his side, sheltering his increasingly ridiculous camera in his arms as he slammed sideways against the stones of Trafalgar Square.

The female cadaver was on him in an instant, her

rubbery intestines wrapped around his ankles. She leaped to sit on his chest. Her hands wielded her intestines, coiling them around Ethan's neck as she reared back, her hideous, partial face howling for her brother dead to join her in the capture of their prey.

The cadaver's head suddenly exploded as lightning arced from the direction of the cab.

Ethan unwound himself from the gory coils, regaining enough footing to lunge through the open door and onto the floor of the cab.

Collette slammed the door shut just as several of the cadavers reached the cab, their plastic fingernails clawing at the paint.

"Let's go!" Ethan yelled.

Valja threw the cab in gear as the cadavers began piling onto the roof.

"Go north—up Charring Cross!" Dr. Benoit shouted, slipping a blue fountain pen back into the pocket of his jacket.

"I thought you lost your pen!" Ethan said as the cab began to accelerate, lurching sideways from the impact of another of the determined dead.

"*A* pen, yes…and I am most upset at its loss." Benoit shrugged. "But one can never have too many pens."

"You nearly killed us!"

"Not nearly—that was Sojourner. But not to worry. I know someone," Dr. Benoit said. "He'll take care of us—keep us safe."

"Why should we trust you at all?" Ethan exclaimed, letting go of his camera and dropping it to the floor. He struggled up and grabbed the doctor by both lapels of his sports jacket. "You're a sorcerer!"

The cab bounced violently front to back as it bounded over one of the cadavers that had fallen under its wheels. Ethan shot upward, banging his head against the roof. He released Benoit's coat, sprawling on the floor.

"I know a man who can better explain the answers to you than I can," Dr. Benoit replied. "You'll know the truth soon enough, Ethan Gallows."

The cab careened up Charring Cross Road, losing the last of the furious cadavers before they reached Covent Garden.

*****

"This is *safe*?" Collette exclaimed, staring out the window at an ancient pub with red exterior walls. Crowds of young people, mostly with their heads hung low, shuffled down the sidewalk between them and the pub.

"No, is not safe," Valja exclaimed from the driver's compartment, craning around to face them through the plexiglass portal. "Vonce, maybe, but no more."

"Nonsense, I assure you, I know the proprietor personally," Dr. Benoit said with a smile. "I've done considerable business with him. He is a marvel when it comes to acquiring the rarest of antiquities, and is something of an artist."

"It's called The World's End," Collette griped.

"Charming, isn't it?" Dr. Benoit said pleasantly. "You know it's been here since 1690? It used to be called Mother Redcap and sometimes Mother Damnable. The legend is that the pub and the nightclub under it are haunted by Mother Redcap—a woman named Jinny who had several of her husbands die mysteriously."

"Great," Collette said without enthusiasm.

"Mr. Ethan," Valja implored. "Camden Town is strange place. Valja take you to nice vestern hotel… hot bath and many armed guards, OK?"

"That is exactly where they will be looking for you," Dr. Benoit said quickly. "And I promise you, you won't find your answers hiding in a Marriott.

"You take the pictures and our friend Collette gets an exclusive. Did you come to London, the very epicenter of emerging magic, to get a story or to take a nice warm bath?"

"A story, huh?" Ethan grunted.

"Like you've never shot before," Benoit replied, sitting back against the seat of the cab.

Ethan glanced at Collette.

"I guess you've still got your camera," Collette shrugged.

"And you're still wearing your interview suit," Ethan said, shaking his head. He turned around to face the cab driver, pulling out his wallet. "Valja, I'll give you five hundred pounds for the day and another hundred for the neighborhood the moment we get back. We'll only be an hour at the most."

"I can't park here, Mr. Ethan," Valja complained. "This is loading only zone."

"Well, what street is this?"

"This is Greenland Road, sir," Valja responded at once.

"We'll look for you here on Greenland Road in about an hour," Ethan said, stuffing the bills through the small portal.

"OK, you come back in one hour—but no later," Valja replied. "And Mr. Ethan, don't get confused. This is not Greenland Place or Greenland Street."

"What are those?"

"Two other roads near here."

"All with the same name?"

"Velcome to England, sir!" Valja shrugged. "That is vhy the knowledge is important."

Ethan put his wallet in the front pocket of his jeans, reached down for his camera, and opened the cab door.

*****

"Are you all right?" Ethan said, looking critically at Collette.

She had a distinctly green pallor and seemed to be having a difficult time swallowing. She lied as she spoke. "Yes...fine. What the hell kind of place is this?"

"Hell may be the right word," Ethan said.

The World's End was stiflingly hot. The great square bar beneath the two-story atrium was surrounded by a sea of the most bizarre and eclectic people Ethan had ever seen. Neo-goths with their pale skin and black makeup mingled with gaunt, button-down-collar types, while punk rock refugees and a surprising number of middle-class women floated around the fringes of the crowd. There was a cloying odor in the air—a mixture of beer, sweat, liquor, and something indefinable which Ethan preferred not to guess. Music permeated the room, a slow but driving beat—sentimental in its melody, yet with surprisingly melancholy tones. The subwoofers were in overdrive, and the pounding of the beat felt as though it passed through him, threatening to shake his heart to pieces. It was compelling and depressing all at once.

"This way," Dr. Benoit said, leading them around the edge of the room toward a circular iron stairway. Paintings were everywhere on the walls, each with several patrons gazing at them intently. Ethan slipped past them, following Dr. Benoit, until he realized that Collette was no longer behind him. He stopped and turned to find her several steps behind him, staring open-mouthed at one of the paintings.

Ethan took several steps back to her side. She seemed to not notice his approach. "Collette?"

"It's…it's so sad," she said, unable to move her eyes away from the painting. "The expression on the father's face…the mother receding from the family not in death but emotionally…by her own choice…"

Ethan glanced at the painting.

It was a scene of insanity, a family being torn apart by the madness of the mother and her desire to drag her husband, sons, and daughters into the darkness with her.

And the figures in the painting were *moving*…

Ethan looked quickly away.

"Come on, my little art history major," Ethan said, gripping Collette by her shoulders and turning her away from the painting on the wall. "I think that's enough for now."

They climbed up the circular iron stairs to the landing overlooking the bar below. Mysteriously, the sounds of the bar from just a few feet below them were gone. Indeed, there was a quiet here that was unexpected. Three large, flat screen televisions flickered on the wall, though the sound was muted. Ethan was chagrined to see that one of the televisions was playing his own CNN International; the other two were tuned to BBC News and BBC Four.

The loft was far from empty. There were a great number of women and a few men who were all paying court to a handsome young man seated in a high-back chair at the far end of the area. Seeing Dr. Benoit, the young man's eyes brightened. He flicked his hand as he stood from the chair, and the assembled worshipers quickly dispersed, vanishing down the stairs and leaving the loft space deserted except for the young man and his new guests.

"Rene!" he said, holding his arms wide in welcome. He had a narrow face with striking features, his long hair parted down the middle, falling gracefully on both sides around a carefully manicured goatee. His purple shirt was open at the collar, its slightly puffy sleeves billowing from the sides of his carefully tailored waistcoat. His pants narrowed toward the cuff where they blended into his pointed-toe black boots. He was, to Ethan's eye, a ridiculous figure—overly romantic and dramatic. Still, it was a good image, he realized, so he raised his camera up to his eye, switching the power on.

"Joseph!" Benoit replied, stepping forward to embrace his friend.

"Damn!" Ethan swore as he recorded the scene.

Collette glanced over at Ethan. "What is it?"

Ethan pulled his camera away from his eye, holding it to his side so that Collette could see through the viewfinder.

"Hey," Collette frowned. "Where is he?"

"He's a vampire," Ethan huffed, then shouted at Dr. Benoit. "You brought us to see a *vampire*?"

The young man stepped back from his friend and held up a single finger as though to make a point. "Reformed!"

"A reformed…you're a 'reformed' vampire?" Ethan said in disbelief. "Just what the hell is that supposed to mean?"

"Well, for one, it means that I'm *not* some moldy old corpse who spends his days underground and only comes out to enjoy the nightlife," Joseph said, falling back to lounge in his chair, one leg hooked over the armrest. "All that nonsense is just Hollywood piffle."

"But not the hunt," Ethan said evenly. "Not the stalking of prey, the drinking of their blood, and the draining of their life."

"Oh, please," Joseph responded, as though he had just smelled something foul in the room. "That was *before*. We had to survive somehow when karma fled from the world. What choice did we have?"

"Sure," Ethan sneered. "Pity the poor monster— not his prey."

"Things are different now," Joseph insisted. "We don't need to feed on living blood any longer—well, except for occasional medicinal purposes or just to keep my teeth in, so to speak. There are far better ways we have today to get what we need—not nearly so crude or vulgar."

"You mean like those paintings downstairs," Collette said in realization.

"How perceptive of you, my dear!" Joseph said, smiling wide, his long canine teeth flashing. "Music, art, film, television, dance…they have all been used since time began to uplift spirits, inspire, and enlighten. But!" Joseph leaned forward in his chair, excited to speak. "If you twist it just right, turn it just so…the arts can be a wonderful tool for draining the spirits of mortals—especially powerful when they give it to me willingly."

Joseph, seeing the look on Collette's face, leaned back, his voice casual. "But you have no need to fear me, child. You're here with Rene and I'll not bother you. He has appealed to me to help you both, and so I shall, as is my magnanimous nature."

"Your magnanimous nature," Ethan said. "As a vampire?"

"Reformed!" Joseph noted once again. "All who come are members of our band, our Velvet Underground. Romantics, artists, poets—their sweet souls are all welcome here. I am the home they long for—a home only I can offer them."

"And will never provide," Ethan finished quietly. "Why do you bother watching the news, then?"

"Oh, *that*?" Joseph shrugged, gazing at the televisions fondly. "It's because I love a good fantasy story—don't you? I was watching just now about a publicity stunt at the National Gallery involving actors dressed as cadavers. Jonas Farben himself was there, commenting on the brilliance of the stunt—and how there was something *funny* about it."

Joseph's smile was full of sharp teeth.

"Come, my friends," Benoit said, gesturing toward a side door. "Why don't you wait in here while I finish making a few arrangements with Joseph. It will only be a few minutes, and then I can get you the answers to the questions you are asking."

"Sounds good," Ethan said with a sudden smile.

"Come on, Collette."

"What?" she squeaked.

"You heard the nice doctor," Ethan said, urging Collette toward the open door. "He'll take care of us…and give us the answers we're looking for."

Ethan and Collette stepped into the large, spacious office. The furniture was of supple leather and everything in it was perfectly arranged. Even the objects on the desk were carefully aligned.

"I'll be right back," Dr. Benoit said with a gentle smile as he closed the door behind him.

Ethan held his smile until he heard the latch on the door click home. At once he grabbed for the phone on the desk.

"Are you insane?" Collette said urgently.

"Damn! The phone's not working," Ethan said. He pulled out his cell phone. "Blocked signal. They want us trapped and quiet about it."

"What's the matter with you?" Collette continued. "We can't trust this Joseph guy! We should have gotten out of here while we had the chance."

"Have you ever fought a vampire, Collette?"

"Have I ever…?"

"I haven't either, but I did watch while one tore apart five Special Forces commandos without breaking a sweat," Ethan said, examining the room, looking for something…anything. "Everyone in that pub was in his control or thrall or whatever you call it. They seem to want us alive, or they would have done us in by now…but why?"

"Well, if we knew *that*, then we'd know what to bargain with. But since they haven't bothered to explain it to us..."

"Wait!" Ethan said. "Maybe they will."

Ethan held up his camera. The Sennheiser receiver was still attached. He switched the power on again, unspooled the earbud headphones from the back of the camera, and pressed one of them into his right ear, handing the left bud to Collette.

In their rush to escape the National Gallery, Ethan had not retrieved the lavalier microphone from Dr. Benoit's lapel.

It was transmitting with perfect digital clarity.

CHAPTER 8
MR. DEMISSIE

Sojourner Lee? It was Joseph's voice. *What was she doing at the Gallery?*

Causing me to lose one of my channeling pens. Benoit's voice this time, clearer and closer. *I suppose it was inevitable that she would make an appearance. She is a very old friend of ours.*

What did she want?

Why, to save us, of course.

Ethan glanced over at Collette. Of all things, she had taken out her notebook. Ethan shook his head, pointing down at the record light on the camera. Collette nodded and put her notepad back in her purse.

Truly? She thinks she can save you and me? The sound of a glass being set on a table carried with Joseph's voice.

Not you, Benoit said, *that cameraman in the office and me. Not even I recognized him at first. It was the artifact that called him out. He just couldn't resist it. What a stroke of luck that he should come to us first.*

I don't believe in luck.

You don't believe in anything.

Not entirely true, my friend. That is why I've called Mr. Demissie.

Mr. Demissie? Ethan could hear the rising tension in Benoit's voice. *Was that really necessary?*

Those were his instructions to me, and you should know better than to question him.

He's coming here?

I have already arrived.

Ethan and Collette looked at each other. This was a new voice. It was deeper and more resonant, despite being furthest from the lavalier microphone. There was a smoothness to its tones that made Ethan think of drowning in honey.

Mr. Demissie! Benoit chirped. *What an honor to see you again, sir.*

Perhaps so, Rene...we shall see, shall we not? The voice faded slightly as Demissie turned away from the microphone. *You were right to call me, Joseph.*

Tell us what you want done, Mr. Demissie—there was a groveling quality to the vampire's voice—*and we'll see to it at once.*

Get a car—a common sedan, if you can manage it— and a driver from among the comely of your minions. Rene and I will take—what name is he wearing now?

Ethan Gallows, Dr. Benoit responded.

Ethan Gallows? A good name.

He wears it well.

Then we shall take Ethan Gallows and the girl to the White Tower and down into the Chamber below. There, in the warm darkness of the taint, he shall forsake, forget, and surrender his will. Is there not comfort in that, Rene?

Yes, sir…but the Chamber of Sorrows itself?

What better place for the taint to embrace such an ancient wanderer? said the cloying voice of Mr. Demissie.

Ethan furrowed his brow. The White Tower was not only the centerpiece of the Tower of London, but the epicenter of all the bizarre happenings in England, and generally rumored to be the place from which all the world's eruption of magic and monsters originated. But "the taint"? "The Chamber of Sorrows"? These were new to him…and by the look on Collette's face, new to her as well.

Most puzzling of all to Ethan: why were they talking about *him*?

I'll have the pub cleared, Joseph said. *Most of them are heading to the Underworld anyway. What I don't understand is why take the girl? You could leave her here with me. I'd be happy to take her off your hands…*

She comes with me, Demissie said curtly.

But I don't see why…

Because you are two-year-olds who have found Daddy's guns and don't know better than to play with them. I'll put this to you in terms you will understand,

Demissie responded. *You weary me, and she will make a meal beyond the appreciation of your crude palate.*

Ethan stood up, facing Collette. "If we're not playing for the wrong team, we're definitely sitting on the wrong side of the field."

"Is there a *right* side of the field?" Collette asked.

"The enemy of my enemy is my friend?" Ethan shrugged.

"Well, that would be the witch that got us into this mess in the first place," Collette said. "If you're suggesting that we go looking for that bleach-haired woman who sent plastic cadavers after us…"

"Where's her card?" Ethan asked suddenly.

"What?"

"Her card…the one she gave you at the Gallery. Where is it?"

Collette started patting down her jacket, stopped, and then pulled the card out of her pocket. She looked at it and groaned. "I'll say this for her: she has a sense of humor."

Ethan took the card from Collette. It was a standard business-sized card printed on both sides. On one side it read "Chance." On the back, it featured a small illustration of a familiar round-headed man with a handlebar mustache in a morning coat leaping out of a pit of fire. The text next to the image read "Get Out of Hell Free Card. Discard to Play."

Ethan handed the card back to Collette. "Great. Look, we can't get into that car with them. Valja should still be waiting for us outside the pub."

"If he didn't just run off with the fare!"

"Just be ready…if we have to make a break for it, we can't hesitate. If we get split up, find a way back to the London Bureau offices and I'll meet you as soon as…"

Ethan heard the lock on the door click. He reached over at once and switched off the camera, the ear-buds reeling into the back automatically, and set it on the desk.

The door to the office opened. Ethan turned with dread to face what was coming into the room.

At first, he almost laughed in his disappointment and relief. An entirely nondescript man wearing a grey suit entered the room. He wore a striped tie over a white button-down shirt. The grey suit was well-cut but not particularly well-tailored, with only the vague suggestion of a pinstripe in its fabric. His shirt cuffs extended a proper quarter inch beyond those of his coat. His shoes had only a dull polish to them.

Ethan studied the man's face—or tried to do so, but found he was frustrated in his attempt. The man was just tan-skinned enough that he could have been of almost any ethnicity. He was clean shaven, his hair neatly cut and trimmed above the ears, but the cut was generic, as though he had gone to any one of a dozen franchise hairstyling places and never paid more than ten dollars for a trim. He was not particularly hand-some, nor was he homely. His eyes were a cloudy grey color, but even that seemed to shift slightly de-pending on the light. His features had a strangely soft quality, as though he were slightly out of focus. The most remarkable thing about him was that there was absolutely nothing remarkable about him.

Ethan was accustomed, as part of his job, to seek out the unique features that appear in everyone's face—either to bring out its uniqueness or to cover it up to make a better shot. But this person had no distinguishing characteristics, even to Ethan's trained eye. He was the most common individual Ethan had ever encountered. But it was this very commonness that made Ethan distinctly uncomfortable. He could be any one of millions of faceless corporate or government bureaucrats one might meet anywhere in the world—at once familiar, yet distant, and in every way forgettable.

A chill ran through Ethan. There was something terribly wrong about a man who was completely nothing.

"Please pardon my intrusion," said the man in grey, nodding his head slightly toward them. "My name is Mr. Demissie. I'm with the government. Dr. Benoit called me and asked that I assist you at once."

Mr. Demissie held out his hand.

Ethan cautiously took it.

In a flash, a totality of nothingness, horrible in its void, filled him. It washed over him like a nihilistic tide, threatening to drown his own existence. Horrible shapes formed in the emptiness, coalescing into the blank face of Demissie standing before him.

Ethan withdrew his hand.

"How kind of him," Ethan said evenly, "considering we just met today."

"Ah, but you are wrong there," said Demissie, his dark voice pouring over them. "We've all known each other a very long time. You just don't remember. But that is part of why I am here—to help you remember."

"I don't know you, man," Ethan shook his head as he picked up his camera.

"But you will."

Demissie gestured for them to move through the open door of the office. Ethan put an arm around Collette's shoulders as they passed through the door and back onto the loft space overlooking the bar. As they had heard, the entire place that had been packed less than half an hour before was now completely empty. Only Joseph and Dr. Benoit remained, both standing near the circular iron staircase.

Collette suddenly spoke. "Where are you taking us?"

Mr. Demissie gazed at the woman as though she were a child interrupting the adults in conversation. "Why, I never said I was taking you anywhere…but as you ask, we will be transporting you to a secure government facility. You'll be safe there while we sort all of this out."

"I appreciate the offer," Ethan said, pulling Collette closer to his side. "But I think we've had a long day. We'll just go back to our hotel and call it a night."

"Ah, but that is where you are wrong." Demissie closed the door of the office and turned to face Ethan. "As you have been wrong about so many things, Ethan Gallows. You've been running all your life, but now—*now*, my old friend—it is time to stop running at last. It is time for you to rest."

"Sounds nice," Ethan said and turned toward Collette. He pressed his face into her hair next to her ear. She squirmed against the implied intimacy, but Ethan held her firmly in his grip.

"Play the card," he whispered.

"What?" she whispered back. They were nearing the stairs.

"Toss it…toss the card now!"

Collette reached down into the side pocket of her jacket. They were at the top of the stairs, Dr. Benoit and Joseph in front of them with Mr. Demissie right behind.

Collette pulled the card out with her fingers and flicked it away over the iron railing. The card spun in the air out into the atrium space over the bar.

Joseph saw it. He cried out, lunging forward, "No! Not here!"

The card exploded with a deep thrumming sound into a blazing, brilliant miniature sun. The light filled every corner of the pub in a shining, pulsing radiance that was completely without heat.

Ethan instinctively turned away from the light. Behind him, he heard an unearthly, high-pitched scream—a sound which passed through his heart with deadly cold, dragging all warmth from his bones.

He had never wanted to get away from anything so badly in his life. He shouted both to himself and to Collette, "Go! Go! Go!"

Ethan reached out with his left arm, wrapping it firmly around Collette's back at the waist. He lunged forward toward the stairs, nearly impossible to see in the blistering light. They ran into Dr. Benoit, and Ethan felt more than saw the man tumble over the railing of the staircase. He would concern himself with that later, he thought; all that mattered was that their way was cleared. He nearly stumbled on the tight spiral of the stairs but kept his feet under him. He and Collette dashed toward the main doors and burst out onto Camden High Street.

Ethan looked around frantically, trying to get his bearings. Though it was late evening, the central thoroughfares were eerily deserted.

"This way!" he shouted, pulling Collette to their left and turning the corner onto Greenland Road.

There, sitting in the loading zone, was a black London cab.

Relief flooded through Ethan as they dashed up to the cab, looking intently at the driver.

"Vell, hello and velcome back, Ethan Gallows!" Valja smiled. "As promised, Valja vaits for you."

Ethan glanced back up at the façade of The World's End. A flashing pillar of light still shone through the glass atrium above the bar and into the clouds overhead. He opened the door for Collette and followed her in at once. "Thank God you're here!"

"Yes, I vill gladly pass along your recommendation," Valja laughed.

"We're off, Valja!" Ethan urged, settling into the back seat of the cab and patting his camera. "Turner House at 16 Great Marlborough Street."

"The Bureau?" Collette sighed.

"I've got some footage for the uplink." Ethan smiled.

But the cab was not moving.

"Valja," Ethan said, leaning forward. "Let's go!"

The huge cab driver held still, turning his head slightly to reply. "Patience one moment. I must wait for the rest of my fare."

"Rest of your fare?" Ethan sputtered. "What are you—"

The cab door opened again.

Dr. Rene Benoit flew head first into the cab, landing with a dull thud on the floor.

He was immediately followed by a long, shapely leg. A moment later, a tall, graceful figure had slipped into the cab and slammed the door behind her.

"Now we can go!" Valja said as the cab roared into the night.

Ethan could only stare.

Sitting on the fold-down seat in front of them, the stiletto heel of her left boot firmly planted in the middle of Benoit's back, was Sojourner Lee.

"I don't suppose we're going back to Turner House," Ethan said, his mouth dry.

"No," replied Sojourner, her gaze as cool as frost. "Not hardly."

CHAPTER 9
NOT BROTHERS

"Park Crescent at Portland Place, Valja," Sojourner said through the opening in the plexiglass, though her eyes shifted only between Ethan and the gasping figure of Dr. Benoit beneath her heel. "How long?"

"Is not long," Valja replied cheerfully. "Traffic is not so much tonight. Few minutes…no more. Did you search Dr. Benoit for more toys?"

"I did," Sojourner nodded, the corners of her brilliant violet eyes turned downward in a sleepy sadness, her small, bowed mouth in a frown. Dr. Benoit drew his hands up under him, trying to push himself up from the floor, but the white-haired young woman dug the tip of her stiletto heel into his back, forcing him to collapse again to the floor with a sharp cry of pain.

"What do you want with Dr. Benoit?" Collette blurted out. Her tone was tinged with false bravado.

Ethan quickly reached over with his hand and grabbed Collette's knee. The shock of it had his desired effect: it rendered her momentarily too embarrassed and surprised to speak.

"Now, Collette, let's not bother the nice lady who animates the dead," Ethan said with studied casualness. "If she has a problem with museum curators who associate with vampires and men in grey suits, I think we should just ask politely to get out of the cab and walk away from something that really isn't any of our business."

"None of your business, Ethan?" said Sojourner, the corner of her mouth twitching with the hint of an inner smile. "How very unlike you. You were always the one who was engaged with every cause, regardless of the odds. I'm sorry to see you so changed, but it does not matter. It has become your business now—it has become all of our business now."

"I suppose we are your hostages. What are your demands?" Collette asked. "Ouch! Ethan, stop that!"

"My demands?" Sojourner asked, arching a pencil-thin eyebrow.

"Yes, your demands," Collette continued. "You've kidnapped all of us. It's obvious that you've targeted Dr. Benoit. Politics? Extortion? What is it your organization is after?"

Sojourner Lee smiled with genuine amusement. "So you think we are terrorists?"

"Nearly there," Valja said from the front of the

cab. They were driving along the most aptly named Park Crescent, a road that made a great, symmetrical curve to the right around a large park with a beautiful building of cream marble and ornamental columns following the arc of the road on the left.

"There they are," Sojourner said. "Put in behind them on the left."

Valja put in just behind another black London cab parked and apparently waiting for them at the curb. Two large men in black t-shirts emerged from the car as they came to a halt.

"This is your stop, Miss Montrose," Sojourner said, opening the cab door on the left side toward the curb.

"No," Collette said, holding her ground.

Sojourner's eyebrow rose again in condescending surprise. "Did you say something?"

"I said we're not going," Collette said, planting her feet apart and crossing her arms over her chest. "If my brothers taught me anything, it was never to go anywhere with anyone until you knew who they were and what they—"

Sojourner rolled her eyes up in exasperation. "Very well, if you insist. As you have brilliantly surmised, we are terrorists, Miss Montrose: evil, evil terrorists with terrible, story-worthy demands of the most lurid fiction you can devise. You have found us out. I will foolishly tell you our demands which you will convey to the authorities and, no doubt, put on your news broadcast as some sort of special bulletin. You, Miss

Montrose, will be the link between us and the outside world and at the very center of this ridiculous tale starting immediately. Satisfied?"

"What?" Collette looked as though she had swallowed her gum. "Now?"

"We will call you on your phone in exactly," Sojourner looked at the large-faced watch on her right wrist, "twelve hours and thirty-seven minutes. We have multiple explosive devices rigged in highly populated areas all around the city," Sojourner continued as Collette grabbed for her notepad and hurriedly began writing. "These locations have all been determined from an ancient formula which I have brilliantly discovered based on mystical symbols found in Lord Nelson's column, Big Ben Tower, and the Greenwich Observatory. If we discover you have not waited for twelve hours for my call, we will detonate these devices causing massive death and destruction—which will all be your fault."

Collette's notebook was open but shaking so badly that Ethan wondered whether any of her notes on this would make sense. "My fault?"

"Yes. These two…henchmen…I will foolishly reveal as being called Uriah and Gideon. They will take you to—where did you say?—oh, yes, Turner House, and leave you there with the rest of the myth-makers. Your cameraman will stay with me to record and deliver our manifesto…"

"No!" Collette said even as the henchman named Uriah was reaching into the cab through the open door and taking a firm hold of her arm. "Ethan! Tell her! I've got to stay with you. You *need* me!"

"Go on, Collette," Ethan said quietly. *One of us needs to get out of here alive.* "I'll be fine."

"No!" Collette wailed, struggling with little effect against the large man dragging her out of the cab. "This is wrong! You don't know anything about these people yet...you don't know if they can be trusted! You *need* me here..."

Henchman Gideon slammed the door of the cab shut as Uriah dragged her to their waiting vehicle. In moments the second cab was rushing away, Collette's urgent face pressed against the back glass.

Valja put their cab in gear once more and continued driving around Park Crescent. He turned right onto Marylebone and crossed the park to the east, continuing until the road became Euston. They entered a canyon of modern high-rise buildings.

Ethan looked out the window. They had just passed the British Library and were coming in front of St. Pancras International Station, its Victorian façade all but hiding the enclosed platform yard. Just beyond, Ethan could see the twin glassed-in arches of King's Cross Station. He remembered that Harry Potter always left for Hogwarts from King's Cross Station. He wondered what J.K. Rowling thought of the world in which they now lived.

They never reached King's Cross, however, as Valja slowed the cab on Euston Road and pulled into the turning lane for Belgrove Street. The car waited

momentarily for a pair of oncoming vehicles—a
London cab and a lorry—before lurching down the
side street and quickly coming to a stop in front of
the neat but otherwise undistinguished face of the
Belgrove Hotel.

"After you, Ethan," Sojourner said, with a gesture
of her long, ivory hand.

Valja opened the door, and Ethan stepped onto the
curb. He gazed up at the innocuous-looking hotel.

"I apologize for accommodations!" Valja said.

"I've been in worse," Ethan replied, trying to take
in the street around him. Though he could see several figures standing under the streetlamps on both
corners of Euston Street, and more down the road,
the streets were nearly deserted. The men appeared
casual, but Ethan caught furtive glances in their direction. They were doing their best to blend in and
look disinterested, but it was obvious to Ethan that
the street was being watched. Two men with arms
as thick as thighs stood on either side of the hotel
stairs.

"These are our guardians," Sojourner said to Ethan
as she emerged from the back of the cab. Behind her,
Valja was dragging Dr. Benoit from the floor of the
cab, twisting his arm behind him, his hand gripping
the elder curator's throat.

Sojourner walked up the steps between the spear-
headed wrought-iron railings on either side, her
heels clicking on the cement squares of the sidewalk.
"Follow me."

"What was all that nonsense about?" Ethan asked. "That bull you handed Collette back there?"

Sojourner turned slowly at the top of the short flight of stairs. The lit entrance through the open door behind her cast her in silhouette as she offered a cold smile. "The truth is so much harder to believe than a story, Ethan. I told her what she wanted to hear: a nice, scary little bedtime fable. You're a television journalist. Isn't myth-making what you do every day? Isn't that what sells?"

"Sojourner," Ethan said quietly, "don't try to sell me. Who are you? Why are we here?"

"The real issue here is who *you* really are." The tall woman drew in a deep breath. "And believe me, Ethan…you are here because we need you."

"And why do you need me?" Ethan asked.

"Because what's going on here isn't a crime," Sojourner said. "It's a rescue."

"Rescuing whom?" Ethan asked.

But Sojourner had already passed through the door.

Valja, with Dr. Benoit still firmly in hand, nodded for Ethan to follow.

*****

They passed the front desk. There was no one on duty. Indeed, they saw no one at all in the small foyer. No one came out of the tiny elevator that barely held them all at once, either. Nor was there anyone in the narrow third-floor hallway where there was barely enough room for two of them to stand side by side.

"It was fortunate that Valja was able to pick you up," Sojourner said as she pulled out an enormous old-fashioned room key from her coat pocket. "He had instructions to follow you once you arrived at Heathrow. That he was able to take you as a fare was a stroke of fate. You hiring him for the day was beyond our hopes, since he was able to let us know to find you at The World's End."

"So he told you where we were," Ethan said.

"Yes," she replied. "I am beginning to think that fate may be one of your talents, Ethan. Time will tell."

"The card you gave us…"

"Oh, *that*," Sojourner smiled as the key grated into the old door lock. "Just an edge if you needed it. There is a war going on, Ethan, a quiet war that the world is trying hard to ignore. Everything depends upon its outcome—everything—and we have to fight this conflict with whatever weapons we may find. Never go into battle unarmed or unprepared. Never give quarter. Never, ever, underestimate the cunning power and insidious nature of the taint."

"The taint?" Ethan asked.

Sojourner turned the key and the lock clacked open. "It is the opposite of karma—the positive magic at the heart of the world's life and soul. Taint is a corruption, a pollution, the result of improper manipulation of karma. It is a disease poisoning the world. Both have been sleeping down through the millennia. Now both have awakened, and the final conflict for the world has begun."

"Armageddon?" Ethan scoffed.

"Armageddon. End of Days. Ragnarök. Day of Judgment." Sojourner shrugged. "Choose whatever name you like."

"What has any of this to do with me?" Ethan asked as Sojourner opened the door and stepped into the small suite.

Ethan noted that it did, technically, qualify as a suite, but the rooms that comprised it were so small as to be more like a single room cut up by too many walls. There was a window in the opposite wall looking out onto the street below. There was a small couch with a floral pattern to one side of the room and a pair of chairs, one in front of the window.

Seated in the chair by the window was a young, short teenage male with closely cropped, straight black hair and dark brown skin. Ethan guessed he was either Filipino or Malaysian by the look of him. It was difficult to tell, as his features were obscured by duct tape over his mouth, his hands tied behind the back of the chair and his ankles tied together and to the back legs of the chair.

"What the hell is going on here?" Ethan asked as he stepped into the room.

The Asian youth looked up with dark chocolate eyes as Ethan stared at him. Valja pushed Dr. Benoit past both Ethan and Sojourner, releasing the curator and propelling him slightly into the end of the room near the tied up young man. Dr. Benoit turned at once, reaching inside his sports jacket. He seemed to fumble about his pockets for a moment. In frustration, he dropped his hands.

"Need a pen, Rene?" the woman asked through a thin smile.

"It will never work, Sojourner!" Dr. Benoit raved, running his fingers back through his grey hair. He stared in hatred toward them through his round-rimmed glasses. "The taint comes like a tide without an ebb. It tears down the walls of an unjust domination and breaks the shackles that have been slowly choking the life out of free men for ages beyond memory! The taint will free me and everyone like me, clawing the scales from our eyes and liberating us from your false laws, morality, and ethics! Time is my ally—and what precious little is left to you is fading fast. You think this little mystic room of yours will stop the taint? Run while you can, Sojourner— you and all your kind. You only provide us with amusement as you try to avoid the madness that will inevitably take you!"

Sojourner stood still, her imperious features unmoved. "It is madness that I am trying to cure, Rene."

Ethan stepped forward toward the young man in the chair.

"I wouldn't do that if I were you," Sojourner said with a quiet smile just as Ethan reached out suddenly, ripping the tape from the youth's mouth.

"*Oweh!*" the teenager cried out. His eyes darted about as he spoke, a torrent of words erupting from him. "*Tolonglah! Tuan, saya nggak tau apa sebabnya orang-orang ini memberikan saya kesini! Munkin saja untuk mematikan saya langsung! Tolonglah memerdekakan saya dan tonong saya kembali ke tana-air ku langsung dan saya akan berikan kepada anda satu harganya yang besar sekali!*"

"He doesn't stop vonce you get him started," Valja said with a laugh, as though this were all just a game.

Ethan held up his hand in front of the teen. "Wait! Do you speak English?"

"*Saya tidak akan berbicara dalam bahasa ingris dehadapan orang-orang ini!*"

"Great!" Ethan said, tossing his hands up in front of him in frustration. "This is pointless!"

"No," Valja said. "It is everything. Three of you together is everything if there is any hope."

"Really?" Ethan said, standing up as the anger rose in him. "Why?"

"Because," Sojourner said, "the three of you are brothers."

Ethan cocked his head to one side in disbelief. "Brothers?"

"Yes," Sojourner said. "Brothers."

Ethan was suddenly convinced that someone in the room was absolutely nuts. "A black cameraman from Washington...a magic-wielding French antiques nut job...and an Asian kid who doesn't speak

English…and we're *brothers*? I think I like that nonsense story you told Collette better…"

"It is a story," Sojourner said, "and a very old one. You have just forgotten it, is all."

"I've *forgotten* it?" Ethan scoffed.

"You forgot this, too," Sojourner said, reaching into the pocket of her coat. "You left it at the Gallery."

Her creamy hand flicked out of the pocket, tossing a small object in Ethan's direction. Instinctively he reached up to catch it.

His hand closed around the small bronze figure of the winged man.

Once again, an unbidden vision bloomed in his mind.

CHAPTER 10
THE GATHERING

G reetings, Abraxas," the fae woman said, her high-pitched voice cutting across the rumble of destruction permeating the air. The winged bronze figure hanging about her neck shifted slightly at her throat. "It has been a long time."

"Not nearly long enough, Andretsanya," the great dragon roared. The flame of karma, perhaps the last that was his to command, roiled between his claws. "What treachery is this at the end of the world, Apogean? We come at your summons and you show us a thief?"

"No, Abraxas!" the Grand Master Priest cried out, raising both his hands in supplication to the enraged creature. "Tsanya has come to help you."

"Help me?" Abraxas sneered, baring his long, sharp teeth. "She stole that very icon from my horde—and all its memories with it!"

"And what use might a dragon's memories be to the fae?" Tsanya shouted back. *"They were put to better use, perhaps, than you deserve...but there is no more time! We must leave now!"*

"I would rather die here than save you," Abraxas bellowed.

"It is the death of dragons that we are trying to prevent," Tsanya shouted back. *"The Seelie Courts have found a way that you and we together might survive—but we need your help as much as you need ours."*

The fire in Abraxas's claw grew brighter, stronger, and more threatening.

"The world will die if we do not act," Tsanya said. *"Will the great Abraxas destroy the life of all the world for his own pride?"*

The dragon reared back his head, trumpeting toward the orange underbelly of a lowered sky. The fireball in his claw vanished in a clap of thunder. Abraxas fell forward on all fours, his head coming within a few feet of the cloaked Seelie female and the priest.

"What must be done, Apogean?" Abraxas asked.

"You must take Tsanya with you—you and your two brothers," the priest said quickly. *"Fly northward, beyond the boundaries of Pythia and the Kurgan Tribes. There on Mount Olygeas you will meet your help to carry you on to the Midgard."*

"Midgard?" Apalala snorted. *"The Seelie lands? Why doesn't she just ask us to leave her at Tír na nÓg!"*

"*Everything depends upon this!*" Apogean screamed in sudden rage. "*Tsanya will tell you the rest…now go!*"

"We came to save you, Apogean," Abraxas said.

"*And you will, my friend,*" the priest said, tears drawing streaks down his soot-smudged face. "*Go. Go!*"

Abraxas eyed Tsanya, then lowered his head to the ground. The Seelie female quickly climbed up the side scales, settling her legs across the dragon's back just ahead of the wing roots and behind the shoulder ridge. Abraxas drew back his lips. The female had ridden dragons before.

"Until the dawn, my old friend," Abraxas said to Apogean.

"However long the night," the priest replied. "Farewell until the dawn."

Abraxas threw open his enormous wings, drawing them downward with his remaining strength. He slowly rose above Apogean, the other Seelie, the temple, and the mountaintop, with Apalala and Fafnir rising into the smoke-choked air behind him. His flight was just easing on his third downstroke when the foundations of the mountain shattered below him. The great temple atop the mountain dissolved into dust, fire, and smoke, sliding sideways into the raging sea.

Then the clouds surrounded Abraxas and his brothers as they climbed higher, veiling their eyes from the wracked agony of the world below.

*****

"What place is that?" Abraxas asked in quiet respect.

"Ask me what it was," Tsanya said into the chill wind.

They stood next to the remains of a glacial lake. Fafnir had asked to stop and drink of its waters, their throats parched from the dry skies and ash. They had landed only to find that the foundations of the mountain had tilted, its peak had vanished and been replaced by fire spewing from its summit. The lake had largely drained, but enough of its waters remained to douse the thirst they all felt. Rivers of fire moved down the mountain. One tendril passed down the gorge they saw below them, winding into the city that stood—or had once stood—at its feet.

The entire city was engulfed in flame.

"What was it, then?" Abraxas asked.

"In the time before the Kurgan tribes came to our land, we called it Novana. It was part of Arcadia not six hundred years before. A beautiful city—nothing to compare to Atlantis or any of the greater human cities—but it had a beauty of wood and stone craft that was elegant and compelling all at the same time."

"You have been there, then?"

"It was my home."

Tsanya turned away, looking up the steep mountainside to its fire-gushing summit. "The mountain will change again. The column of fire will collapse, *and death more terrible than any we have seen will descend down the mountainside. We must not be here when that happens."*

"Where then can we go?" Fafnir asked, standing at the edge of the nearly drained lake. "The world is truly ending. The very magic that sustains us is fleeing from the world."

"We should face our enemy," Apalala said with fierce conviction. "If we cannot outrun or outfly the death throes of our world, then we must confront the power that cuts at the throat of all creation!"

"To do so we must confront ourselves," Tsanya said bitterly. "The karma that wells up from the world was a blessing, and was kept in balance when we respected it—and you three dragons do, by all accounts. But where there is power, there is the potential for advantage. At the root of it all were those of our respective races who did not respect the power that they wielded any more than they respected our brothers and sisters around us. We used the karma to bend reality to our will—and our will was all too often selfish and prideful. Reality itself was twisted with too much force until it snapped, and the taint slowly crept through the cracks into our world.

"The Seelie have heard rumors that several of the high level wizards in old Avalon were planning some great spell to push the taint from the world. Others said that the spell was to elevate the taint...triumph in its darkness at the banishment of karma."

"The dragons learned of this, too. Could such a

terrible spell have gone wrong? Causing the end of the world?" Fafnir asked.

"Perhaps," Tsanya replied. "But one spell alone—no matter the darkness of the wizard's heart who wrought it—would not be enough to tear down the world. I have heard reports that many of your own kind—dragons who had learned of this terrible incantation—had rushed to stop it. Perhaps they failed—or perhaps their success caused this; who can say? It does not matter now. That one spell, regardless of the power of its wizards, would not have brought down the world. No, we are all to blame for centuries of bending the world to our will against the nature of its foundations. We are all responsible in some measure for the taint and the weakening of the world that brought us to this final, terrible day."

"You are quite a philosopher for a thief."

Tsanya turned to face the towering dragon. "And the day may yet come when you thank me for my skills in taking from your horde, great Abraxas."

"Should there be another day," Apalala said.

"There may well not be unless we act," Tsanya said. "So let us speak of the death of dragons. What happens when a dragon dies, Fafnir?"

The dragon snorted a puff of smoke from his nostrils. "The body dies and rots back into the earth."

"And the soul?"

"The soul is of karma," Fafnir replied, shrugging his massive shoulders. "It is re-formed of the elements within the brood clutch of eggs and reborn anew."

"But in its rebirth the dragon's mind is clear—a clean slate as yet unwritten. The soul of the dragon remains asleep within the new, young dragon—its memories lost to it. Tell me, Great Abraxas of Trocea," Tsanya demanded, "why your horde—or that of any dragon—is so important?"

Abraxas pulled his head back, his great eyes narrowing beneath his bony brow. "The horde is the repository of a dragon's greatest wealth."

"Which is?"

"The dragon's former thoughts, his memories, and his experiences," Abraxas rumbled. "The objects are imbued with the dragon's past. A young dragon is drawn to its former horde so that it may remember again who it is and who it has been in countless lives before." The great dragon's nostrils flared. "To take something from a dragon's horde is to steal not just treasure but knowledge, wisdom, and a connection with his former lives. It takes a part of his soul."

"Which is why I came and took this from you," Tsanya said, touching the winged icon hanging just below her throat. "We, too, are creatures of karma—our immortal bodies and souls are bound inexorably to its force. Like you, the end of karma means that death—the true death of mortals—will fall upon us, and where our souls will go then, we have not been able to know."

"Then death has come to claim us?" Fafnir asked.

"No," Tsanya said. "I have come to offer you and your kind a hope. Thanks to your borrowed treasure, *we have discovered how we might create scions."*

"'Scions'?" Apalala repeated.

"Meaning what?" Abraxas sneered.

"We are going to preserve life," Tsanya snapped. "We have found a way to graft the souls of noble dragons and Seelie into the race of men."

"You are insane!" Abraxas asserted.

"Listen to me!" Tsanya pleaded. "We have debated long on this course, and it is not lightly taken. Man is short-lived and disposed to selfishness, cruelty, and temper—but they are proven survivors. Of all the races across Erebea, only man is assured to survive the coming night…a night without karma or taint that will last millennia on end. Your souls—the seeds of who you are—will pass from father to son, from mother to daughter—sleeping within the scions born of mortality and grafted within their lives. Your sleep will be troubled; not all of you will survive the journey down the centuries. But one day the foundations of the world will turn again, karma will return, and with it your souls will be awakened."

"We would be children," Apalala scoffed. "Mortal! Vulnerable!"

"We would not know ourselves," Abraxas said. "All that we are or have ever been would be forgotten."

"Yes," Tsanya said, looking away, back down the mountain, toward the fires of the city far below them. "But one day there would come a rebirth and an awakening. The light of karma would again rise above the horizon of the world."

"And the taint," Fafnir said. *"It, too, would return."*

"Yes," Tsanya agreed. *"Which is why you must be there to stop it when it does."*

"You ask us to pass through a nightmare from which we might never awaken," Abraxas said, shaking his head.

"It is a long journey, indeed, Great Abraxas of Trocea," Tsanya said. *"It is a journey that not all of you can survive."*

"Are there others?"

"Many others...from different broods," Tsanya said quickly. *"But I have come for you, Abraxas— you and your brothers."*

Abraxas gazed for a time in silence at the Seelie female.

"How does this profit the Seelie?" he asked at last.

"I don't know what you..."

"The Seelie do not do this thing for the sake of the dragons," Abraxas said, his voice shaking the ground. *"How does this benefit the Summer Court?"*

"We will need you in that future time, Abraxas," Tsanya said. *"Should you awaken and dragons again come into the world, we will need your help."*

"Our help...to do what?"

"To find our way back into the world," Tsanya said simply. *"The Courts are removing to Tír na nÓg before the karma in the world falls. There, the fae will be beyond the circles of the mortal realms. Only a handful of us will stay here, sleeping through the*

ages as you will, hidden among the souls of men. When you awake to your true nature within the scions who walk the earth in that future time, we will need you to help us forge a gate, a path, a bridge back home for the fae to return to the world."

The mountain shook beneath them.

The three dragons and the faery woman looked up. The top of the mountain exploded, with great shoots of fire and rock arcing away from the summit. The edges of the peak began to shift.

"It is a chance," Fafnir said to his brother dragons.

"It is a hope," Abraxas answered.

He lowered his head down, leaning it toward Tsayna. The faerie woman smiled with relief as she once again quickly clamored up to sit on the back of the dragon's neck.

Abraxas pushed off from what had once been a beautiful alpine bowl, gliding down the face of the mountain, his brothers behind him off either wing. Gathering speed, they soared upward, just as the mountain collapsed behind them, its searing hot ash driving down the mountain toward Novana. Anyone who had survived in the city had but moments left to live.

The world was coming apart beneath them as Abraxas and his brother dragons wheeled to the northwest and began beating their wings toward the lands of Pythia and the lost lands of the Arcadian Alps.

There they would find Mount Olygeas...and their fate.

CHAPTER 11
GREY GENTLEMEN

Ethan dropped the figurine. The world of the present flooded back as the small statue bounced on the thin carpet at his feet.

Sojourner reached down quickly, snapping up the bronze figure and slipping it into the pocket of her coat. Her violet eyes blazed. "Welcome back, Ethan Gallows."

"Nice to be back," Ethan said carefully. He was keenly aware that he was sweating profusely, and wished with all his soul that this woman didn't see it. "I'd be interested to know just what brew of chemicals you've been using to coat that bronze in your pocket. I'll bet it could fetch a good street price in some urban areas. It's got quite a kick."

Sojourner shook her head. "Still enjoy playing the skeptic, do you, Ethan? Hiding from the world behind your camera, never participating or taking responsibility for what you see through that lens of yours—all very convenient and easy on the ethics. But now I'm afraid the time for such luxuries has passed. We've got a job to do—all of us—and we need you and Rudi here," she pointed to the bound teenager, "to manage it."

"Sorry," Ethan shrugged. "I've already got a job, and by the looks of your friend tied to that chair over there, he's not going to be much help to you, either."

Sojourner's coifed hair bounced slightly as she laughed. "You were always this stubborn. Lucky, continually. Adaptive, certainly. But stubborn was your defining characteristic."

"As though you know nothing about stubborn," Dr. Benoit snarled. "You will walk into your own grave for spite."

"Cheerful to the last," Sojourner answered with a tight smile.

"So can we get down to it?" Ethan asked. "What do you want?"

"I want to help you fulfill an old promise, Ethan," Sojourner replied. "And a destiny."

"I'm not interested in destiny," Ethan said, shaking his head. "My own or anyone else's."

"It won't matter," Dr. Benoit said through a grin. "They're nearly here now anyway. They are trying to warn you, Ethan, but you will not listen. It won't be long."

Sojourner cocked her head to one side as though listening. "He's right. They're coming."

"For dinner, I suppose?" Ethan commented dryly.

"And you're the main course," Sojourner responded. She moved to the window, looking down the street below. "The Grey Gentlemen—they're sweeping the city."

"And I take it that is *bad*?" Ethan quipped.

"You met Mr. Demissie earlier tonight," Sojourner shot back. "He is one of the Grey Gentlemen—the human disguise too often adopted by Those Who Dwell Below. What did you think of him?"

Ethan shuddered. "I couldn't stand being near him. When he shook my hand—"

"What?" Sojourner looked at Ethan in open astonishment. "You mean you actually *touched* him?"

"I've never experienced anything so horrible in my life." Ethan grimaced.

Sojourner's face twisted into a crooked smile. "You don't like being touched, do you, Ethan? I mean, brushing against other people's clothing doesn't bother you, but skin to skin with strangers upsets you, doesn't it?"

"It's not a problem," Ethan answered. "It's a quirk, is all. Most of the time it doesn't even bother me."

"I know," Sojourner said, walking slowly toward Ethan. "I feel the same way. It's a good thing, too, Ethan…because the last thing either of us want is to be found by those Grey Gentlemen. And you're going to help us get past them."

"Me?" Ethan asked.

"Sorry," Sojourner said. "Like it or not, you're going

to have to wake up now, friend—as in *right now*."

With that Sojourner reached out and clasped both her hands around Ethan's.

*****

Abraxas stood gazing toward the opposite side of the reflecting pool, considering the form of Adalinda.

The sight of two dragons standing on either side of the great pool in the center of Atlantis under the warm midday sun would have been a cause for concern, had either of them retained their true forms. Both of them had been summoned by Apogean and the temple priests to compete for the position of Guardian; now they were awaiting the council's decision and—more problematic still—the blessing of the Sun-King.

So, as both were talented form shifters, they had adopted the guise of humans, willing their shapes to collapse into the more common shapes of Atlantean citizens, and had decided to pass the afternoon's wait by visiting the stalls and shops that lined the great wall surrounding the pool.

Adalinda was watching Abraxas as well, a wry smile on her beautiful face—or what passed for beautiful among humans. She set down the beads she had been examining at a vendor's stall and strolled across one of the bridges toward Abraxas.

"You wear that look well," Adalinda called to him as she approached.

"As do you," Abraxas replied. "Perhaps you

should keep it."

Adalinda smiled. Her skin was pale for most humans, and her horns had been transformed into a shockingly white color, but the gown she had chosen was a vibrant violet to match her eyes. *"Thank you, but I'll not be needing it once I am appointed Guardian. Look at you, however. Have you seen yourself in the pool, or did you fall in trying?"*

"So I look that good, do I?" Abraxas asked, folding his massive human-shaped arms across his broad chest.

"Oh, yes," Adalinda cooed in jest. *"I'm all in a swoon...and just whose form did you steal?"*

"I borrowed this form from a warrior in Avalon," Abraxas said with a slight bow. *"Touched him before battle, gratefully—or, I must say, the form would not have turned out nearly so well afterward."*

"Only once?" Adalinda remarked. *"I am impressed, Abraxas. Your talents as a shape adapter are formidable indeed. Should I need a comely escort to the Sun-King's Ball, I should be delighted to bestow the honor on this form of Abraxas."*

"I regret that I may not be available," Abraxas answered.

"And why not?"

"Because as Guardian," Abraxas answered through a wide human grin, *"I would be on duty. But until that day, would you do me a favor?"*

"You?" Adalinda chuckled. *"And just what sort of a favor did you have in mind?*

"Would you show me how you form that hair of yours to look so perfect?" Abraxas asked, running his large hand through his rough hair. *"I always have trouble with the hair."*

*****

They came down the street as one—a line of grey-suited men swaying back and forth with each step. The line stretched east to west across the city, moving down every alley, opening every door, and passing through every room. Couples slept fitfully but remained asleep as the grey-suited men with the blank faces passed through their bedrooms. Insomniacs fell unconscious before their televisions as they passed through their living rooms. Children cried out and then went silent as the faceless figures gazed down into their cradles and moved on. They never stopped or paused but moved relentlessly from locked house to house, shop to shop, and pub to pub.

They moved down Belgrove Street. Without a word spoken between them, the grey figures moved to the doors on either side. Each opened silently before them and they passed in, emerging moments later to move further down the street to search another building, room, hall, attic, closet, or cellar in turn.

The door of Belgrove Hotel opened at the approach of the Grey Gentleman—but the figure stopped.

One of its brothers stood in the shadows of the doorway.

The gentleman was confused. There was an order to what was being done and the appearance of this brother gentleman in the doorway was outside the sequence. The Belgrove Hotel was to have been his to search for Gallows and his co-conspirators.

"Brother," the gentleman said.

"Not here," the other responded from the shadows. "Continue."

"This was to be my path," the gentleman said. "You are out of order."

The grey gentleman in the shadows stepped forward, the light from the street cascading down past the brim of his bowler hat.

"Mr. Demissie!"

"This is my path. It is *you* who are out of order," Demissie said. "What name do you use?"

"Mr. Smythe," the gentleman responded at once.

"What are you doing on this path, Mr. Smythe?"

"I seek Gallows, Lee, and Benoit."

"Find them, Mr. Smythe," Demissie said in low, menacing tones, "but this is my path. Continue on your own."

Mr. Smythe bowed his head slightly, tipped his bowler hat, and continued to the next door down Belgrove Street.

*****

Mr. Demissie climbed the stairs slowly and then walked directly to the door of Sojourner's suite. He considered it for a moment, his right hand shaking before reaching down, twisting the knob and throwing open the door.

Sojourner stood up at once. "Well?"

"They have moved on," said Mr. Demissie.

Valja let out a long, relieved breath.

"Very well done…for an amateur," Sojourner said with a rakish grin. "You're a quick study."

"Funny," Demissie answered, shivering. "Now tell me how to let this go…I feel like throwing up."

"It's really very simple," Sojourner said. "All you have to do is—"

"Wait!" Demissie said, holding up a gloved hand. "First, I want my clothes back. Then you tell me."

"Your clothes?" Sojourner scoffed. "You didn't use to be so prudish…at least, not when I was around."

"Look, lady," the figure of the Grey Gentleman said with an angry inflection in his voice quite out of character for Mr. Demissie. "I don't know what kind of voodoo you've talked me into, but this skin is *way* too pale a shade for my liking."

"Relax, Gallows," Sojourner said, sitting down in a chair and leaning it back in order to swing her long legs to rest, crossed, on the table in front of her. "You're the one who created this form, not me. Besides, you just outwitted the Grey Gentlemen. They'll have to search all the way to Croydon before they figure out they missed us. That should give us plenty of time."

"Plenty of time?" Ethan—in the shape of Mr.

Demissie—asked. "No. No more time and no more games. I'm leaving right now."

"Out there?" Valja scoffed. "Vith gentlemen still in search of you? Have you any idea vhat they vill do to you if they find you?"

"And I'm supposed to trust you?" Ethan shot back. "You've kidnapped all three of us under this ruse of being brothers, but none of us seem to want to be here. I've been chased by walking dead, snowed on, betrayed by a vampire—a *reformed* vampire, thank you very much—and hunted by some Grey Gentlemen goons from hell. I'm tired! I want my clothes back, I want my camera back, and I'm leaving so that I can get my bed back and sleep off this nightmare in a hotel guarded by heavy weapons."

"That sounds very reasonable," Sojourner nodded pleasantly.

"Where's Benoit and the other guy?" Ethan demanded with a little less heat than his previous rant. Sojourner's calm reaction had taken him off guard.

"Oh, they're resting comfortably," Sojourner answered in a matter-of-fact tone. "Anything else?"

"Well…yes!" Ethan said. "You were going to tell me how to get back to looking like me again."

"But you have such a talent for form shifting," Sojourner said through a playful pout. "With a little more practice, I think it could all come back to you."

"I don't *want* it to come back to me," Ethan answered.

"As you wish, Ethan," Sojourner said through a

cool smile. "But we all have talents. One of mine is the gift of a pleasant night's sleep."

Her violet eyes looked at him from beneath her thin eyebrows.

Their color was the last thing Ethan remembered that night.

CHAPTER 12
TANDEM JOURNEYS

Ethan awoke slowly, his head lolling gently back and forth to the rocking of a train, the quiet rushing sound gradually growing in his consciousness.

Light flared suddenly in the window next to him as they emerged from a long tunnel. Squinting, he turned his head away from the light and sat upright.

The chair he occupied was elegant and wide, and for a moment he thought of first-class on an airliner—not that his assignment editor would allow him that luxury ever again. Across from him was the teenage boy from the hotel suite sleeping sideways in his chair, the side of his face pressed against the back of the plush seat. The youth's mouth was open, and a short stain of drool inched down the back of his seat.

Outside the window next to him, the English countryside was flying past at an incredible pace. Farmland fields under low grey skies seemed to vanish as soon as they appeared.

Ethan looked quickly around the ultra-modern rail car, taking it all in, his trained eye fixing on framed image after image. The Eurostar logo fixed to the front door of the car was flanked by one of the most heavily armed troopers he had ever seen. The man wore a green camo helmet, ballistic vest, and full battle gear, his face hidden behind a combat faceplate. He carried a Heckler & Koch G36 assault rifle fitted with an AG36 grenade launcher and enough ammunition to start and end a war. A quick glance toward the back of the car revealed the trooper's twin standing next to his own doorway connecting to the cars further back.

The rail car itself was filled to capacity, the hum of conversation filtering over the quiet rush of the train. The talk was subdued—no one took travel lightly any more. But since the increase in incidents on-board commercial aircraft, rail travel had seen a dramatic increase everywhere.

Across the aisle sat Valja, his enormous size taking up two seats. His large arms were crossed in front of him as he slept. His feet were stretched out onto the two seats facing him as he snored loudly. This meant that the giant cabbie was taking up four seats, but no one seemed inclined to bother him for them.

Next to Ethan sat Dr. Benoit, his stare fixed on the nonchalant, willowy Sojourner sitting across from him.

Ethan rolled his head around on his neck and checked out his arms and legs. He was himself again. He stretched. "So I see we're on another enforced outing. And just where are we today?"

"We're in Kent. We just crossed under the tunnel at Mersham," Sojourner replied. "Does that help you at all?"

"No," Ethan said. "Not really. But this is a Eurostar high-speed train, so I take it that we're not going to be in England for very long."

"Really, is this the best the great Sojourner Lee can do?" Dr. Benoit mocked, nodding toward Ethan and the sleeping teenager across from him. "These two have no idea who they are, let alone what they will have to do. Would they even perform the rites willingly if they understood them?"

"We have a little time to explain it all, Rene," Sojourner replied.

"Not enough," the doctor countered. "The darkness comes, the night falls, and your time runs out sooner than you think."

"Is he always this cheerful?" Ethan asked.

Sojourner surrendered a frosted smile. "He is. Here, I brought something of yours."

The woman reached down and picked up Ethan's camera from where it sat next to her. He was surprised by the elation and relief that he felt at the sight of it. She handed it to him casually, but her eyes remained fixed on his features as he took it.

"I charged it for you," she said. "All your footage is intact."

Ethan checked the playback anyway. "Thanks. So it is."

"You hide behind it, don't you," Sojourner said.

Ethan did not look up from the camera he caressed in his hands. "I don't know what you mean."

"Let me offer you a bit of parlor magic," Sojourner said, drawing in a deep breath. "You never feel quite right without a camera in your hands. You never feel more alive than when you are capturing image after image. When you go home—and that's rare, indeed—you spend much of your time with your collection of cameras, carefully preserved photographs, and video files. Not movies; no, your tastes don't run to such bland and commercial fare—but the sights, sounds, and experiences that you've captured with the equipment in your own hands. Some might think that narcissistic, but they would be completely and damnably wrong, wouldn't they, Ethan?"

The rumble of the train lay for a moment between them as Sojourner leaned closer.

"You watch to remember," she said through a wicked smile. "You want to hang onto life without ever once being involved in it. The time is coming, Ethan, when you won't have that luxury any longer. You'll have to take sides. You'll have to act."

"That's not my job," Ethan said.

"It's everybody's job." She sat back with satisfaction. "You're compelled to collect things, you know. You collect images and the cameras that capture them—even though in your mind you realize that some of them are completely worthless to anyone but you. Rene here collects bizarre artifacts of all kinds and displays them with corpses. And our friend here…"

She placed her left hand on the teen's shoulder who jumped awake at her touch.

"This is Chahaya Rudi Atmoprayitno, an Indonesian internet hacker—excuse me, security specialist—who collects information, stores it, and sifts it, trying to always get his hands on it. Don't you, Rudi?"

The teenager grinned uncertainly. "*Permissi, bu! Saya ngok mengerti bahasa goblok anda.*"

"Eloquent as always," Dr. Benoit said with dry dismissal. "Fascinating as all of this is, I have to piss."

"I'll take you," Sojourner said, standing.

"You've hobbled me—stripped me of all my artifacts," the doctor said with thinly veiled anger. "You've cut me off from the taint and now I'm no better off than the rest of you stupid cattle. But how long before the darkness catches up to you, Sojourner—before it catches up to us all? Besides, do you really think I would jump off of a 300-kilometer-per-hour train in a mortal body while I was powerless?"

"You've done worse, Rene," the woman said, pulling the man up out of his chair by his arm. "Indulge my suspicious nature."

Ethan watched as Sojourner moved toward the lavatory at the front of the rail car. Ethan let out a long sigh, turned the camera over in his hands, and caught the dark eyes of the Indonesian boy sitting across from him staring at him.

"Well…Budi or Rudi…or whatever your name

is," Ethan said, more to himself than his companion. "I don't suppose you know what this is all about, do you?"

The teenager leaned forward, a bright expression on his face as he spoke. "*Munkin anda juga seorange yang bisah menolong saya?*"

"Yeah," Ethan said. "Whatever you said. I guess that's about as much help as I can expect. Rudi to the rescue."

The teenager leaned further forward in his seat, glancing sideways across the aisle toward the still sleeping Valja. He then flicked his fingers and hand toward him repeatedly in small gestures.

Ethan leaned forward. "Look, I don't understand—"

Rudi suddenly spoke. In English.

"*You've got to get me the hell out of here!*"

Ethan stared, his mind momentarily unable to connect the clear, English words with the boy whose face was only a few inches in front of his own. "What? Did you just—"

"That woman is crazy, man!" Rudi said under his breath. "She was telling that Valja goon some weird-ass bedtime story about—like, the end of the world and dragons having their spirits hoodooed into scones or something."

"Scions," Ethan corrected. "You've been listening in this whole time?"

"Look, man, it pays sometimes to be a foreigner, you know," Rudi said, shooting a quick glance back toward Valja. "Nobody expects some dude from backwater Asia to dig their rap."

Ethan choked down a laugh. *"Dig their rap"?* What movies did this kid watch to learn his English, anyway? "And just what did you hear…Rudi, isn't it?"

"Yeah, Rudi will do." He nodded.

"Well, Rudi, if you don't mind, can we start with who the hell are you?"

"Like she said: I'm an internet security specialist."

Ethan smiled, shaking his head. "Sorry. You're not old enough to be a specialist at anything."

"Oh, and like you can even remember the pass-word to your Facebook account," Rudi said, folding his arms across his chest. "There isn't a corner of the web dark enough that I can't reach."

"Let me guess," Ethan replied. "Someone found you poking around a corner that was so dark and buried that they preferred to hire you rather than keep looking over their shoulder for you."

Rudi looked at Ethan out of the corner of his eye. "Not bad, old man…you read that just about right. B of A found me digging around in some of their less than public accounts. Now they pay my bills and keep me in hi-tech heaven, too, long as I do all my scrounging for them."

"Sweet gig," Ethan nodded. *Keep this kid talking.* "So what brings you on this railroad trip, Rudi?"

"Man, my boss in Jakarta hands me a first-class ticket and tells me to hop a flight to London," Rudi whines. "All expenses and the whole bit. Says there's this secret conference on network ghosting accounts and deep encryption double-blinds. It's old stuff to me, but I figure I'll take the gig, spend their money, and see some of the world before it all spins down to hell. Only I get here, and there's no conference… just this insane chick and her ape dragging me away in his cab and spewing a bunch of whacked-out junk to each other. They talked about you, too, man! Said you were coming and how they had to put the bag on you, too."

"OK, Rudi, I can help you," Ethan said, "but you've got to help me first."

"What do you mean?" the youth replied suspiciously.

"I can't help either of us until I know what's going on here," Ethan said. "Tell me what you've heard… the stuff you heard when they didn't think you were listening."

"Aw, man!" Rudi's face looked as though he had just been robbed.

"Help me and I'll help us both," Ethan urged.

"They'll be back any minute now!"

"So give it up quickly," Ethan said as straight-faced as he could manage. "What did you hear?"

"The lunatic chick, she went on and on all about these dragons from, like, crazy ancient times," Rudi spoke quickly, his words smashing together. "They were supposed to be the police of the world or something, watching over their magic power karma dope. Only the whole thing crashed on account of this stain or whatever they call it. Story is, these wizard dudes were bending reality with this karma, right, only they got greedy and kept bending it too much. You know, like bending a soda can back and forth too many times until it breaks. Only when this karma breaks it leaks out this awful stuff called stain—"

"Taint, they call it taint."

"Whatever. This taint begins corrupting the souls of ancient dudes and even takes over some of the dragon souls. So then karma and taint start tugging at the world. Or maybe it wasn't that stuff—maybe it had to do with some magic dudes pulling some crap that they wasn't supposed to do. I don't know. Anyway, the whole world crashed and burned and both karma and taint go down the drain completely and pretty much take all the ancient dudes with it. That was bad news for the dragons since it was karma that kept the dragons going."

Ethan shivered suddenly. There was something close that was making him uncomfortable—something that felt too familiar and dangerous. It was like déjà vu but stronger. *"I feel a disturbance in the force, Luke."* He shook himself.

"So…goodbye dragons?" Ethan urged.

"Right," Rudi went on. "Only now there are these elves or faeries or gnomes or something that took the souls of these dragons and put them asleep in human babies so they could survive—like that monster thing in *Alien*—only they would be all asleep-like, see—passing from generation to generation, just waiting until karma comes back and all hell breaks loose."

"And what does that have to do with us?" Ethan asked, checking the front of the train compartment.

"Right, like *I* know," Rudi replied, his agitation growing by the moment. "She thinks you and I are some of these ancient kick-ass dragons—or that we're carrying their souls or something inside us. She says we're from the same brood."

"Brood?"

"Yeah," Rudi said. "These dragons were born into broods—whole clutches of eggs hatched at the same time. She says the bond between these 'broodmates' is close—something about their souls being in, like, harmony. A brood that's tight is powerful, and…hey, man, what do you want all this info for now? We gotta go!"

"We *are* going somewhere—about three hundred klicks an hour. Look," Ethan said, "we're heading toward the Chunnel. Can you think of any reason why they would want to take us into France or the continent?"

A familiar shape sat down suddenly next to Rudi. "I've always wanted to go to France."

"Collette?" Ethan nearly choked. "What are you doing here?"

"Looking for you," she said. "It was hard, but I had good help."

"You know me," said the all-too-familiar voice standing in the aisle. He moved with elegant ease into the seat next to Ethan, swinging his courier bag onto his lap. "I'm always searching for something…

funny," Jonas Farben said through his broad, even-toothed smile.

In that moment, the English countryside vanished as the Eurostar train plunged into the tunnel under Shakespeare Hill and began its descent below the English Channel.

CHAPTER 13
JUST LIKE MAGIC

"You brought *him*?" Ethan said.

"Well, I couldn't just leave you in the hands of these desperate terrorists, could I?" Collette shot back, folding her arms across her chest. Her green eyes had a particular fire in them as she spoke. "Those goons dropped me off at Turner House and nobody at the Bureau was very helpful."

"So you called Farben?" Ethan's tone was accusing.

"No," Collette said. "Someone from the Bureau called Dr. Farben. He was most concerned and came at once to help."

"I'll bet he did," Ethan said.

"Ethan, this man worked all night to find you," Collette snapped. "Why, it was only because of him and his contacts that we were able to find you at all! As it was, we barely made the train."

"Now, Collette," Farben smiled with professional

148

humility, "you need not worry about Ethan. He just doesn't understand."

"True," Ethan agreed, "I don't understand you at all."

"Who's your new friend?" Collette asked, nodding to the youth in the chair next to her.

"Oh, forgive my bad manners." Ethan's words dripped sarcasm. "May I introduce Rudi. Rudi, this is Collette Montrose and her most peculiar friend Jonas Farben."

Jonas extended his hand and a counterfeit smile.

Rudi hesitantly took Jonas's hand as he affected a confused look. "*Maaf! Tidak mengerti saya.*"

Ethan continued, "He's from Asia."

"Does he speak English?" Farben asked.

"Not so far," Ethan said with a shrug. He glanced toward the front of the car. *What's taking them so long?* "As you can see, however, we're a little busy here, so if you would kindly shove off to your own seats, I'm sure we'll have plenty to talk about once we reach Calais—"

"We've got a little time to talk right now," Farben said, waving his hand to indicate the window next to Ethan. "We're in the Chunnel now…so we've got thirty-one miles of tunnel ahead of us and nothing to relieve our boredom."

"What are you doing here, Farben?" Ethan asked.

"As Collette told you: looking for you," Farben said easily, relaxing back into the chair, though his melting charm was doing little to thaw the man next to him. "You're famous again."

Farben pulled an iPad from his padded courier bag and showed Ethan a browser window. The video began playing on the CNN web page at once.

"...*in London where reporters Collette Montrose and her cameraman were caught up in a dramatic publicity event at the National Gallery in Trafalgar Square. Hundreds of specially costumed actors portraying the plasticized bodies from Dr. Rene Benoit's new exhibit chased our reporter into the square to the delight of the initially startled onlookers. It was all in good fun, as Dr. Jonas Farben—on hand for the event—explained—*"

Ethan reached over and turned off the tablet. The image and sound disappeared.

"My good friend, we really need to put this little thing behind us," Farben said as he slipped his iPad back into the case.

"Little thing?" Ethan snapped. "You rigged my Hanoi footage and claimed that I was the one who faked it! You know damn well that my footage was authentic, that it was a legion of the walking dead that tore down Hanoi, and yet you purposefully rigged my footage to make it look phony and then 'exposed' me as a fraud to every media outlet on the planet! Now it looks as though you've done it again."

"You're absolutely right," Farben nodded.

Collette's jaw dropped.

Ethan blinked. So did the record light on the camera cradled in his hands. "What did you say?"

"You're absolutely right, so why don't we talk about it, the two of us together? You seem like a reasonable man. You and I really should be on the same side on this issue. So I thought we might talk a little sense."

"You want to talk about why you sold me up the river on the Hanoi story," Ethan said. The audio meter LEDs were bouncing on the back of the camera. It was picking up the sound just fine.

"There are bigger issues involved here than perhaps you have fully appreciated," Farben said, switching smoothly to lecture mode. "Issues bigger than you and me; issues having to do with the preservation of reason and truth."

"Truth!" Ethan nearly laughed. "What do you know about the truth?"

"I know that it is all too easily overwhelmed by superstition, fear, and ignorance whenever we are confronted by the unknown," Farben said, speaking in clear, exaggerated tones as though Ethan were taking a lesson. "Since the time of Heraclitus more than twenty-five centuries ago, mankind has been on a journey to understand the truth—and that truth is science. It is a truth of reason and of rational foundations. It is the denial of the ancient caveman—the superstitious, mindless primitive huddling in fear from that which he does not understand, and spinning religious bandages to cover over the gaps in his understanding. Science, reason, cause and effect that is testable and verifiable—that is what elevates man above the common primitive. That is what holds our modern civilization together. That is what makes man noble."

"And so you nobly lied about me?" Ethan said.

Farben smiled with affected embarrassment. "It was necessary…desperate times require desperate means, and even those will be justified in the results. You've been many places, Mr. Gallows, and seen a great many things…*shared* a great many things with the world audience. You are a seeker—searching for truth on which you can report and expose to the world. But you, perhaps more than nearly everyone else on the planet, knows that there are new forces at work in the world—things which are, *as yet*, un-explained.

"The ancients saw an eclipse of the sun and made up tales of great monsters swallowing the light in the sky—sacrificed their own men and women to appease the gods against this terrible event and were glad they had done so when the sun reappeared. Now we know the real causes of an eclipse—that it is a celestial event caused by the relative motions and positions of the sun, the moon, and the earth in their orbits. We know when an eclipse is going to take place in advance and have done away with human sacrifice to this perfectly understood astronomical event. The supremacy of reason and science did away with all that unthinking, superstitious nonsense."

"What does that have to do with me?" Ethan asked.

"It has to do with all of us," Farben said, leaning in toward Ethan. "Something happened—something fundamental and extraordinary—that changed the way things worked in the world. Every scientist in the world is working on just what that fundamental change actually is, but thus far the roots of it are a mystery that we simply do not yet understand. We all see the symptoms—what appear to be monsters, ghosts, vampires, beasts, and the manifestation of so-called magical powers."

"So all of this is because of *magic*?" Ethan asked.

"No! It just *looks* like magic to us because it is not understood," Farben said in earnest, his hands now animated as he pressed home his point. "Don't you see? Arthur C. Clarke once said that 'any sufficiently advanced technology is indistinguishable from magic.' It was the third of his three laws of prediction. All the things we've been seeing recently— the apparitions, these so-called monsters, and what most of the uneducated and superstitious people of the world are calling magic—*all* of these things can and will be explained by science, given sufficient time for rational examination. The scientific method will strip away all this mystical nonsense and, as it has done throughout the centuries, expose these dark mythologies as simply natural and scientific processes which have, until now, either been dormant or undiscovered."

"Science will explain the walking dead, vampires in North London, werewolves at Heathrow, and Dr.

Benoit casting fiery spells in the National Gallery with his pen?" Ethan's skepticism was obvious in his tone.

"No, you're missing the point," Farben said, shaking his head. "Science will explain what *appears to be* walking dead, vampirism, lycanthropic behaviors, and either the natural or, more likely, illusionist tricks of Dr. Benoit and his kind."

"Do you have an explanation for all of this?" Ethan retorted, ignoring a glare from Collette.

"Not yet," Farben said with special emphasis. "That, dear Ethan, is the complete and entire point. Research takes time and—given the large number of strange phenomena that have recently been reported—it is taking considerable effort and resources. Meanwhile, our civilization of reason and enlightenment is faced with things that science cannot yet explain, and the results could be disastrous. We are on the verge of a second Dark Ages, when the scientific foundations will be tossed aside in favor of superstition and anarchy. That is why it is so important to keep everyone calm and, more importantly *rational*, through this lag time between mystical illusions and the truthful, real, and scientific principles underlying these phenomena. There are, admittedly, new forces at work here—forces that have yet to be understood by science—but until science can properly understand, harness, and control these forces on behalf of mankind, then the hysteria must be kept to a minimum. That's what I and like-minded scientists around the world are doing in a concerted effort in the service of humanity—keeping everyone calm long enough for the hocus-pocus magic trick to be explained and understood in rational, logical terms."

"So you're saying that you're preserving the truth and integrity of science by lying about what you don't understand." Ethan was not buying it. "You're going to save the world by making me look like an idiot for filming the truth."

Farben smiled again. "A small price to pay for such a lofty goal."

"Sorry, not feeling that honored," Ethan sighed.

Ethan sat back in his chair. He watched a number of people move up and down the crowded aisle.

One of them was dressed in a modestly tailored grey suit.

Ethan frowned.

The man turned to face Ethan. There was a vaguely disturbing menace moving beneath faceless pleasantness in his features which Ethan could not place. A thin smile played at the corners of the man's mouth before he turned away, moving past the armed soldier. He closed the frosted glass door behind him and moved further forward in the train.

Ethan struggled to remember his features, then realized with a shock that it was in the man's absence that he knew him.

"How did you find us?" Ethan asked urgently.

"What?"

"How did you find us—exactly?"

"A tip, actually, from one of my sources in the British Government," Farben said smugly. "He told me that you might be in the company of either a cab driver named Valja Lonchakov or a woman named Sojourner Lee. Once I had the names from Demissie, it was simple enough to use the researchers at CNN's London Bureau to track you to…"

"Wait!" Collette said, turning suddenly toward Farben. "You didn't tell me his name was *Demissie*!"

"Yes," Farben replied. "He's very well-connected with the foreign office and…"

"Damn! Where's Sojourner?" Collette said to Ethan.

"She took Benoit to the john. But they should have been back here long before now. We've got to find them and get off this train."

"We're under the English Channel!" she replied.

"What is the matter with you two?" Farben asked, more irritated than concerned. "We'll be in Calais in less than ten minutes."

Ethan and Farben were thrown suddenly forward. The train was decelerating rapidly, the squealing of the wheels under the carriage carrying up through the frame of the car. Collette shoved Farben off of her and back into his opposing seat even as the deceleration continued. Ethan climbed back into his own seat, his foot braced against Rudi's seat across from him, his left hand gripping the arm rest and his right gripping his still-recording camera.

"We'll never make it to Calais, you idiot," Ethan said urgently over the rising screams in the cabin. "They couldn't find us on their own so they let you find us for them—you and the renowned researchers of CNN. You've probably led them right to us!"

"Who?" Farben shouted over the din. "Led who to you?"

"I think we're about to find out!"

There was a groaning and shrieking of tortured, sheering metal. The Eurostar carriage lurched suddenly, the lights flickering for a moment as the rail car suddenly twisted madly off the tracks and began to flip. In the next instant, darkness fell around them, but the sound of wrenching steel continued into what seemed like eternity.

At last the motion stopped. The tunnel lights were shining through the shattered windows of the twisted rail car.

The grinding sound had stopped but was now replaced by something unearthly and unholy.

More than two hundred feet below the surface of the Channel, the sound echoed over them from outside the train, ahead in the tunnel.

CHAPTER 14
CHUNNEL

TC: 00:27:33:15 / GALLOWS, ETHAN (RAW/NFB)[1]

LN-7 CLASSIFIED ULTRA / NEED TO KNOW

No video. Audio track continuous. Sounds of unidentified persons screaming. Loud scraping and banging sounds as the camera is jostled.

"Oh God! Oh God!"[2]

GALLOWS: "Shut up, Farben!"[3]

FARBEN: "Please, my leg...oh God, my leg."[4]

A shaft of light swings from side to side. A tall,

---

1 Hindsight™ Real-time Video Documentation Software. Under License.
2 (Unidentified A)
3 ID positive: Gallows, Ethan (CNN-Atl)
4 ID A link positive: Farben, Dr. Jonas (Fox News Net)

obscured figure holds the flashlight, drags something/
someone between the seats. Figure stops, swinging
the light toward the camera. Lens flare obscuring the
image.

"Ethan! What happened?"[5]

Camera rocks slightly, then twists suddenly,
blurring the image.

TC: 00:27:45:24 / CAMERA LIGHT ON

The face of the woman comes into view. Tall with
close-cropped white hair.

GALLOWS: "I don't... They know we're here, Sojourner.
That stain or taint or whatever it's called."

SOJOURNER: "HOW?"[6]

Camera swings downward. Farben lies in the broken
remains of his train seat. Holds up his hands,
shielding his eyes. His left leg below the knee is
twisted at an angle.

GALLOWS: "Mister Nancy Drew[7] here was good enough
to do Demissie's[8] work for him. They followed him to
us."

---

5 (Unidentified B)
6 ID B link: Sojourner — Background reference:
Searching...
7 Drew, Nancy: Fictional female, youth detective
created by Edward Stratemeyer and largely
ghostwritten by various authors under the pseudonym
of Carolyn Keene.
8 (Unidentified C)

Sound of metal tearing and twisting cuts across the voices. Camera shifts quickly toward what remains of the front of the rail car. Glass forward door is shattered. Main cabin lights are extinguished. Some dim incidental light from globes in the tunnel outside. A uniformed soldier lies in the glass from the doorway, struggling.[9] Several bodies strewn about the forward cabin also struggling to get up.[10] Three not moving.[11]

Unknown person called Sojourner lifts up the person[12] she has been dragging by his collar. His hair is disheveled and coated in dust. His suit is torn. He pushes his glasses onto his nose. Sojourner pushes the man to her right. Camera pans to follow as the man is caught by another man,[13] large, muscular, who holds him in an arm lock.

Camera shifts wildly again. Woman with short, dark hair struggles to her feet.[14]

GALLOWS: "Collette, get up. We've got to move."

---

9 ID positive: tagged IFF — Phillips, Dallin, Lance Corporal, 3rd Battalion, Royal Anglian Regiment / HMAF-UK
10 (Unidentified D, E, F, G & H)
11 (Unidentified I, J & K)
12 (Unidentified L)
13 (Unidentified M)
14 (Unidentified N)

MONTROSE: "I'm moving..."[15]

Violent shaking. Ceiling comes briefly into focus under the light from the camera. Two seconds later, emergency lights flash on, illuminating the scene of injured passengers and twisted carriage.

Camera twists suddenly. A howling distorts the audio. Then: a rush of sparks outside the shattered windows. Also, large flaming pieces of debris.

GALLOWS: "What the hell is that?"

SOJOURNER: "They're called Dwellers — Those Who Dwell Below — like one of the Grey Gentlemen but in its monstrous, natural form. And it's coming for us."

"I know what else it is."[16]

Camera pans and focuses on Benoit. His teeth are stained red with blood from his split lip. He grins. "It's the end of the line, Gallows. The end of a very long line!"

A wrenching sound fills the audio, drowning out Benoit's words. The camera blurs, pans, fixes momentarily on the aft section of the train. Passengers are trampling one another in their rush to the back of the car. The camera blurs in sudden movement to the right. Focuses as the roof of the rail car is peeled

---

15 ID N link positive: Montrose, Collette (CNN-Atl)
16 ID L link 85% positive: Benoit, Dr. Rene

open from the center toward both sides of the car by what appears to be two enormous clawed hands.

The stark glare of the emergency lights shine up into the face of the creature, a canine-shaped snout with four rows of razor sharp teeth tearing at the steel and plastic of the rail car. Its glistening humped shoulders press upward against the roof of the tunnel nearly twenty-five feet above the rail bed. Six eyes set back beneath bony ridges of the head search the cabin while long, black tentacles — some thick as tree branches while others are thin and whip-long — reach forward from either side of the ridge plates running down its back. The tentacles have black, obsidian ridges and barbs at their ends. The camera's focus keeps shifting in and out as it tries to track the creature —

Camera unable to focus on its black skin.

TC: 00:29:14:18 / AUTOFOCUS OFF

Camera shifts down to Phillips. He rolls onto his back, his HK AG3617 now free. He flips the cocking handle out from under the hand grip, pulls the bolt back, and aims the muzzle toward the creature. The creature sees the movement and slashes its tentacle

---

17 Weapon ID positive: Heckler & Koch G36 with AG36 grenade launcher, standard-issue assault rifle for HMAF-UK

downward, plunging through Phillips's ribcage. Just as suddenly, the tentacle retracts, dragging Phillips upward through the opening in the ceiling, slamming his upper body and right arm against the twisted roof framing overhead, before hurling the body backward down the tunnel.[18] The HK AG36 falls back into the cabin.

Sojourner steps between the camera and the monster and begins to change shape. Her long leather coat drops. Leathery wings erupt from between her shoulder blades, claw-like hooks jutting from the thumb points of the wings.

SOJOURNER: "Get them out of here, Valja!"

Camera swings left, focusing on Lonchakov,[19] his arm still around Benoit. A long sword is held in his right hand, double handguard above the grip with one set arching back toward the grip and the other arching forward. Its blade burns with a blue flame.

LONCHAKOV: "We go together!"

Camera swings back to Sojourner.[20] Her skin has taken on a white scaly quality, her short spiked hair coalescing into long, white horns. Her face has

---

18 Phillips, Dallin, Lance Corporal — KIA / Notify NOK
19 ID M link positive: Lonchakov, Valja (Cab Operator, London) — Documentation suspect
20 ID 45% positive: Sojourner

elongated into a muzzle with sharp fangs.

SOJOURNER: "I'm unimportant! They are everything! Get them there, Valja...I'll meet you there!"

The rattle of automatic gunfire explodes from the end of the rail car. Tracer bullets flash across the screen. Camera shakes. View suddenly obscured by a chair.

FARBEN: "Argh! Get off my leg!"

Camera moves up and shifts angle forward over the seats. The creature rears back against the assault, the bullets ripping into its enormous, black, shifting mass. The unearthly howl of the beast shakes the walls of the rail car. Shattered glass cascades out of the frames. The tentacles of the beast lash forward, thrusting like spears overhead. A terrible cry rings out from camera left. The camera spins toward the sound, catching the image of a second security soldier,[21] his body pierced by the narrow, barbed tentacles of the beast, being thrown upward, slamming against the steel crossbeams bracing the top of the tunnel. The second soldier's body is bent impossibly backward against the framing, his cries suddenly silenced.[22]

---

21 ID positive: tagged IFF — McConnel, Llewelyn, Private, 3rd Battalion, Royal Anglian Regiment / HMAF-UK
22 McConnel, Llewelyn, Private — KIA / Notify NOK

SOJOURNER: "Ethan!"

The image pulls down and the startling image of a white-scaled woman's face with a pronounced muzzle fills the frame, its hair now horns sweeping upward and away from her face.

SOJOURNER[23]: "Take Rudi and the doctor! Go with Valja and get out of here!"

GALLOWS: "Go? Where can we go?"

SOJOURNER: "Out on the platform! Find a cross passage to the service tunnel between the main tracks and get out."

GALLOWS: "What about you?"

SOJOURNER: "I'll join you later...Valja knows where...now go!"

Sojourner stands up. Her hands are claws, reaching up in front of her. Lightning crackles between her fingers and she turns to face the beast. Light flares blindingly off the camera's right as the beast howls again.

Collette Montrose into frame. She is carrying one of the HK AG36 rifles. Across the aisle and crouching between the facing seats is Lonchakov, his sword aflame in one hand, Benoit's collar in the other.

MONTROSE: "You heard the lady...well, whatever she is. Let's get out of here!"

---

23 ID 23% positive: Sojourner

FARBEN: "You can't leave me here!"

Camera swings down to show Farben. Gallows's voice is heard behind the camera.

GALLOWS: "If that thing is after us then it's better for you to stay here. You don't want to be near us when that thing gives chase. That goes for you, too, Collette."

A hand reaches across the lens, dragging it to face the CNN reporter.

MONTROSE: "No, Ethan! You're not leaving me behind again! You need me!"

An explosion of blue shoots over the tops of the seats. The beast howls again. Sojourner's wings appear briefly in the frame. She steps forward out of the frame.

"Wah-doo! Wah-doo!" A young man[24] yells to the left of frame.

GALLOWS: "It's time to get off this train!"

Camera swings suddenly, the image blurring substantially.

TC: 00:36:16:23 / DIGITAL IMAGE BREAK UP: 46 FRAMES

Sounds of shattering and falling glass.

Exterior of train: Engine and three cars forward are devastated. The creature nearly fills the width of

---

24 (Unidentified O)

the tunnel. Arms and tentacles flail about a radiant ball of lightning arcing inside the cabin of the rail car torn open before it.

Lonchakov pushes Benoit forcibly through the frame of the shattered rail car window. Benoit falls heavily next to the derailed train. The face of Montrose momentarily passes the frame as she climbs onto the evacuation walkway running along the side of the tunnel, helped up by Atmoprayitno.[25]

The creature turns toward camera, its tentacles cracking through the air in its direction. Lonchakov turns, the second HK AG36 now slung across his back, his sword tearing through the air with the sound of a torch. It slices cleanly through a narrow tentacle, severing it completely just as several more shoot through the air in his direction. Benoit struggles below the platform, trying to get to his feet. A hand comes into frame, grabbing Benoit by the arm and shoving him into the access passage with Montrose and Atmoprayitno.

The camera swings again, showing the train illuminated from within, sparks flying up in the face of the beast. In the center of the storm stands Sojourner, her brightly illuminated, winged figure

---

25 ID O link positive: Atmoprayitno, Chahaya Rudi (Interpol) — File damaged

clearly showing through the broken window frame in
the car. The lightning in the beast's face panics it.
The tentacles reaching for Lonchakov suddenly retract
and lance down toward Sojourner.

GALLOWS: "Come on!"

Lonchakov turns, sword still in hand, and leaps
up onto the platform. He runs past the camera, which
follows him into the access passage. Lonchakov —
Benoit again in hand — runs down the access passage.
Montrose and Atmoprayitno are at his heels. The camera
swings back again to the mouth of the tunnel, taking
in a wider shot of the savaged rail car and the scene
of the wreck. In that moment, the lightning stutters,
falters. The figure of Sojourner falls back as the
beast lunges downward, its black form engulfing the
glowing figure and extinguishing its light.

END SEQUENCE — TC 00:37:14:21

CHAPTER 15
SACRIFICES

W hich way?" Valja called back, pushing Dr. Benoit through the access doorway into the service tunnel beyond.

"Right," Ethan shouted. "We have to go right."

Ethan followed Collette and Rudi into the service tunnel. After the expanse of the Chunnel, the service tunnel felt cramped and narrow.

"Over there!" Ethan pointed to the left side of the double roadway running down the center of the tunnel. There was an alcove with an emergency electrical vehicle plugged into the wall. It had two seats and a large flatbed on the back. "Will that thing run?"

Valja was already dragging Benoit toward the vehicle, but Rudi was quicker on his feet. The youth passed them both, jumping into the right-hand seat and quickly bringing the cart to life. Valja pulled Benoit around the front and into the passenger's seat on the left side, planting himself on the back between the seats, flaming sword still in hand. Collette, gripping the automatic assault rifle by its handle, threw herself over the low railing and onto the flatbed of the vehicle. She had barely managed to sit up and plant one foot against the low back gate when Ethan leaped onto the truck next to her.

"*Awas! Awas!*" Rudi shouted.

Collette had gone pale, looking up at Valja and his blazing sword. "Where…how did you find that?"

The electric vehicle lurched forward twice, nicked the edge of the alcove, and then darted out onto the roadway.

Collette, jostled out of her stupor, shouted in alarm. "Ethan! We're heading for—"

"France, I know! We were in the tunnel around fifteen minutes," Ethan shouted over the rising hum of the electric motors. "The trains are in the tunnel for about twenty minutes…that means that we're a lot closer to France than we are to England. Nobody wants to spend more time in this tunnel than they have to with that—"

They had just passed another access passage when the sealed door exploded across the service tunnel, its deformed steel slamming against the curved wall of the tunnel opposite it.

"We've got company!" Ethan called out.

The creature poured into the tunnel, its movements sliding faster than Ethan thought possible. *Monsters in the movies always move so slowly,* he thought. *I always used to wonder why people didn't just get out of the way. Now I see the truth...great...*

The maw of the creature opened in rage, its ranks of teeth glistening in the lighting of the service tunnel. Its roar rushed down the hall behind them as it charged after them, its massive appendages pushing its tentacled mass forward like a bullet propelled down the barrel of a gun.

"Oh, I've had about enough of that!" Collette snarled. Ethan glanced over at her and was astonished as Collette swung the folding stock into place and flipped the cocking handle out from under the gun's handle. With a single motion, she pulled the bolt backward, glanced at the safety fire selector switch on the right side, and flipped it to auto. She had barely raised the gun stock to her shoulder before she squeezed off a short burst from the gun.

The creature howled, its barbed tentacles writhing with the impact of the projectiles.

Two more bursts rang from the gun before Ethan could ask, "Former military, Collette?"

"No. Four older brothers in Georgia," she replied, her cheek down on the rifle stock, aiming through the built-in scope as she squeezed off another round.

More rounds fired above Ethan. Valja had pulled out his weapon and was now firing into the creature as well.

The creature staggered from the fusillade.

"Keep going, Rudi!" Ethan called out. "I think we're—"

The electric car suddenly lurched sideways and began rocking back and forth. Valja reached down, gripping the back of the seat to keep his balance. Five rounds from Collette's gun chipped the tunnel ceiling in quick succession.

"Rudi!" Ethan growled, twisting around.

"*Goblok! Jangan! Jangan saja!*" Rudi was yelling. The young Indonesian was wrestling for the steering wheel with Dr. Benoit.

The car was rapidly decelerating.

The demonic creature surged forward, its eyes fixed on its prey.

Ethan set his jaw, pulling himself over the seat and wedging himself between Benoit and Rudi. The French curator screamed with fury, clawing at Ethan. "It's come for *me*! Its power! Its majesty! It's all for me!"

Ethan quickly gathered the front of Benoit's jacket in his left hand, drew back his right fist, and slammed it into the face of Dr. Benoit.

Skin striking skin—

*****

Abraxas reeled backward from the collision, instinctively folding his wings tight about his body as he rolled. Fafnir rolled with him, his claws digging tightly into the scales of his brother dragon. Their massive bodies tumbled as one through the air, plummeting in a great arc across the hills of the eastern steppes. Villages passed beneath them, closer and closer, as they fell.

"It's a lie!" Fafnir screamed in rage and agony. The shrill sound of his voice was a screeching thunder across the land below. "It's all been a lie!"

The two dragons, locked together in fierce embrace, plunged downward, rolling slowly in their meteoric descent. Behind them, a third dragon struggled to follow them downward toward the sweeping landscape.

"You have drunk of a poison well," Abraxas roared, hoping that his words would penetrate the dark veil over his brother's mind. "You have been taint-tempted, brother!"

"There is no taint!" Fafnir snapped. "Only the lying stories told by the sorcerers! Only death in a harness of chains!"

The dragons crashed into the ground, their impact throwing an enormous plume of dust and rock into the air. Their momentum pushed them across the grassy field, dredging a long furrow up the hillside. Near the crest, enough of their speed remained for them to smash into a barn and three smaller houses. The buildings crumbled at once under the terrible weight of the dragons as their occupants—and any remaining villagers—fled into the surrounding fields in panic.

Abraxas set his hind legs into his brother's flanks, pushing upward sharply, his back against the ground. Fafnir scrambled with his claws, unable to find any

leverage or to maintain his grip on his fellow dragon. He tumbled backward and spun, rolling up onto
his feet, his long claws digging into the ground.

Abraxas also sprang to his feet and faced his
brother, their bellies hugging close to the ground.
The first to spring into the air would expose their
unprotected abdomen to the other, and neither dared
risk it. They were both on the ground facing each
other, circling around the ruined beet field with the
shattered human buildings to one side, their eyes
never leaving the sight of the other.

The third dragon alighted just beyond the ruined
field. "What is the matter with you both?"

"Apalala," Abraxas said, his eyes still fixed on
Fafnir, "our brother seems to have acquired a taste
for the taint."

"You speak as though you know something about
it," Fafnir replied, his long fangs exposed in a sneer.
"Abraxas the Great—protector of the law! Never
questioning, never deviating. So bound up by the
chains of other people's rules and morals and ethics
that he cannot lift his wing without their permission.
They were the ones who caused this, brother—not me!
They brought this power into the world and I have
tasted it. It is more than you will ever know, Abraxas,
and I am the one who found it! I, the lesser dragon
who cowered in the cold shadow of your wings. I did
it! I found something great! I found a power that you
don't have and cannot even understand."

"It has hold of your mind, brother," Abraxas said,

limping slightly from a gash in his left leg. Fafnir was so engaged in his opponent that he did not notice he was being maneuvered toward where the astonished Apalala had landed. "It will enslave you."

"It will free me," Fafnir snarled.

"Free you? Free you of what?"

"It will free me of you!"

It was then that Abraxas saw it. The chain around Fafnir's neck had been hidden by his scales, but the writhing darkness gathered about the amulet at his throat was unmistakable.

All three dragons sprang at once.

Fafnir drove powerfully toward Abraxas, the pulse of debilitating night, filled with despair, discharging from the magical icon. Abraxas had already spent his leap. He saw the onrushing darkness about to engulf him when the magic shifted suddenly, slamming down into the field. Apalala had pounced on Fafnir's tail just as he had pushed off from the ground, and so the wayward dragon suddenly fell downward, betrayed by his own momentum, and slammed into the ground.

Abraxas acted at once. He pounced on his brother, driving his shoulder deep into the other dragon's side. Holding him against the earth, he snatched the dark amulet from his brother's throat.

In that moment, the darkness called to him, beckoned him with a seductive song and promises of power, freedom, and passion.

Abraxas cast it away, a shiver wracking his body.

"What do we do?" Apalala begged.

Abraxas kept his shoulder down, firmly pinning Fafnir to the ruined field, despite his brother's thrashing panic to escape. "We take him home, back to the Western Isle. We keep him away from the taint and watch over his recovery. Rest him, Apalala—do it now."

The dragon obeyed, summoning the karma from within. He placed his talons to his brother's writhing head.

Fafnir went suddenly limp.

"They say," Apalala murmured, "that once a dragon has been tempted by the taint, they never lose the taste for it."

"Then," Abraxas replied, "we must see that he is never tempted again."

*****

Ethan pulled his fist back from Benoit's face. The curator still held his grip on the wheel, refusing to let go.

Ethan's fist slammed downward again.

*****

Abraxas pushed into the sky above the clouds, the end of the world veiled below him. His brothers flew beside him, Apalala and Fafnir. He looked up at them, wondering if they would always shine, if they were looking down on his world, and if they cared whether or not it died.

As he watched, the stars began to vanish behind him.

Startled, he looked back.

Darkness, palpable and terrible, was rising like a wave into the night sky behind them.

"It is the taint," said Tsanya, watching from his back. She gripped the hilt of her Seelie weapon, a long sword with a double handguard. "It, too, is being dragged from the world, but it does not wish anything to survive it—especially dragons, Abraxas. Especially you."

"What are we to do, brother?" Apalala asked across the sky.

"We must out-live the darkness, brothers," Abraxas replied. "We must surrender our better selves and sleep among men."

"And we must hurry," Tsanya shouted. "There is little time remaining before karma shall leave the world and this hope is closed forever to us all."

"Then we must use well what time we have," Fafnir replied.

The shadow was getting closer.

*****

Ethan drew back his fist a third time, but the doctor had gone limp in his left hand. Rudi pulled his own hand away from the back of Benoit's neck, a pale, golden glow fading from his palm.

"Thanks, Rudi," Ethan said. "Keep driving! This

is a race we do not want to lose!"

Rudi slammed his foot down on the accelerator, and the cart began picking up speed quickly.

"Hey, guys!" Collette called out.

Ethan looked back anxiously.

The tunnel was empty.

"Where did it go?" Ethan said.

The tunnel sped quietly by around them.

"Collette?" Ethan asked. "What happened?"

Collette drew in a breath, raising the muzzle of her weapon toward the ceiling. "I don't...I don't know. One moment it was there, and then it took a turn and vanished."

"A turn?" Ethan said.

Collette nodded. "I think it went back down one of those access passages, like we came through to get—"

"Rudi!" Ethan said quickly as he clambered back over the seats next to Collette. "We've got to go faster, right now!"

The electric car responded immediately, suddenly accelerating again. Collette reached out, gripping the rail along the side of the flatbed. The lights of the service tunnel were ripping past at a terrific rate.

"Ethan?" Valja asked, his own weapon raised against the cab driver's massive shoulder. "Is problem?"

"I think that thing moves quicker in larger spaces," Ethan said in a rush. "It's going to try and—"

Another access door blew into the tunnel, clipping the back of the cart and causing it to swerve. Rudi managed to keep the cart on the road, but now the creature was right behind them, rushing down the tunnel in its full fury.

Valja and Collette both lowered their weapons at once, firing simultaneous bursts into the black, shifting monster. They peppered it around the eyes and head as its jaws opened to engulf them.

Collette reached forward on the barrel, flipping the safety off on the grenade launcher. She fired its single round into the maw of the beast.

The dull thud of the explosion splattered pieces of the creature against the walls. It dropped back several feet, weaving in its agony. The jaw hung broken and slack, the eyes on the right side completely missing along with a large part of its head.

But as they watched, the eyes began to grow back and the creature pushed the jaw back into place even as it continued after them.

"It's regenerating!" Valja yelled.

"Give me that!" Ethan shouted, pointing at Valja's gun as he set his camera down between the front seats.

"Why?" the huge cabbie demanded.

"Because I'm pretty sure I can't use a flaming sword!" Ethan yelled back.

Valja handed him the HK AG36. Ethan gripped the handle and put his finger on the trigger.

Valja grabbed Ethan's shoulder and turned him until they were face-to-face.

"Vhen you get to France," Valja said, "you must take Benoit vhere he needs to go, vhere you all must be by midnight tonight. Your lives are at stake!"

"Our lives?" Ethan said. "They're rather at risk now!"

"Benoit vill be out for only few hours," Valja said. "Pray it is enough time to see you there."

"See us where?"

"Mont Saint-Michel," Valja shouted. "The Mountain of Saint Michael!"

"Where?"

"I know it," Collette said after three more shots.

"And what do we do when we get there?" Ethan asked.

"Remember!" Valja growled, his pale eyes bright. The strange sword flamed in his hands. "Mont Saint-Michel tonight! Sojourner vill find you there. I'll meet you there if I can."

"Where are you going?" Ethan asked in astonishment.

"To purchase you some time," Valja said.

"No!" Collette reached up too late to stop him as Valja leapt off the back of the vehicle, his flaming sword raised. He plunged the blade into the face of the creature. It folded under him, skidding along the length of the tunnel as Valja rode on its chest. The demon's tentacles lashed at Valja, tearing bleeding wounds in his flesh, but Valja continued to battle, plunging the blade again and again into the creature's throat.

"Short bursts," shouted Collette.

Ethan took aim, pulled the trigger, then released.

The gun jumped in his hands.

"Are we there yet?" he shouted.

The tunnel began to rise quickly. They were moving away. He could no longer see Valja, but the creature was still there.

Ethan pulled the trigger again and again. After each burst he shouted, "*Are we there yet?*"

*****

The cart burst out of the emergency service tunnel into the sunshine of Calais, suddenly skidding to a stop on the roadway ramp that paralleled the Chunnel rails on the north side.

"Rudi! Why the hell are we stop—"

The cart was immediately surrounded by French armed soldiers, their assault weapons all lowered and pointing directly at the occupants.

Ethan slowly raised his hands above his head, tossing the assault rifle from him and onto the ground. "Play nice, Collette," he said in a calm voice. "Let the nice French soldiers have your gun."

"But Ethan…"

"We just entered their country with armed automatic weapons," Ethan said quietly through a smile. "I think they have the right to ask us a few questions."

Ethan placed his hands on his head and looked slowly around. There were armed soldiers lining the top of the tunnel entrance, and possibly an entire infantry battalion situated in prepared positions on either side of the tracks. They were mixed in with heavy armor, as well, and he thought he could see several lines of artillery beyond the terminal.

"Besides," Ethan said. "I don't think they're here for us."

The Dweller burst out of the service tunnel in a gush, rising up in the open air and expanding to nearly fifty feet in height. Its tendrils shot outward, lancing the soldiers around it, flinging them in long arcs of screaming terror.

The French weapons shifted to the creature, erupting into a cascade of small-arms fire.

All eyes were on the demon that had emerged from the tunnel.

"Let's go, Rudi!" Ethan shouted over the din.

Rudi hit the accelerator pedal once again, driving madly along with the retreating ranks of the French soldiers around them seeking a more defensible position.

The demon waded through the soldiers, rushing for Ethan's cart, but in that instant the French tanks opened fire, their explosions driving the enraged creature backward with sheer force. The soldiers continued to fall back, trying to get clear of the artillery rounds that were sure to drop next.

Rudi drove madly down the road, weaving between the soldiers as explosive rounds started falling all around them in a rain of death and fire.

"Welcome to France," Ethan shouted at Collette through the horrific roars, the screams, and the flying dirt.

CHAPTER 16
NIGHTMARES

The electric cart shot down the roadway, rushing through the hail of small-arms fire, the thump of mortar rounds, and the thunderous concussion of the direct-fire tank rounds. Rudi, eyes wide and both hands with a death grip on the steering wheel, threaded the small vehicle between the soldiers. The road was unbearably straight, following the east side of the rail tracks directly away from the round portal of the service tunnel.

Ethan gripped the slumping form of Dr. Benoit by the jacket collar, trying to prevent him from falling out of the careening vehicle. The Dweller behind them reared up to nearly one hundred feet high, its black, shining hide glistening in the bright noon over Calais. Its enormous tentacles were tearing into the soldiers around it, its claws gripping the battle tanks and tossing them aside as it tried to surge forward.

The artillery blasts and the explosions from the tank rounds continued to press it back, however, preventing it from moving forward.

It was looking for them, Ethan realized. It had come for them.

They sped, barely under control, passing beneath a small bridge and then a second, much wider pair of road bridges overhead—a freeway, Ethan realized. On their left, Ethan could see an emergency response building next to a helipad. There were a pair of security gates but both were opened wide as armored personnel carriers rushed through the fencing.

Ethan tapped Rudi on the shoulder and pointed to the left.

"That way, Rudi!" Ethan yelled over the continuing bombardment behind them.

Rudi pulled the steering wheel hard. The tires bit into the roadway, tipping dangerously before he relaxed the wheel slightly. But then he pulled the wheel back in the opposite direction to avoid an onrushing ambulance. They missed the gate entirely, swerving back onto the road they had just left, continuing down the main road parallel to the tracks.

"What the hell are you doing?" Ethan yelled.

"Get off my back, man!" Rudi yelled back. "I didn't ask for this gig!"

Collette was gripping the low rails surrounding the bed of the truck with white hands, her feet wedging her in firmly. "What? You mean he speaks English?"

"Only when he has to," Ethan answered.

More APCs were roaring up on the opposite side of the roadway. At least for the time being, the French military drivers were following the rules of traffic.

"We need to get out of here," Ethan said, the wind rushing past them. "Make our way into Calais. Get in touch with the Paris Bureau, maybe, or the consulate. Let them know what happened and get some help."

"But what about Benoit?" Collette asked. "Valja said he had to be at Mont Saint-Michel by midnight. He said our lives were at stake."

"Collette, our lives weren't all that 'at stake' until we met these people—or whatever they are," Ethan said. "They're all running some big game, and we don't even know the rules. They're playing us, Collette—and I just don't want to play anymore."

"You don't want to play?" Collette's eyes flashed with anger. "Those people back there probably died just on the chance that you might take the doctor to Mont Saint-Michel! Half the French army seems to be putting their lives on the line, too, by the way."

"No thanks to you," Ethan shot back. "If you hadn't called in Farben to track me down, that demon-monster might not have known where to look for us!"

"I wouldn't have had to look for you if you hadn't sent me away!"

The cart rocked back and forth suddenly.

"Would you two mind chilling for a while?" Rudi called back over his shoulder. "We're not going anywhere in these wheels. If you can manage to just keep your pie holes shut for a few minutes, I think I can arrange for an upgrade."

Rudi slowed the vehicle and pulled into a small parking lot next a set of buildings near the auto loading ramps. The smoke columns continued to rise behind them, while the thunder of the French barrage persisted unabated. Rudi stopped the electric vehicle so quickly that the unconscious Benoit nearly flew forward over the dash, kept in his seat only by considerable effort on Ethan's part.

"That's what I'm talking about," Rudi smiled. "An upgrade."

"That's an upgrade?" Ethan said doubtfully.

"That," Rudi said, clambering out of the electric vehicle, "is just what we need. A Citroën C4 Picasso with all the candy."

"It looks like every SUV I've ever seen," Collette said as she climbed gingerly over the side of the cart. Ethan noticed that her business suit was considerably worse for wear, torn somewhat up the right thigh and spotted all over with greasy, dirty patches. Her hair, despite its truncated length, was definitely not camera ready.

"They're called MPVs here—multi-purpose vehicles," Rudi said with a broad grin. "This one has it all—satellite navigation, Bluetooth hands-free, WiFi, and an HDi 16 engine."

"It's a family van," Ethan said, lifting the limp Benoit out of his seat.

"That's the best part," Rudi grinned. "*Sechantik munkin!* Who's going to give this a second look on the road?"

"Look, I want out of here as much as the next guy, but how are you going to bypass security on that—"

Rudi put his hand to the door, spreading his fingers against the side just below the handle.

The Citroën chirped merrily as the door gave a satisfying thunk. Rudi opened the driver's side door, hopped into the driver's seat, and, pressing the same palm against the steering column, grinned as the engine turned over and spun up to life.

"Don't sweat it," Rudi said, stepping out of the running vehicle. He opened the rear driver's side door, gesturing toward Ethan. "Give the man a seat."

Ethan bundled the doctor into the rear seat. The interior of the car had space for seven—which was, he had to admit, remarkable in a car that size. As Ethan stood up, Rudi leaped back from the car.

"*Awas, deh!*" he said.

Collette had slipped behind Rudi and jumped into the driver's seat, slamming the door behind her. "I'm driving! Get in."

"What do you mean, 'you're driving'?" Ethan asked, wrestling with the seatbelt around the limp Dr. Benoit.

"I'm the only one here who has an international driver's license," Collette said, a fierce determination in her green eyes.

Ethan slammed the door shut and moved to Collette's window. "We're stealing a car and you're worried about one of us having a *license*?"

"Yes!" Collette said, her voice growing louder. "I've been chased by dead museum displays, kidnapped, threatened, nearly eaten by some monster underneath the English Channel, and I'm tired of being told what to do! The steering wheel's on the left side and so am I, so grab your damn camera, get in the car, and shut up!"

A flight of six Mirage 2000 jets shrieked overhead, just barely above the roof of the building across the road. Ethan ducked involuntarily and raised both his hands in surrender to the woman he was supposed to be babysitting on this "simple assignment." He had seen enough people under stress to know that they sometimes would cling to anything they could control when everything else was uncontrollable. "Anything you say, Collette."

"I call shotgun!" Rudi exclaimed, grabbing a courier bag from the electric vehicle.

"Where did you get that?" Ethan asked, snatching his camera from the vehicle before climbing into the back next to Benoit.

"Oh, just something I picked up," Rudi said, running around the car and hopping into the front seat. "I thought it might come in handy."

"Well, Collette," Ethan said. "Where are we going?"

The shriek of ripple-fired rockets tore through the air overhead.

"Anywhere but here," she said as she quickly pulled out of the parking lot, the car wonderfully agile and quick to accelerate. It pushed them quickly down the road as a wall of fire erupted at the mouth of the Channel Tunnel entrance nearly a mile and a quarter behind them.

Ethan, sitting in the rear passenger's seat, drew his hand down his weary face. He had not really slept since the flight into Heathrow. Sojourner had done something to him to get him on the train—there was a gap in his memory—but for a woman capable of animating the plastic dead, playing Ethan like a puppet must have been easy. Whatever that had been, it had not been sleep. Sitting in the relatively familiar surroundings of a car—even a stolen one—left him feeling suddenly drained.

He tilted his head down as he rolled his neck. Dr. Benoit's glasses had fallen off his face and onto the floor. The frame had sprung out from when Ethan had hit him during their escape up the service tunnel. With a weary sigh, Ethan reached down to the floor, picking up the glasses.

They felt familiar to him, comfortable in his hands, although he could scarcely guess at why. He had always had perfect eyesight and often eschewed even wearing sunglasses, as he felt they changed his perception of color around him. He preferred to squint under a hat visor than alter his view. Yet here he held another man's bent glasses and they seemed entirely natural in his hands.

He adjusted the bent wire slightly and then, without thinking, he raised them up and put them on.

He was looking into another world.

*****

These were not his eyes.

He saw himself—Abraxas—laboring above the high peaks. His great chest was heaving with the effort, his long wings dragging his body with enormous speed through the sky. He saw, too, the diminutive form of Tsanya astride his back leaning forward against the rushing wind in their desperate flight.

These were not his memories.

These were Fafnir's eyes. These were Fafnir's thoughts. This was Fafnir's soul and destiny.

He felt a great love for his brood brother well up within his heart. Abraxas the true. Abraxas the honorable. Abraxas who had always placed his own life between the taint and karma.

Now, thought Fafnir, they were on their last and longest of journeys. The world was ending around them, but Tsanya had spoken of a dawn beyond the fall of the sky and a hope beyond death. He understood the journey of the scions and how desperate a chance the Seelie Court was taking in sending their souls to sleep among the children of men. More desperate, perhaps, than the Seelie knew, for once they had been transmuted into human hosts, the dragons would be far more vulnerable to the taint, especially in its final death throes. The taint itself was aware that it, too, was being dragged from the world.

The eyes of Fafnir looked behind him. There, against the failing stars, he could see their forms:

dragons who had become taint-taken—their souls lost to the darkness, now devoid of the karmic light. They desired above all else to drag the soul of the great Abraxas and his brothers into the long, tormented night with them—to make them as miserable as they. The taint had expended its last, dying fury upon the taint-taken dragons—driving them across the sky that they might murder the scions before they had a chance to live and thereby thwart all the plans of light.

And such was the speed of their fury that they would overtake them all before they reached the summit of Mount Olygean and the transmutation would never be.

Such were the thoughts of Fafnir—thoughts Abraxas had never known—as he gazed with growing resolve upon his brood brother, who struggled before him through the thin, high air. Fafnir knew Abraxas was better than he. Fafnir knew Abraxas would survive.

And Fafnir thought, in the dawn beyond the night, that Abraxas would somehow remember and save him.

But only if Abraxas lived through this night.

Fafnir drew in a deep breath.

These were not his eyes. These were not his wings. Yet it was Abraxas's heart that broke as Fafnir turned in the night to take on the taint-taken dragons alone, for the sake of his brood brother's hope.

*****

Ethan pulled the glasses violently away from his face.

He looked over at Dr. Benoit. The older man's grey hair was disheveled, his eyes closed, but Ethan could see them moving under the eyelids. His lips were quivering, trying to form sounds in his deep, mystical slumber.

Ethan carefully folded the somewhat fixed glasses and slipped them into the breast pocket of Benoit's jacket. He sat back, thinking for a few interminable minutes.

"Collette?" he finally said.

"Calais's the next exit," Collette answered. "I'm not stopping for a bathroom before then."

"We're not going to Calais," Ethan said.

"We're not?"

Both Collette and Rudi glanced back at him.

"No," Ethan replied, his voice husky. "Rudi, tell that GPS to show the way to Mont Saint-Michel."

CHAPTER 17
ROAD RAGE

The A16 was closed around the vicinity of the Channel Tunnel entrance, requiring that they navigate the surface streets for a while before the GPS could provide a route around the carnage still taking place there. At last they managed to find the A16 and headed south, roughly parallel to the French coast.

The A16 proved to be a toll road. The first few toll plazas had their gates open due to the evacuation request from Calais, and they were hurriedly waved through along with a considerable number of other refugees. The demarcation lines on the road proved to be largely suggestions, and the speed limit something beyond safe and prudent. Just outside of Abbeville, Collette followed the GPS instructions and merged onto the A28/E402. Ethan read the words "Le Havre" on the road sign—a name that had some meaning to him from his study during his youth of World War II, but its location was still a mystery to him. It was soon afterward that Collette pulled over into a rest area on the long and seemingly interminable A28 for a bathroom stop. Ethan objected at first, but the suggestion itself proved too much for him, so he took his opportunity in the cone-shaped bathroom building.

The confusion in Calais would eventually come to an end, and with it might also come the awareness that a Citroën owner in Calais was missing his Picasso automobile. But no one bothered them, and they continued until the GPS directed them to the A29/ E44 exit and their first closed toll booth. There was an awkward scramble for a few moments as they approached the toll since there was a distinct lack of Euros among three of the conscious passengers in the car. Fortunately, thanks to Rudi's quick hands, Dr. Benoit's wallet provided the required funds before they arrived at the toll gate.

Exact change was not an option, so Collette approached one of the manned toll booths. Ethan held his breath as Collette negotiated the change. An African American man, a Southeast Asian youth, a Caucasian woman, and an old, unconscious Frenchman in the back seat sounded like either a joke or a very high profile. Yet the French toll operator made the exchange with little comment, the gate swung open, and once again they were back on the road. With each successive toll booth, Ethan began to relax a little more.

In time, the long farmlands and quaint towns of the French countryside gave way to more modern construction, storage tanks, and light industrial buildings behind the lush trees. They crossed the Seine over the Ponte de Normandie suspension bridge east of Honfleur just as the rain began to fall, following as it curved around to the southeast, then taking the right-hand exit on the interchange onto the A13 tollway.

The rain started coming down in earnest as the Citroën hummed along the four-lane tollway. It had been over two hours, and only now was Ethan starting to actually relax. It appeared they were ahead of the law for the time being and had a lot of road ahead of them. It was time to have a nice long talk with Rudi.

"Where did you get the iPad?" Ethan asked from the back seat.

"Oh, this little thing?" Rudi looked back over his shoulder from the front seat with an impish grin on his face, turning the iPad back and forth in front of Ethan. "It was just lying around, you know, and not doing anyone any good."

"It's got *J. Farben* etched into the back of the case." Ethan pointed at the back.

Rudi flipped the pad over, feigning pleasant surprise. "Why, yes, I believe it does. But come to think of it, I don't believe he is going to be needing it for awhile."

"You're right. I suppose Mr. Jonas Farben has

other things on his mind about now…if anything," Ethan said, his elbows on both seat backs as he leaned in from the back seat. "Does it work?"

Rudi just shook his head. "Oh, man, you don't know me very well if you're asking that question."

He touched the edges of the device and the screen lit up at once. The security login flashed for a moment and then the home screen came up.

"Anything you want to know?" Rudi asked, flexing his fingers over the touchscreen.

"Yeah," Ethan answered. "How did you do that?"

"Ancient Chinese secret, man!"

"Yeah, you're not Chinese," Ethan said and shook his head. "Who are these Grey Gentlemen we keep running into?"

"You want the official story or the real one?" Rudi sniffed.

"The real one, I guess," Ethan answered.

Rudi opened a browser window and began typing on the touchscreen. The number of keystrokes his fingers made, however, were fewer than the number of letters appearing in the search bar.

Ethan grimaced. "*Wikipedia*? That's where you're getting the real answer?"

Rudi scoffed. "The net's been redacted, man. Anything you see on official sites is just whipped cream and cherries covering up the real thing. The Wiki's the only place where the info comes straight from the people—and now it's the most reliable place for the honest dope. It's not filtered by the Man. Governments have tried shutting it down, man, but they've gone all voodoo underground and their servers keep moving. You want it undiluted—this be the place."

"Fine," Ethan surrendered. The world was upside down, and he just had to get used to it. "What have you got?"

"Check this out," Rudi said, and read aloud, "'Grey Gentlemen: Derived from the phrase "men in grey suits" referring to men in business who have a lot of power and influence though the public does not see them or know about them. In the modern context, the term refers to the insidious forms in which Those Who Dwell Below have chosen to masquerade in the modern age. The Dweller compresses its form into a close approximation of a man, then uses its intrinsic alien power to ward the minds of those who see it against its true appearance. However, the Dwellers have difficulty maintaining details and may be discovered through minor inconsistencies that generate a feeling of unease in those who view them. To casual observers, however, there is nothing extraordinary about these men in their grey business suits and bowler hats. They appear, apart from their outmoded hats, no different from the tens of thousands of similarly attired businessmen who work in London or its environs each day.'"

"Well, that certainly sounds like the Jeeves following us."

"Is there a cross-link to those Dweller things?"

Ethan asked.

"Yeah, here it is." Rudi tapped and the screen changed. "Oh, you're not gonna like this one bit: 'The Great Enemy, the Dwellers, the Oqalay'ta, the Deep Terrors, Siths, Firbolg…' Well, they have a lot of cheerful names. Anyway: 'Shapeless, insidious evil that has moved beneath the earth since mankind's first emergence. In earlier times, the Dwellers had forms that might have been considered beautiful. Legends tell that they could become whatever they believed themselves to be and took on shapes both graceful and natural. Changes in the world, however, caused them to flee underground where they lost their ability to maintain specific forms for long. They sought refuge in an underground abyssal region known as Catham. With the coming of a new age they attempted to return to the surface.'

"Apparently that didn't go very well 'cause here it says: 'One by one they left the tainted mass of their collective hive, and as they emerged, took on the forms of beasts terrible and unique, each one shaped from shards of the dreams and nightmares of the ancient race. These forms were as efficient as they were horrific: they bore tentacles and claws to pull the bulk of the creatures through the lightless caverns, as well as countless eyes and orifices to see and prey upon the primitive life that made its homes in the tunnels…'"

Ethan let out a low whistle. "Well, that certainly

sounds like what we met in the Chunnel."

"Hey!" Rudi said cheerfully. "It says here the Dwellers discovered that their forms were not only malleable, but could mimic others' shapes. All that was necessary for any of the individual Dwellers to attain a shape was for 'that creature to be brought, living, to Catham, and there be immersed in a living lake and fed upon by the Dwellers' many minds…'"

"Thanks, Rudi," Ethan said quickly. "I think we get the picture."

"So what do you have on scions?" Collette asked. She was tired of driving, and it was showing in her eyes and the sound of her voice. The rain pounded the roof of the MPV and showered down the windshield as she subconsciously hunched over the wheel in order to see better.

Rudi drew in a deep breath. "Well, we've got a reference to kinship, as in a descendant from a noble house or family…that sounds promising…something about a twig and grafting…there's this shoe-box-on-wheels car by Toyota, some comics, a couple of computer game references…oh, here's the money entry: 'Scions: A living vessel for dragon souls.' That sound like what you're looking for, boss?"

"Read it out," Ethan said.

"We got time," Rudi said. "'Scion (*dragon lore*): A scion is a mythic character type from Seelie lore of Ireland combining story archetypes of Norse and Vandal legends and is closely related to fae changeling tales. Scions were said to be living, human vessels for the containment, transportation, and survival of the immortal souls of dragons. While the legends differ in details, most agree that the souls of the dragons lived within their human host until that host reproduced, thereby allowing the transfer of the dragon's soul to the growing body of the infant child. Thus, scions are most often described as being in their youth. The main stories revolve around dragon souls sleeping until magic again enters the world and the final conflict of the End Times takes place. (*SEE End Times, Armageddon, End of Days, Qiyamah, Kali Yuga, Ragnarök*).'"

"Scions are supposed to be connected to the end of the world?" Collette asked skeptically.

"Yeah, that's about it," Rudi said, gesturing at the screen. He craned his neck around to look at Ethan. "So, you got a name in this dream, Mr. Scion?"

"Abraxas," Ethan said quietly.

"Abracadabrax?" Rudi said.

"Don't be a smart ass." Ethan nodded toward the iPad.

Rudi typed again across the screen. His eyebrows rose.

"Well, look at this… 'Abraxas (*dragon*): Legendary dragon of Trocea (*need reference*). In *The Book of Fomador*, he is the dragon referred to as "fireborn," first of his brood, and master of flame and light. Said to have sunk Atlantis and stolen magic from the world. He was most often accompanied by his two brothers, Fafnir and…'"

Rudi's voice trailed off.

"And who, Rudi?" Ethan said.

"Apalala." Rudi looked out the window for a moment, taking in the green trees behind the rain as they blurred past. "Weird, huh?"

"Why?" Collette asked. "Who's Apalala?"

Rudi continued to look out the window as he spoke.

"Me," he said. "I'm Apalala. At least, that's what my dreams are all about."

"So this second dragon," Ethan said, grabbing the iPad out of Rudi's hands. "Is there a reference to… hey, it died!"

Rudi turned around, an irritated look on his face. "Of course it did! Give me that!" He snatched the device away from Ethan, and it instantly sprang back to life.

"I see you've got a talent," Ethan said.

"And it's *my* talent, so lay off," Rudi snapped.

"What about the reference to Fafnir?" Ethan nodded again to the tablet.

"Fine!" Rudi grumbled. "There's a lot of stuff here about some Norse mythology and some Icelandic legends…blah, blah, blah…hey…wait a minute, there's something here about that Fomador book… 'In *The Book of Fomador*, Fafnir is said to be the brother of Abraxas and Apalala. In the twenty-second canto of that work, he is said to have stayed behind to protect his brothers at the Turning of the Wheel and the Change of the World. He saved the souls of his brothers before he was taint-taken, his own soul sacrificed for their sake. He was condemned to his own scion fate—but the seeds of his darkness carried over with his soul down through the ages.'"

"Taint-taken?" Ethan frowned. "What the hell is that?"

Rudi rolled his head around, trying to loosen his neck muscles. His fingers flitted against the touchscreen display.

"The reference comes from here... 'Taint: The corruption of karma and considered its opposite. Created when the flow of karma is damaged or overused. It is most often associated with the general concept of the negative. For example, it is associated with and said to induce feelings of heaviness, rage, despair, or fear. It is an unnatural force contrary to life... Souls or spirits who have been taint-tempted or taint-trapped can choose to embrace the taint rather than strive against it. These are said to be "taint-taken." The individual becomes an unnatural creature, his will subverted to the perverted forces of the taint.'"

"Well, that's cheerful," Ethan said. "So is that what's happened to the professor back here?"

"Seems so," Rudi shrugged. "But it says that he had to willingly embrace the taint. So any way you look at it, the dude called it on himself. It ain't nobody else's problem, man—and that especially includes me."

"Does it say anything about getting rid of it?" Collette asked.

"It says here they can be 'rescued,'" Rudi said. "It takes…"

Rudi suddenly stopped mid-sentence.

"What?" Ethan urged.

"Well," Rudi started speaking again slowly, his tempo increasing as he managed to force out the words, "excuse me while I quote: 'The taint-taken can be rescued from their state. They must be removed from all areas already affected by the taint and taken to a place of high karma. There, only their broodmates will be able to affect the taint-taken's state and wouldn't you like to know how to do that, Ethan Gallows?'"

"Very funny, Rudi," Ethan said.

"You can think so if you want, man," Rudi said, holding up the iPad. "But that's what it says right here."

Ethan gaped at the screen. At the end of the paragraph appeared the words "and wouldn't you like to know how to do that, Ethan Gallows?"

Collette interrupted. "Uh, guys—"

Ethan ignored her. "How did you…what does the citation read?"

Rudi took the tablet back and checked the reference. "It says the modification of the file was made by 'Sojourner'—no last name."

"When?"

"Six days ago."

"Seriously, Ethan," Collette called more urgently. "We may have a problem."

"What?" Ethan asked irritably.

"I don't know if anyone else has noticed," Collette said, doing her best to stay calm, "but there are no other cars on the road."

The GPS indicated exiting to the right. Ethan managed to catch the signs over the deserted roadway pointing the direction to Rennes and Cherbourg. They were on the outskirts of Caen, and all he could see was what looked like fierce and almost continuous lightning flashing from the direction of the city center through the falling rain.

"What is that?" Collette asked urgently.

"Just keep driving," Ethan said. "This is a belt route around the city…maybe if we stay on this we can avoid—"

His words were drowned out almost at once by the roar of a four-engine vintage bomber skimming over the top of the car, two of its starboard engines on fire and trailing thick, black smoke.

"It's a Lancaster, or maybe a Halifax. I never could tell them apart," Ethan shouted, craning to see better through the passenger window in the rear of the car. "It's got RAF markings and looks big enough to be a Lancaster but—"

His words were drowned out by the explosion of the bomber slamming into the gigantic shopping mall complex to the south of the road.

"Is it the Air Force?" Rudi gaped.

"Not since the 1940s," Ethan said. "But who would be flying...oh, nuts! Collette! Watch out!"

It was too late to brake. Collette swerved into the passing lane, narrowly avoiding the column of mud-caked soldiers slogging in formation down the road ahead of her. There were several large vehicles also moving at a snail's pace further ahead, veiled by the rain.

"Who are they?" Collette demanded.

"You mean who *were* they?" Ethan breathed.

Rank after rank of soldiers flashed by their speeding car, all covered in mud-streaked grey. Their stahlhelm-style helmets were as distinctive as the insignia on the dark collars of their tunics. But it was their ashen, blotchy faces with their dull, lifeless eyes and patches of peeling flesh that shocked Ethan nearly as much as their uniforms. They weren't nearly as decomposed as they should have been.

"The 12th SS Panzer Division," Ethan said, swallowing hard. "I guess the war is back on in Normandy."

Ahead of them, the width of the roadway was blocked completely by a line of German panzer tanks clattering and roaring down the toll road, their treads digging into the asphalt. Collette slowed down and their Citroën Picasso fell in line between two ranks of the zombie German soldiers.

Ethan glanced at Benoit. The man was still unconscious, but his arms and legs were making violent, jerking movements. "They seem to be affecting our friend here in the back seat."

"What do I do?" Collette's voice broke at the end of her question. Her hands were bone-white from her grip on the wheel.

Ethan took in a long breath. "They don't seem interested in us. Let's not do anything to change that. We're all one big, happy Nazi army of the undead here, OK? They look like they're taking the exit up ahead. Maybe we can just…pass them?"

The panzers began forming a single line; the lead tank, flying a Nazi battle flag from its radio mast, moved the column down the Mondeville exit.

"The thunder's getting worse," Collette shouted.

"That ain't thunder," Rudi said.

Columns of earth exploded skyward in front of them. The artillery rounds began falling ever closer in a continuous bombardment from the city center.

Dr. Benoit awoke with a start, his eyes wide and arms thrashing where he sat buckled in. He screamed, trying to form words but remaining unintelligible through his terror.

The tank commander in the turret ahead of them suddenly turned in their direction, his sightless eyes fixed on the car.

The ranks of soldiers around them all turned their heads as one in their direction.

"Go, Collette, go!" Ethan yelled. "It's a war zone!"

Collette turned on her blinker, pressing through the line of panzers without making eye contact with the SS tank commander who was now watching her intensely. The commander keyed his throat microphone, and the enormous panzer in front of them came to a sudden, rocking halt.

Collette swerved through the Nazi soldiers, pointed the car down the two-lane divided motorway, and jammed the accelerator to the floor. The Citroën responded at once, leaping forward in a rush down the rain-drenched open road before them. The artillery rounds were falling around them now on either side of the road, dirt and rocks pelting the vehicle as it surged forward.

Ethan turned around, peering out the rear window.

The turret on the lead panzer was shifting, its 7.5 cm KwK 40 long gun dropping downward as it swung toward them. Three of the following tanks were following suit. It had barely stopped its traverse when there was a flash from the muzzle.

"Hurry, Collette!" Ethan shouted. If they could make it through the railway overpass ahead of them, they might get away with their escape. "I think they're—"

The shot from the panzer was not accurate, but it did not need to be. The round exploded into the railway overpass just ahead and to the left of them with an impact that pushed the light Citroën sideways.

Collette instinctively hit the brakes, skidding over the rain-slick road and then overcorrecting. The Citroën flipped sideways, rolling several times before coming to a stop upside down.

The next thing Ethan was aware of was hanging

upside down from his seatbelt in the crumpled car.
Rainwater splashed against his face through the broken window, and ashen-faced, dead-footed soldiers
on both sides of the overturned car looked in at them,
several raising their MP40 submachine guns in his
direction.

CHAPTER 18
IRON CROSS

"What do we do?" Collette asked, her voice quiet and intense, and her words entirely too fast. "What do we do?"

Ethan looked out the side of the antique car, still in disbelief at the Nazi markings on the vehicle as well as the animated corpses in the seats in front of him. One of them drove the *Kübelwagen*, the German equivalent of a WWII-era jeep, while the other held his machine gun on the four of them packed into the back seat—including Dr. Benoit, who was obviously confused and was shivering uncontrollably. Ethan could see to the right side of the off-ramp the remains of a late-model Nissan Titan truck, the driver's side door riddled with bullet holes. The cargo bed was mangled almost beyond recognition by what Ethan could easily imagine as a round from one of the *panzerfaust* anti-tank weapons he could see carried by several of the marching dead around them.

"Just…we just wait," Ethan said, gritting his teeth. "If they had wanted us dead we wouldn't still be here talking about it now."

"Now, why doesn't that make me feel any better?" Rudi asked in a nervous sulk from where he was uncomfortably smashed against the far wall of the vehicle.

The zombie driver followed the column of panzers around the off-ramp, the dead soldiers of a dead Reich surrounding their car, all of whom were matching the pace of the tanks ahead of them. The bombardment had shifted to the west for the time being, and the Nazis were using the lull to move. The column followed the roundabout at the top of the off-ramp, exiting into the vast parking lot of the mall. The end of the huge building was still burning furiously from the crash of the Lancaster bomber.

"We are in big trouble," Ethan said.

The enormous parking lot was being used as a staging area by the Nazi zombies. An SdKfz 10/4 half-track, self-propelled flack gun stood to the side of the roundabout with a full crew of grey-skinned dead congratulating themselves on the downing of the bomber. Several more of the Volkswagen *Kübelwagen* jeeps were pulled into the gas station and refueling from the modern pumps there. Seven panzers were parked in the lot of an auto shop where maintenance crews were repairing the tanks.

In an open patch of parking lot, Ethan saw a company of zombie soldiers marching in the grey rain, their hoarse voices raised in singing the *Panzerlied*.

Ob's stürmt oder schneit, ob die Sonne uns lacht,
Der Tag glühend heiß, oder eiskalt die Nacht,
Bestaubt sind die Gesichter, doch froh ist unser Sinn,
Ja, unser Sinn,
Es braust unser Panzer im Sturmwind dahin.

An entire dead army was working furiously in the rain—while the flash and thunder of explosions came from the center of the city to the west and just slightly north.

An *oberstleutnant* on the road in front of them motioned them to follow a single panzer that had pulled off the road. The tank swiveled into a parking lot, digging great gouges out of the asphalt, and stopped. From the top of its turret, a single corpse—the *hauptmann* in charge of the panzer tank column—pushed himself up out of the hatch, straightened his field tunic, and adjusted his officer's cap so that it would sit perfectly square on his head. He spoke briefly in the rain to the oberstleutnant, motioning toward Ethan, before turning on his heels and striding toward the building behind which they were now parked.

"Rudi," Ethan said quickly. "How's the professor doing?"

"Oh, who cares?" Rudi shot back.

"I do," Ethan snapped. "Don't piss me off, Rudi. You don't have a lot of friends here."

"Chill, man," Rudi said, holding up his arms as best he could in the cramped space. "Look at him! It's like he's on speed and tranks all at the same time. I've never had someone react that way after I touched them. Usually they're just out. Whatever's here is trying to wake him up, I guess. That makes for a confused dude who looks mostly like he needs rehab."

The hollow-eyed Nazi soldier waved the barrel of his MP40 at them. "*Raus! Raus! Schnell!*"

"I've watched enough war movies to know what that means," Rudi said. He gripped Dr. Benoit's left arm and pulled the jerking, confused curator toward the open door of the command car. "Let's go, Alice."

Ethan got his shoulder under the arm of Benoit and then realized where they were going.

The Nazi tank commander stood in the doorway next to the drive-thru, waiting for them to follow him in out of the rain. The zombies had set up their headquarters in a McDonald's.

"Are we supposed to give our name, rank, and number of our order?" Rudi asked.

*****

The argument was deafening.

Ethan struggled through the door assisting the dazed Dr. Benoit and nearly dropping him just inside the entrance.

A group of Nazi commanders were gathered

around one of the central tables in the McDonald's, a
tourist map of Caen spread out on the plastic surface
before them. Their flesh was appalling—a putrid grey
color with deep coagulation blotches in the hollows
of their cheeks and around their sunken, dried-out
eyes. Their pointing fingers were barely sheathed in
any flesh at all. A number of salt and pepper packets
were scattered across the surface of the brochure, as
well as a smaller number of small fast-food boxes.
The argument was heated between them, and Ethan
didn't understand a single word of it. He had always
been fascinated with World War II, especially after
the stories his father had told him of the Tuskegee
Airmen and the black combat soldiers who volun-
teered for duty the moment Eisenhower—desperate
for manpower—had desegregated the front lines during the Battle of the Bulge. But, somehow, that had
not translated into an interest in learning the German
language, which to his ear sounded now both entirely
too fast and too harsh.

The tank commander stepped up to the table,
clicking his heels and offering his Nazi salute in
a sharp manner. Most of the men around the table
acknowledged the salute with a half-hearted return,
while some of the older-appearing *Wehrmacht* gen-
erals did not bother at all.

The hauptmann tank commander then smartly deposited Jonas's iPad computer bag, Collette's purse,
and Ethan's camera, wallet and, passport on the table.
The dead officers all leaned in closer with heightened

curiosity as one of them with *oberst* insignia shoulder boards began gingerly pawing through the items. The man rifled through Ethan's wallet and passport and then picked up the Sony camera.

Ethan did not speak German, but perhaps he knew just enough to get himself in trouble.

"*Kamera, Herr Oberst,*" Ethan called out.

The Nazi commander's dead eyes shifted at once to Ethan. "*Was haben Sie gesagt?*"

Ethan swallowed hard. An army of the dead would have little reservation about shooting anyone, he figured, so their only hope lay in not waiting for their own inevitable firing squad. He pointed at the Sony still in the commander's hand. "*Kamera. Bitte, Herr Oberst,* that's my…damn…*das ist meine Kamera.*"

The oberst stared at Ethan for a few moments— along with the rest of the staff around the table and almost twenty adjutants crowding the room. Then the oberst suddenly smiled, his cheeks drawing his thin skin back away from his yellow teeth. His mouth opened, and he laughed heartily, the sound of it like a ludicrous death rattle. The other officers around the table chuckled as well. The oberst picked up Ethan's passport again, flicked it open under his dead gaze for a moment, and then stepped around the table, the camera still in hand.

"So you are an American cameraman, Ethan Gallows," the oberst said, his voice dry and grating. His accent was heavy but his English very clear. "Your papers tell us that you are working for the CNN. No doubt a division of your OSS and their puppets at MI6, although why your leaders would have thought a *neger* to be able to infiltrate our lines unnoticed is laughable."

Ethan kept a firm grip on his anger. He knew the Nazi was baiting him, but he reminded himself that the man was already dead and no doubt had only memories of a different time. He spoke carefully, "As you say…it is laughable."

"Your name is most appropriate, Gallows," the oberst said, jutting out his prominent chin in defiance. He swung his head back casually toward the officers still standing around the map. "*Herr Galgen!*"

The officers all laughed at the joke.

"Well, Herr Galgen, I am Oberst von Essen, and we know all about you and your little plans." The zombie pushed the rotting flesh of his face a hand's breadth away from Ethan's nose. The stench coming from the creature's putrefied lungs was nauseating. He doubted the monster needed to breathe for anything more than to hear the sound of his own voice. "We were informed of your coming, and now you are in our hands."

"You knew we were coming?" Collette asked in surprise. "That's not possible!"

"Anything is possible for the Third Reich!" von Essen shouted in indignation. "I have been to your Cambridge Universities and your London Theaters! I have studied your weak-willed society and its moral decadence! You Americans sat on your fat asses and did nothing, while we built a Europe that was unified and strong—beating its soft, useless iron into strong steel with our blood and the treads of our panzers. Of all people, you Americans should have been on our side—were on our side—against the English monarchists who you yourselves threw out of your own country! Now you think that you can enter this war in which you have no business, to meddle in the affairs of greater nations than you, undermine their resolve, and conspire with your own enemies to deny the destiny of the German Reich?"

Ethan stood very still. The oberst was building to a blind rage.

"You inferior swine!" The oberst was screaming. "You are everything that I crave to destroy! A *neger*, a dirty Oriental, and this," the Nazi raged as he pointed at Collette, "an obvious Jewess! Three inferior races meddling in affairs far beyond their comprehension! I would shoot you myself in that kitchen, cook your hearts on that grill, and eat them myself if I had my will."

The oberst took a step back. Ethan did not move.

"But we must obey orders," Oberst von Essen said, shaking, as he tried to control himself with such violence that a patch of skin dislodged from the back of his hand. "It is your lucky day, Herr Galgen, you and your conspirators. You are to be questioned by a ranking officer of the *Abwehr* who will be here this very afternoon. It was he, in fact, who ferreted out your plot and alerted us to your coming."

"The man who discovered us?" Ethan asked, coloring his voice with a hint of fear. It was easy enough to fake, considering his surroundings. He hoped that taking on a ridiculously submissive role would make it easier to get close to this oberst and tear his throat out when the opportunity presented itself. Zombies, he decided, he could put up with. Nazis were far worse.

"That's right," von Essen continued. "Generalleutnant Demisch will be arriving from Calais. Once he has you in custody, he tells us that our victory is assured."

"Generalleutnant Demisch?" Ethan asked.

"*Ja*," von Essen said, his putrid eyelids narrowing over his dead eyes. "I see that you are familiar with the generalleutnant."

Disgust flashed across Ethan's face. "Yes, Herr Oberst, but not by that name."

"Then we will get you reacquainted," von Essen said, turning his attention back to the Sony camera in his hands. The oberst turned away, stepping back toward the officers still gathered around the tourist map spread on the table.

"Who's he talking about?" Rudi whispered behind Ethan. "Who's Demisch?"

"Not Demisch. *Demissie*," Ethan said quietly, shaking his head. "That bastard just doesn't give up, does he?"

"A most unusual camera," von Essen said, turning back toward Ethan. "Where do you put the film?"

Ethan was about to answer when a loud voice called out behind him, "*Achtung!*"

A shorter man—barely five feet seven inches tall, Ethan guessed—strode purposefully into the room. He wore a peaked officer's cap—a *Schirmmütze*—with a set of wrap-around goggles resting above the visor. His double-breasted trench coat was wet from the rain, the distinctive epaulets faded in color, but their markings as a general officer were still visible and, to Ethan, shockingly distinctive. That the man was another of the animated dead was unquestionable, though he was more whole than most Ethan had seen thus far. He held the baton of a *general feldmarschall* in his gloved hand.

Every zombie in the room snapped to attention, the heels of their boots cracking together and their backs straightening. Right arms flew upward in the Nazi salute.

The feldmarschall raised his baton in return, then glanced over Collette, Rudi, and Benoit before turning his attention to Ethan.

Ethan stared back into the familiar face. He had only seen this visage in black-and-white photographs, but he was certain that it would not have been this grey-green color when the man had been alive.

The feldmarschall stepped up to the table and examined the objects, then turned to von Essen.

"Who are these people?" the feldmarschall asked, pointing toward Ethan.

"Bitte, General Feldmarschall—"

"Sprechen auf Englisch, Herr Oberst!"

"Spies, Herr Feldmarschall!" von Essen replied at

once. "We have been ordered to detain them!"

"Nonsense," the feldmarschall casually replied. He stepped closer to Ethan, both his hands holding his marshal's baton behind his back. "They are non-combatants in this action."

"But, Herr Feldmarschall—"

"I am telling you that they have nothing to do with our purposes here," the feldmarschall said, his tone more definite and forceful as he turned again to face the oberst. "Did they have any weapons?"

"Their objects are highly suspect, Herr Feld-marschall!"

The brow of the feldmarschall lowered. He spoke slowly, as though to help the oberst understand. "Are any of those objects weapons, Herr Oberst?"

"Nein, mein herr!"

"Then you will return them at once," the feld-marschall said directly, "and release them."

"No!" came a sudden shout.

Ethan turned at once toward the sound in dismay.

Dr. Benoit, shaken from his stupor, was hastily setting his glasses back on his nose to see where he was, his eyes wide. He rushed forward toward the oberst. Several of the soldiers in the room raised their weapons in alarm.

"Do not listen to him!" pleaded Dr. Benoit. "He is a traitor to the Reich!"

CHAPTER 19
GENERAL MADNESS

Oberst von Essen and the feldmarschall both re-acted strongly, but there were few others in the McDonald's dining area who understood English.

"*Dies ist ein Verräter an das Reich!*" Dr. Benoit corrected himself as he pointed toward the feld-marschall.

The remaining Nazi officers at last understood. They glanced at one another for a moment and then broke into a hideous rendition of laughter.

"*Du Idiot!*" The oberst laughed until a piece of his ear fell from his head. "*Dies ist Feldmarschall Rommel!*"

"*Du irrst, mein herr. Ich bin nicht Rommel,*" said the feldmarschall.

The smile fell at once from the face of the oberst, and the laughter from the dead officers in the room quickly faded. The enlisted soldiers along the walls shifted listlessly.

The oberst shrugged, his rotting face contorting in disbelief as though some trick were being played on him. "*Aber, mein herr...*"

"*Nein. Rommel ist tot.*"

The oberst looked back at the panzer command staff, his hands open in front of him as if asking a question. The commanders cast uneasy glances at each other.

"Rommel is dead," the feldmarschall stated again in English. "The 12th SS Panzer Division is dead. Everyone here is dead. You, Herr Oberst, are most definitely dead."

The muffled explosions of artillery rounds rumbled through the room from several miles west of the Mc-Donald's. The sound of the rain filled the silence.

The feldmarschall took off his hat and began removing his gloves as he spoke. "Tell me, Ernst: we have known each other a long time, have we not?"

The oberst nodded. "*Ja*, since North Africa."

"And you have clear orders as to your objective, *ja*?"

"*Jawohl, mein herr!*"

"Humor me, Ernst," the feldmarschall said as he removed his gloves. The hands had such a cadaverous look to them that Ethan wished the general had kept his gloves on. "Tell me your orders."

The oberst clicked his dead heels together. "We are to search for and capture enemy spies—as we have done, *mein herr*."

"That is surely not something requiring an entire panzer battalion," the feldmarschall quipped. "What is your military objective?"

"We are to break through the lines of the enemy, crush the resistance, and blitz westward just beyond La Cambe. Once there, we are to rendezvous with other elements."

"And then?" the feldmarschall asked quietly.

"I do not understand, Herr Feldmarschall," the oberst said.

"Do you have further orders?"

"Those are my orders."

"And who gave you those orders?"

"Mein herr?"

"It is a simple question, Herr Oberst," the feldmarschall said, his clouded eyes narrowing in the direction of the dead Nazi officer standing at attention before him. "Who gave you those orders? Was it General von Rundstedt? Perhaps the division commander. Was it Feuchtinger? No?"

"I…we have received our orders, Herr Feldmarschall!" the oberst answered, as though the reply should have been sufficient justification.

"I see," replied the feldmarschall as he stepped past the oberst to look down at the map. Ethan could see the border embellishments announcing different inns along the Normandy coast. The feldmarschall began pointing at locations around the brightly colored map. "So here we are on the outskirts of Caen. The invasion forces opposing us are here, here, and here, threatening to surround us, and yet your orders are to search for spies and break through these lines to…where did you say, Ernst?"

"To La Cambe, *mein herr*!"

The feldmarschall nodded, his gaze cast down on the map as he spoke. "And do you know what is *in* this place just outside of La Cambe, Ernst?"

"I was not informed," the oberst replied.

The feldmarschall drew in a deep, painful breath.

"It is your graves," he said.

The sound of the rain increased outside the windows.

"We have all been dead for over fifty years," the feldmarschall said, straightening up. "We are puppets fighting and refighting a war that was lost long ago."

"What is this nonsense?" said an oberstleutnant standing on the far side of the table. "Are you telling us that we are ghosts?"

"No, we are not ghosts," the feldmarschall said. "We are that which is left behind when our ghosts depart! Our spirits have gone to God, made peace for the war that we have made, and by the grace of God, perhaps have been forgiven for the things that we have done. But *we*…we are the rotting remnants of what we once were! *We* are the bodies of corruption that have remained behind. *We* are the soulless, stinking shadows of who we once were—with no hope of becoming what we might have been! What is there for us but to find our own graves and crawl back into the welcoming earth, that our parts might rot back into the world that spawned us and hope to be returned in some more pleasing, useful form? But the world awakened us from that hopeful oblivion, and now we walk the world once more, killing again, destroying again, and wreaking havoc again!"

The feldmarschall turned toward Ethan, Collette, and Rudi, his jaw clenched in agony as he spoke. "I have the memories of the spirit that once inhabited this body! I remember this place and these faces! I remember fighting here against these same enemies. I had my car accident not eight miles from this place. And I remember the morning back in my home—in my own home in Herrlingen—when those bastards Burgdorf and Maisel came to my door with a choice to either kill myself with the poison they brought and die a hero of the Reich, or die with my wife and son that same day as traitors. I remember the look on my wife's face when I told her that in fifteen minutes I would be dead. I had to tell my son to not say a word about it!"

The feldmarschall cried out in rage, his dead arm sweeping the map from the table.

"Now my soul is at rest with God. But something— some force of darkness—bids my mortal remains to walk the earth again with all the thoughts of my life, yet none of its hope," the feldmarschall raged.

"Herr Feldmarschall," said Dr. Benoit, "you are not well!"

"Not well!" the feldmarschall raged. "I am *dead*, you idiot!"

"Herr Oberst," Benoit continued, turning toward von Essen, "the feldmarschall has lost his mind! In his insanity, he has conspired with traitors of the Reich and imagines the war to be lost, but you are here, *mein herr!* Your warriors of the Reich stand around you, ready to do battle for the Fatherland! You have your orders from Generalleutnant Demisch. How should it go for you when he arrives, and you have listened to the treacherous ravings of an unhinged mind?"

"Oberst von Essen!" The feldmarschall was speaking in barely controlled tones. "You will release these people at once! I do not know what powers are drawing us out of the ground to fight this war again, but they must be stopped! If these people are allowed to go on their way, then perhaps our bones will be put to rest!"

"Our bones?" the oberst shouted, wheeling on the feldmarschall. "I've seen too many of our bones crushed beneath the unworthy enemies of the Reich! We are the superior race, and it is our destiny to rule the world. I will not be dissuaded from our rightful victory because of some defeatist propaganda!"

"But you are *dead*, von Essen!" the feldmarschall said. "You and your army of rotting corpses parading around as though Himmler himself was kicking at your heels!"

"We have come to fulfill our destiny!" the oberst raved. "Helmut! Franz! *Setzen Sie den Feldmarschall unter einschluss.*"

Two of the infantry men in the room rushed forward, taking the feldmarschall by both arms.

"You are a fool, von Essen," the feldmarschall said. "The war will never end for you. You will fight on forever with no victory and no defeat…only pain."

Oberst von Essen ignored him. He issued orders to the oberstleutnants in the room. Ethan caught words such as "panzer" and "Bayeux" and "La Cambe," but couldn't make out much else until Dr. Benoit spoke up.

"You will turn us over to your Generalleutnant Demisch first, *ja*?" the doctor urged politely.

"Yes, of course!" Oberst von Essen snapped. "We shall turn all these traitors and spies over to the generalleutnant, and be rid of the stinking lot of you! Our undying armies will march over the decadent Allies in fearless devastation. We shall be like a locust of justice, driving all before us in fear!"

"Except that you are probably facing an army of the Allied dead," Ethan interjected. "The Allied cemetery at Colleville is between you and La Cambe. The same mystic forces that drew your dust from your graves seems to have reassembled them as well."

"We will crush them beneath the treads of our tanks!" the oberst bragged.

"And they will rise up behind those same tanks," Ethan said. "And you will never—none of you— have any peace again."

The shrieking sound of a sixteen inch naval shell tore through the air above them, its explosion completely obliterating a small market on the far side of the main road. The concussion shook the glass around the McDonald's dining room. More rounds began falling, their sound overwhelming. The range was long, however, from the naval bombardment, devastating a stand of commercial buildings but landing too far beyond their targets to effect the gathering panzers.

The barrage stopped as quickly as it had begun. Outside in the rain, soldiers were running about trying to prepare for the ordered assault.

The oberst turned to face Ethan.

"We will *never* give up!" he said, jutting out his square chin. "We will fight to the last man. That is our standing order, and that is our honor and our glory. We will fight to the last man!"

"You are all the last men," Ethan replied.

The oberst raised his cadaverous hand to strike.

"Halt, Herr Oberst!"

Oberst von Essen restrained his open hand, turning toward the man who had just entered the room.

"I am expected," said the SS generalleutnant. He was a thin, tall man in a mud-caked uniform, a leather trench coat, and a pair of motorcycle goggles. In his left hand, he held a large briefcase. Ethan could not quite make out his face.

"Ah, Generalleutnant Demisch," the oberst bowed, then gestured toward his prisoners. "Our new friends here have been anxiously awaiting your arrival."

The generalleutnant bowed stiffly in return. "Herr Demisch sends his regrets, Herr Oberst, that he is delayed and cannot attend to the matter personally. He has instructed me to act on his behalf."

The eyes of the oberst narrowed. "May I see your papers please, Herr…"

The generalleutnant set the briefcase down on the table in the middle of the command staff.

"Stauffenberg, Herr Oberst," the officer said, straightening up from the briefcase as he handed a set of papers to von Essen. "Claus von Stauffenberg."

The oberst's eyes grew wide. "Nein!" he shouted.

Ethan's eyes flicked to the briefcase on the table. He turned to warn Collette, but the zombie oberst ran directly into him. Ethan grasped out to steady himself, his hand brushing the oberst's before finding purchase on the hand of Benoit beside him as the bomb in the briefcase exploded.

CHAPTER 20
THE TAKEN

A shiver ran through Fafnir, though whether of fear or delighted anticipation, he could not truthfully tell. Perhaps both, he admitted to himself, as he soared back through the darkened skies directly toward the onrushing wings of his pursuers. Behind him, Abraxas and Apalala continued on through the storm. He had slipped away from them with care—they would not suspect he had left them and had turned about to confront the sweet, beckoning darkness that stalked them all.

He could smell the intoxicating power approaching with every beat of his wings. The taint, Abraxas had called it; but those who drank of it, reveled in it, and wielded it knew it by other names...names that were not laden with disdain. To those who were carried away by its warm, seductive embrace, it was liberating and desirable beyond anything the *world had to offer. It promised to break all bounds of the physical and spiritual, elevate personal desires above the chains of ethics or law, and bend truth to the gratification of every carnal desire.*

All it asked in return was surrender of one's will.

Abraxas had long reasoned in his compassion with Fafnir about the taint. The ability to choose for oneself—to determine the course of one's own soul—was the very foundation of creation, he had said. To give this away was to throw away the most precious jewel at the heart of our existence; it was a denial of our very self and our responsibility to bring order and joy to the universe.

Abraxas was wise, but Fafnir knew that his brother had no experience. He had not tasted the relief that was the taint or the tantalizing power it forever promised and occasionally delivered. His brother had never understood fully—could never understand—the experience that still called to Fafnir, urging him to return to its forgetful, warm embrace.

Fafnir knew that he would fail. His only hope lay in resisting the taint as long as he could. Every moment that he held these taint-taken dragons at bay bettered Abraxas and Apalala's chances of out-distancing them and arriving at Mount Olygeas before the world's end.

He could see their forms now, distinguished from the black tendrils extending darkly from their long wings—tendrils that tied them to the ground below, but through which the power of the taint sustained them. He remembered the feeling he had had of those same streams running behind his own wings as they had seemed to lift him up effortlessly.

Fafnir set his jaw, trying to keep his mind focused.

Five dragons, he counted. Each of them was a dark brother to the others—a brood forged out of their mutual surrender to a new master; Apophis, Nagendra, Shesha, Volos, and Vritra—they had been his brothers, too, in the taint.

Apophis closed on him first, diving below him and then looping upward, the streams of taint dragging into a great, collapsing loop around Fafnir as he tried to bank away. Nagendra and Shesha crossed in front of Fafnir's turn, forcing him to pull up to avoid them. He broke through the tendrils, their touch exhilarating, familiar, and alluring. It cost him his speed, however, and he was forced to beat his wings vigorously to keep his altitude. It brought him nearly to a standstill in the air as he rotated around to face the dragons turning in arcs around him.

"Coming home, old friend?" Vritra hissed, his lips curled back in a vicious smile. "Have you come to drink deeply of the lifeblood of the world?"

"No more!" Fafnir shouted, folding his wings and diving straight downward. The paths of the dragons had crossed beneath him. He sliced through the ribbons of darkness, their black ichor trailing down the veins in his wings, seeping into his membranes as he plunged. His mind reeled with the heady sensation of its power as it pushed at the karma within him and *displaced it.*

Fafnir spun downward through the sky, the other five matching him as he fell. They rolled around him in a barely controlled descent, a dance falling through the clouds as they wove their spiraling cage around him.

"We have missed you, our dark brother," Apophis whispered as they fell through the sky toward the smoke-shrouded ground below. "You have been too long from us."

"Not nearly long enough," Fafnir replied, the wind shrieking about him.

The smoke parted before them, blown apart by a rush of wind. Below them a mountain had been torn open, its summit exploded into the sky and the molten core of the world boiling in a volcanic crater and bleeding down the mountainsides.

"We have come to save you, brother," said Nagendra.

"Yes, save you," echoed Volos.

The cauldron of lava was rushing up to meet them. Fafnir suddenly recognized the place—it was Vulcanis. It had long been a brooding, towering mountain of darkness—a place claimed by the taint. Now the world was spiraling into a different darkness—karma and taint drained from the world together—and the mountain had broken in the straining conflict between the two. It was an open gateway into the warm, promising hell beyond the world into which the taint was being pulled.

Pulling Fafnir with it.

Fafnir spread his wings suddenly, the leathery membranes shaking violently with the speed of the arrested descent. The dragon's muscles ached as they strained against the wind, but he slowed quickly, his wings catching the turbulent, rising air from the heat of the cauldron directly below him.

The tainted dragons rushed past him, splitting below him. They pulled quickly into climbing curves in five different directions at once.

Fafnir looked up.

The weaving tendrils of the taint from the five predator dragons cascaded down on him, coating him in its black stain. Fafnir felt suddenly infused with power, pride, unity, freedom, superiority, and most of all, relief.

"Yes, brother," Apophis urged as he wheeled about Fafnir. "Let go of the moral burden! Let go of the false concern for others and the weight of their cares! You are better than they are…better than him!"

Fafnir thought of Abraxas. Abraxas the Great. Abraxas the Good. Abraxas who cast a shadow in which Fafnir had ever been diminished. Was he not great as well? Did not the dark blood of the world's taint make him great, too?

"The taint! It is the taint speaking!" Fafnir roared, his wings clawing upward, using the rising heat to push him higher.

"Yes, it is the taint speaking," Volos cackled as he climbed beside the increasingly desperate Fafnir.

"Speaking the truth when no other will tell you. The world will sleep and we will sleep with it, but there will be a time when the world will awaken once more. Who will be victorious in that day, brother? Which shall be proven the better path? Will you live your life under the tyranny of another creature's ethics? Will you be a slave to law? Be free of this terrible oppression—be free of your brother's domination— and claim for yourself your rightful place to rule this world! We shall serve our wants...our needs...and be free!"

The air was filled with the smell of sulfur. Fafnir struggled for altitude, the taint coursing through his body. It stripped from him the burdens of the world, empowering him as he had not known for a long time. It surged through his veins, sending quivers through his talons.

"Are you afraid?" Nagendra taunted. *"Is the great Fafnir afraid of the taint? You used to be so powerful...so brave...so sure. Can you not handle its divine power? So weak...so weak..."*

"And to think how we had feared this Abraxas," Shesha said. *"Let us leave this whelp and devour a meal of more substance. If we are to fall, then let us take Abraxas with us as a prize! One of us will take him into the darkness with us!"*

"No!" Fafnir howled.

He connected with the taint, drawing the power within him. He felt the old familiar longing, the craving, and the struggle between the fading hope to *control it and the overwhelming desire to surrender everything to it. He clung to one thought in a sea of desire and yearning surging through his mind—that Abraxas must live.*

Fafnir had to save them—even if it meant falling to the taint to do so.

Fafnir enlarged, the taint growing within him. His physical size doubled to monstrous proportions, and great arcing bolts of lightning surged over his body. The five taint-taken dragons drew back in sudden surprise, trying to scatter, as the monstrous form of Fafnir suddenly turned on them.

The pursued became at once the pursuer, surrendering his rage to the darkness that coursed through his veins once more. One by one, in swift succession, his enormous talons captured the taint-taken dragons in his grip. One by one, he shredded the membranes of their wings, stripping them of their ability to fly and casting them—laughing hysterically—into the cauldron of Mount Vulcanis. There, the reeling tendrils of the taint itself, being dragged from the world, pulled them downward to vanish in the molten stone and beyond.

At last, only Apophis remained.

The enraged Fafnir drove through the skies in pursuit of the giggling dragon, snapping the connecting ribbons of taint, gathering them to himself, each one adding to his heady powers. Fafnir was justice. Fafnir was vengeance. Fafnir snatched Apophis from the air with his foreclaw and felt the bones in his prey's wings snap in his grip.

"Well done," Apophis cackled, blood streaming from the side of his mouth.

"Not finished," Fafnir snarled.

The enormous dragon wheeled about in the sky, returning once again to the seething volcanic crater. He folded his wings and dove straight down toward the fiery cauldron.

"You'll not be taking Abraxas with you," Fafnir said, his eyes tearing with the increasing speed of his dive. "We're leaving with the taint together."

Apophis twisted his head around to face the enormous face of Fafnir. Blood was flowing from his mouth, but he could still speak.

"Together? Oh, I think you've misunderstood," Apophis gurgled. "Abraxas will be taken—but not by us."

Fafnir looked sharply down at Apophis wrapped in his powerful talons. They had nearly reached the cauldron.

"It will be you who brings him into the darkness," Apophis grinned. "You're not going anywhere!"

And then the taint withdrew.

Fafnir's form collapsed back to its natural size. Apophis, his wings still shredded, was now suddenly larger than Fafnir, his black form hysterical with glee. Apophis kicked hard against the stunned Fafnir, sending the dragon spinning away.

Fafnir was shocked. The sudden loss of the power and comfort of the taint stunned him with its with-

drawal. He reacted out of instinct, his wings suddenly deploying to arrest his fall.

Apophis arched his back, his laughter echoing with that of his brothers from the cauldron walls, as he plunged into the lava, the taint dragging him downward. In that instant, the summit of the volcano collapsed downward, imploding with the withdrawal of the taint. The mouth of the volcano fell into a caldera, capping the volcano from the world and sealing the passage of the taint's withdrawal with it.

In the smoke-filled skies above the remains of Vulcanis, Fafnir shivered uncontrollably. The taint had abandoned him. He would remain in the world. Yet he felt the taint imbedded within him.

Fafnir turned in the sky and began pulling himself through the air toward Mount Olygeas.

Abraxas and Apalala were safe.

And to save them, Fafnir knew, he had sown the seeds of all their fall.

Fafnir was taken once more.

And someday, they would be, too.

CHAPTER 21
RESISTANCE

Ethan held still, anticipating for a brief moment the effects of the blast, and then the orange light engulfed him.

There was only a short silence in the glow, followed by the clattering sound of objects falling to the floor. Ethan turned around quickly as the glow faded from the McDonald's dining area.

Grey dust floated in the air, drifting down to settle on the dining surfaces, plastic chairs, and benches. Rotted German uniforms were collapsing everywhere, each filled with piles of grey ash. MP40s and Karabiner rifles lay scattered about where they had fallen. Only one figure in a Nazi uniform remained intact and standing in the room: Generalleutnant Claus von Stauffenberg.

Dr. Benoit, standing beside Ethan, suddenly lunged for the floor, an MP40 lying in front of him. He grabbed the weapon, bending over it, as he tugged at the bolt, trying to arm it. The general-leutnant dropped down to his knees, snatched up the Karabiner rifle next to him, and drew the bolt.

Ethan glanced from one to the other, then dove for Benoit, wrapping his arms in a flying tackle and driving them both across the floor. They hit the ground with a heavy thud, the grey dust billowing around them as they slid through the crumbled dead and their remaining uniforms, boots, and belts.

"Rudi!" Ethan coughed through the dust. Benoit was flailing beneath the cameraman like a cornered badger and Ethan was having trouble holding him. "Get over here!"

Rudi shook his head. "*Tidak munkin, tuan!*"

"Don't try that with me!" Ethan was trying to yell and spit the dust of the dead out of his mouth at the same time. "Put the professor out again before he gets us all killed!"

Collette's eyes were fixed on the kneeling gener-alleutnant as the muzzle of his rifle shifted back and forth between where she and Rudi stood and where Ethan was grappling with Dr. Benoit. She gave Rudi a shove, and he jerked forward. He reached gingerly into the billowing dust obscuring both Ethan and Benoit and plunged his hand toward the curator's head. Benoit shuddered violently then fell still once again.

Ethan shivered, the dust sifting off his frame as he stood up. He rubbed his hands violently through his close-cropped hair, shivered again, and realized he was looking down the muzzle of the generalleutnant's steady rifle.

"Generalleutnant, eh?" Ethan said, his face souring at the taste in his mouth. He spat the vile dust again out onto the floor. "I thought it was *Oberst* von Stauffenberg."

The generalleutnant's eye down the sight of the rifle remained as steady as the muzzle pointed at Ethan's face as the man spoke with a French accent. "We could not find a colonel's uniform quickly enough. One must make adjustments. Please, identify yourselves."

"My name is Ethan Gallows," Ethan said evenly. "This woman is Collette Montrose and that is Rudi Atno…Atono…well, his name is Rudi."

The muzzle of the German Karabiner did not waver. "And the sleeping gentleman on the floor with the death wish?"

"Ah," Ethan answered, glancing backward. "That would be Dr. Rene Benoit…a Frenchman with dubious allegiance."

"You are American, yes?"

"Yes…that is, Collette and I are Americans. Rudi is from Java, I think."

Still the rifle remained rock steady.

Ethan thought for a moment then spoke. "Jean has a long mustache."

The eye behind the weapon's sight blinked.

Ethan thought for another moment. He let his next sentence dangle at the end, inviting completion.

"The violins of autumn…"

"Wound my heart with monotonous languor," answered the generalleutnant with a deep chuckle. The muzzle lowered and the generalleutnant stood up. "You watch too many movies, Ethan Gallows!"

"And you have a flare for the dramatic," Ethan responded. "You are certainly not von Stauffenberg, though I thought the name appropriate, considering your choice of weapon. Just what kind of bomb was that anyway?"

"We call it a KLD," the generalleutnant said, slinging the Karabiner onto his shoulder by its strap. "Karmic Liberator Device. It's a low-proximity, high-yield karmic pulse device. It temporarily establishes an area of pure karma, forcing the taint and its effects out of an area for a time."

"In this case, this taint stuff was the glue holding these walking dead together, I take it," Collette said.

"Maybe you should call it a 'Zomb-bomb,'" Rudi said, brushing the dust off of his arms with disgust. "Or, I don't know, a 'Zombie-bombie'?"

"Are you sure he is with you?" the generalleutnant asked.

"He says he is," Ethan answered, eyeing the generalleutnant. "And you? Are you with us?"

"Lois François du Lac," the generalleutnant said, extending his right hand. "*Resistance du la Vivre.*"

Ethan took his hand. "Resistance of the Living?"

"Perhaps Living Resistance is better," Lois said with a shrug. "Caen was our city before this abomination returned. Now the entire Normandy coast is being ravaged again by armies who have risen from their graves. We are trying to take back our homes from the dead. I am sorry that we were not able to intercept you sooner, but Sojourner did not give us much time."

"Sojourner!" Collette exclaimed. "You've heard from her?"

"She contacted us just a few hours ago," Lois replied. "Unfortunately, the Germans were also informed by the dark ones and were looking for your coming as well. It was unfortunate that they found you before we could intercept you. Now we must hurry. We do not have much time to get you out."

"Uh, Ethan?" Rudi said.

"Just hold on a minute, Rudi," Ethan said. "What do you mean we haven't much time?"

"I really think you need to listen to me," Rudi said, his words exaggerated as he spoke.

"It is the KLD," Lois said to Ethan. "It's powerful but extremely limited. The duration of its effects are—"

"Ethan!" Rudi shouted.

"What?"

"The dust is moving!"

Ethan looked at the floor. The grey dust was shifting under his feet, gathering itself together toward the piles of antique uniforms. Hands began coalescing out of the particles, their partially formed fingers undulating across the tiles, reaching for the weapons as the attached mounds shaped into eye sockets and partial heads.

"We're moving, too," Ethan shouted. He snatched his camera from the table then threw the messenger bag with the iPad back to Rudi. Reaching down at once, Ethan grabbed up the feldmarschall's peaked cap and tunic. He had to pull it away from the emerging hand clinging to the coat's hem. "Quick! Rudi, you and Lois grab two uniform jackets and caps. Shake them out, put one on Rudi and one on the professor. Then climb into the back of that nice-looking Mercedes out there."

"What are you doing?" Collette asked.

"Grab a couple of those MP40 grease guns, and toss as many clips as you can find into your bag." Ethan glanced around again and found an infantry tunic and a soft cap. He dragged them from the clutches of what was rising from the floor and plopped the hat down on Collette's head, pushing the tunic into her hands. "You're the driver."

"Well, I don't want to *be* the driver anymore!" Collette said with indignation.

"Don't worry, it looks like the rain has stopped. And, anyway, I can't be the driver," Ethan said.

"Why not?"

And then, as Collette watched in horror, Ethan began to transform. He shrunk down inside his jacket, his face growing sallow and pale. His eyes drew back and his face began to change. Then his skin turned a sickly gangrene color.

It was the face of the dead Nazi commander that spoke to her in a rattling voice as he jammed the peaked cap on his head and traded out his jacket. "I'm the feldmarschall. Lois—you're the aid. We're going to walk out that door, get into that car and drive out of here like we're all one big, happy Nazi family on a picnic, OK?"

A grey hand reached up from the dust, wrapping its cold fingers around Collette's ankle. Startled, she kicked the hand back to dust, jumping back slightly.

"Sure, whatever you say," Collette answered.

*****

They did not stop until they took the exit to the A84. The sign said "Vire / Saint-Lô / Le Mt-St-Michel / Rennes" before they circled around, passed below the overpass, and Lois told them to pull over to the grassy area on the side of the road.

Lois jumped out of the car.

"Hey," Ethan said, once again looking like himself, "where are you going?"

"My fight is here, my friends," Lois said, pulling off the hat and tunic. "Your fight is still ahead of you."

Lois began moving around the open-topped Mercedes-Benz 770k, pulling the command flags from the bumper posts as he spoke. "Do not stop for another forty kilometers or so. The fighting around Saint-Lô has been particularly heavy this week between the American 1st Airborne and the 21st Panzer Division. There are no reports of troop movements between here and Villedieu-les-Poêles. Beyond that you should be fine through Avranches. Follow the signs from there, and you should have no trouble reaching the *mont*."

"Can I take off the uniform now?" Collette groused.

Lois looked up. "But of course, *mademoiselle*! My apologies."

Collette offered a tight smile as she tore the hat from her head and started pulling at the tunic.

Ethan stepped over the seat back to stand with his arms folded over the windshield of the car. "Lois, can you tell us something?"

"*Oui, monsieur,* if I can."

"What are we to do when we get there?" Ethan asked. "When we get to Mont Saint-Michel?"

Lois pulled the last command flag and squinted at Ethan through one eye for a moment. "Sojourner said that you are a scion, yes?"

"That's what they tell me," Ethan said with a deep shrug.

Lois thought about this for a moment before he spoke. "No one can tell you, Monsieur Gallows. Scions carry their burdens deep within them from the times long gone. Their scars run as deep as the dreams of man. It is not for others to tell you who you are or what you must do. It is up to you to remember who you are and what you must do."

"You know, when you said that just now," Rudi said, his face a mask of rapturous thought as he sat on the upper edge of the back seat, "I realized that while it sounded obscure at first, it turned out to be absolutely meaningless."

"Sojourner said she would meet us there," Ethan continued, ignoring Rudi.

"Then you have nothing to fear," Lois nodded. "She will guide you. She, too, after all, is a scion."

"So you're in league with the scions, eh?"

"But of course," Lois smiled. "Surely you knew that we are all fighting more than some dead soldiers on a Normandy beachhead?"

Ethan reached down and shook Lois's hand. "Thank you. *Bon chance* with those Germans."

Lois's smile broadened. "We defeated them once before. I suspect we can do so again."

Collette pressed the starter on the floor, depressed the clutch, and shifted the vintage Mercedes into gear.

Ethan held up one of the submachine guns they had taken. "What about these?"

"Take them with you," Lois said. "I suspect you'll need them."

The French countryside was soon drifting past them on the abandoned divided motorway. The sounds of the bombardment of Caen slowly faded behind them. Ethan kept his hands occupied cleaning the case and lens of his camera, but his thoughts were far from the task.

"Hey," called Rudi from the back. "Can we just

leave the Nazi uniform on Herr Benoit back here?"

"It is a pretty good look on him," Ethan agreed, glancing back. Benoit still wore the hat and tunic of a panzer officer. "You don't suppose there are several Nazi zombies running around naked in a Mc-Donald's about now, do you?"

"Take it off him," Collette ordered.

Ethan looked at her in surprise. "What?"

"Take that uniform off of Benoit," Collette said firmly, her hands gripped around the wide wheel of the Mercedes as they thundered down the road.

"Why?" Rudi asked.

"Because he may wake up in it," Collette replied. "And I wouldn't want him to get any ideas."

CHAPTER 22
MONT SAINT-MICHEL

He lay with his back against a small, solitary mountain of stone, the sun beating with warm rays upon his outstretched, relaxed wings. The rush of the tide sounded in his ears across the floodplain, moving almost faster than flight as it surged around the pile of stone, cutting it off from the flat expanse of the mainland beyond.

This was his favorite time. The foundation stone of this place was a focal nexus of karma—a wellspring of peace and joy. The sands surrounding it had been touched by the taint and hovered menacingly about it, but when the tide came in around its base, it cut off the darkness, driving the taint back deep into the sands and letting the stone rest.

His little mountain—the place where he and his broodmates had first hatched from their clutch—became an island twice each day. He fancied both it and himself as things apart and free of the world's cares—glorious under the warm sun and the blazing blue of an expansive sky.

"Are you pleased to be home, Abraxas?"

The dragon opened one eye, twisting his scaly head toward the interloper. "I am, brother. Pleased to leave the strife of the world for a time, albeit short."

"Too short, I would agree," responded Fafnir. The dragon perched on an outcropping next to where Abraxas continued sunning himself. "Apogean has called us back to Atlantis. We have made a vow to come to his aid and we must honor it."

"We shall," Abraxas agreed, twisting his shoulders slightly where they lay against the warm rocks, "but must we do so immediately?"

"The taint is spreading like a blanket over the Fomodorian holdings in the north," Fafnir said with uncharacteristic impatience. "It is everywhere on the continent, and there has been no message from across the river in old Avalon for nearly a month. Something terrible is brewing there, I can smell it. If Apogean calls us, it bodes ill."

"And we will act, brother," Abraxas said, closing his eyes. "But this is a perfect moment, and you would toss it aside so easily? We who have clenched our fists against the darkness of the taint for so long—should we not spread our wings beneath the sun for a brief moment? A fist once clenched cannot clench again until it is opened and relaxed, is this not so?"

Fafnir chuckled, deep and heartfelt. Then he curled his wings, rolled over onto his back, and spread the great leathery expanse open against the sun.

"How I have missed this, brother," Fafnir said, craning his neck back against the top of the mountain and breathing in the ocean air. "Will there be another perfect day? Will you bring me back here?"

"Someday, brother," Abraxas said. "Someday in the sunlight."

*****

Ethan let go with a shiver, his fingers shaking slightly as they pulled away from the skin beneath Benoit's collar. He stepped quickly out of the Mercedes-Benz.

As he turned to take in their destination, he exclaimed suddenly, "Wait!" His camera immediately went up to his eye, the record button already pressed. "I know this place! I've been here before." *In fact, I was just here.*

"You and about three million other visitors each year," Collette said from the driver's side of the antique convertible. She slowly stood up, stretching out the kilometers of road from her frame. "It's the second most popular tourist destination in France. Though by the look of it, there's been a definite downturn in attendance."

The waters of the Bay of Mont Saint-Michel and the English Channel cut grey across the horizon, a thin sliver of orange beneath the lowering clouds the only remnants of a sunset. The image in the viewfinder swung with a practiced smooth motion until Mont Saint-Michel—the Mountain of Saint Michael—filled the frame. It was an imposing and inspiring island of granite surrounded by tidal flats of sand, currently exposed. An old causeway, built to allow cars to travel across the sand to the base of the rock, was now impassable, long sections of the causeway either buckled or vanished, taken back by the sea. The parking lot closest to the island was now nearly gone. The mount itself stood in enormous silhouette, an island of granite nearly half a mile wide at its base and over eighty feet high. This stone surface was capped almost entirely by the magnificent and imposing Romanesque and Gothic edifice of the abbey and the smaller buildings of the walled town built around its base. Not a single light shone from its black windows; in fact, there was no illumination at all coming from the brooding mass of the tidal island.

"No, I mean before," Ethan said, panning slowly along the horizon line and then following the towering fortification walls of the abbey up to the tower at the top of the abbey's cathedral, its peak piercing the sky like a black lance. He stopped recording and lowered the camera, taking in the enormity of the vista with his own eyes. "There were no buildings then—only the stone warming my back."

"Ethan," Collette said, her eyes fixed on her cameraman, "the first of the chapels on this island was built in the tenth century. Most of it was built in the sixteenth and seventeenth centuries. And you say you remember this place without buildings?"

"Hey," Rudi called from the oversized back seat of the car. "The old guy is coming around. What's the plan, man?"

Ethan turned back to the car. "Have a nice nap, Professor?"

"*Doctor*," Benoit responded with a sullen, dismissive sneer. "Get Sojourner. I don't deal with cattle."

"Gladly," Ethan said, gathering the curator's coat up in his fist and pulling him out of the car. "We're meeting her here."

Benoit looked down at Ethan's vice-like grip, thought for a moment, then smiled. "Of course, Mr. Gallows. No need to concern yourself with me. Go and fetch the bitch. I have a few things I'd like to say to her myself."

Ethan threw Dr. Benoit forward toward the towering edifice and the ragged edge of the parking lot. The curator staggered, struggling to keep his feet under him. Reaching up, he adjusted his coat and ran his hand back once through his hair. He glared at Ethan as he pushed his glasses back up his nose.

Rudi was out of the car, as well, his hoodie pulled up over his head and his hands pushed down into his pockets. The temperature was dropping quickly around them with the fading light. Farben's iPad case, bulging with thirty-two-round cartridge clips, hung across the young man's back, and he had one of the MP40s slung over his shoulder. "So do we just wait here or what?"

"We go in," Ethan said. "There's got to be a way to—"

"Back in the Middle Ages," Dr. Benoit interjected, "this place was known as 'Saint Michael in Peril of the Sea.' This was due in large part to the tidal waters and the sands that surrounded the mount. Pilgrims used to cross those sands on foot to reach the mount as a testament of their spiritual faith, an emblem of their journey to heaven."

Rudi frowned. "So, like, we just walk over then?"

"It was a *trial* of their faith," Collette said with emphatic warning. She pulled her MP40 out of the car, checking the bolt and clip as she spoke. "There are unpredictable pockets of quicksand that surround the mountain. The tides can come up over forty feet deep and are so fast that they can outrun a man. You might also have mentioned that, Dr. Benoit."

The curator shrugged and smiled again.

"If we stick next to the old causeway," Ethan said, "we should be all right. A little pilgrimage of our own, Doctor?"

"I refuse," Benoit stated flatly.

"But you used to love this place," Ethan continued.

"Love it?" Benoit scoffed. "This hateful place of ignorance and superstition? Never!"

"You've just forgotten," Ethan said, stepping up to the curator. "Haven't you, *Fafnir*?"

"What?"

"That's your name, isn't it?" Ethan said.

"I've had many names," Benoit answered in disdain. "Too many, each one lost in the next, time piled on time, age upon age. Who can remember their names in dreams?"

"Then let me remind you," Ethan said, shoving the old man's shoulders, twisting him around, and propelling him down the steep bank toward the soft sands below. He turned to Collette and Rudi. "Come on! I don't think we've got much time left, and we've still got to find Sojourner."

They crossed the cool sands next to the shattered and ruined causeway, occasionally having to circumnavigate sections of the road which had crumbled across their path. The sand felt spongy in places. The Couesnon River—the heart of the estuary—wound past them on their left. The remains of a wooden foot bridge ran across the face of the ancient battlement wall, ending nearly ten feet up the sandy slope at a small heavy door and a larger, heavier door.

The larger door was partially open.

"Someone's been here ahead of us," Collette said, shivering slightly.

Ethan pushed Dr. Benoit up the slope toward the opening. The doctor, however, stopped at the threshold.

"You—I can't," he pleaded. "I won't do anything. I'll just wait here, I promise. Just please don't make me—"

Ethan shoved the doctor again, propelling him

through the opening into the walled courtyard beyond.

"Coming?" Ethan asked Collette as he stepped through after the doctor.

Collette glanced at Rudi, who shrugged, gesturing for her to precede him. "Age before beauty, girl."

In the fading light, it was obvious this was the old ticket entrance for the island. The fees and tours signs hung at awkward angles on the walls, one of them banging slightly against its loose mountings in the evening breeze. The archway on their right was open, leading to the narrow, main street of the mount. They passed an abandoned restaurant on their right, its tables covered in dust and dried leaves, while the hotel was on their left, dark and forbidding. Ahead of them, the main arch gateway lay open, its portcullis drawn up and its short drawbridge lowered. Beyond the arched passage, the narrow, main street of Mont Saint-Michel ran like a curved canyon between the towering dark façades of closed cafes and curio shops. The paint had faded on the once-ornamental signs, each of which creaked slightly in the wind. The street itself wound its way upward, curving to the left with occasional steps.

Ahead of Ethan, Dr. Benoit had begun to shiver. Ethan continued to herd the curator ahead of him up the road. "You will pay for this! I will eat your beating heart out of your torn chest, Gallows!"

Ethan nodded and gave the reluctant curator another shove. He was feeling better than he had in quite some time, he realized, despite the gloomy, gothic atmosphere and the bizarre circumstances that had brought him here. There was a sense of home in the middle of this gothic horror that was inexplicable—like he belonged to the place if not this particular time.

"Hey, the town is, like, closed," Rudi said from the back. "Someone want to remind me where we're going?"

"Up, apparently," Collette replied, pointing with the muzzle of her grease gun.

La Grande Rue became even more narrow and climbed at a steeper angle. They passed a small chapel and cemetery on their left. Ethan eyed it momentarily, but the graves seemed to all be intact and undisturbed. The stairs of the *rue* became even steeper now, the shops disappearing and the path taking a sharp turn to the left. The stairs turned again and rose precipitously up a long, straight flight at the foot of the abbey wall. Ethan pressed Dr. Benoit ahead of him through the archway, up another flight of stairs, and into the Guard Room entrance to the abbey itself.

"Gallows, stop! You've got this all wrong," Benoit pleaded. "We've gotten off on the wrong foot, you and I."

"Keep climbing," Ethan said, pointing through the archway and up the stairs to their left.

"Look, I've got a lot of money—a lot more than you might suppose," Benoit said quickly. "And there's more still I can get for you. Why risk an easy future? This is dangerous—both for you and for everyone here. You just don't know how dangerous it is!"

"Probably not," Ethan said, climbing the steps closer to Benoit.

"But it doesn't have to end badly for any of us," Benoit continued in a rush. They were moving up a long, curving staircase inside the confines of the abbey itself now, a narrowing stair between the abbey rooms on their left and the foundations of the cathedral on their right. A rusting sign on the wall proclaimed it to be the *Grande Degré*. The slit of sky above the walls was filled with dark clouds and dim flashes of lightning. "We can all just walk away. Gallows! Listen to me. You can go back to your life, and no one will get hurt. No one will be any the wiser. You can forget—"

"Ethan!" Collette exclaimed. "There's someone at the top of the stairs."

"Yes," Ethan said. "Sojourner said she would meet us here."

"This is getting too weird, man," Rudi said with a nervous edge to his voice, his hands shaking as he held the German machine gun. "Maybe the man's right. Maybe we should just forget about this and split."

"No!" Ethan said emphatically.

"Why not, man?" Rudi whined. "What's in this for you? Why do you care?"

"Because I'm sick of the dreams!" Ethan yelled, turning on Rudi on the long, seemingly interminable staircase. "I'm sick of half-remembered lives, joys, and pain! I've forgotten who I am anymore, Rudi. Maybe you never knew. But I have to know. I have to."

"Be careful what you look for, Abraxas," Dr. Benoit said quietly. "You may not like what you find."

Ethan wheeled on the stairs, growling at Benoit. "Let's find it together! Get moving, Benoit. We've got an appointment to keep."

They moved through the Saut-Gaultier passage at the top of the stairs and stood in a wide terrace. The low walls afforded an unobstructed view of the wide sandbar below, the English Channel to the northwest and the broad expanse of French countryside to the south and north. On the east end of the terrace, Ethan could see the entrance to the cathedral; the great spire at its transept rose toward the sky, a statue of St. Michael the Archangel gracing its topmost peak.

"Sojourner?" Ethan called out quietly, but the terrace was deserted.

"Where the hell did she go?" Rudi asked.

In the northeast corner of the terrace, a single statue of a kneeling angel was set in the center of a turret overlook. Ethan considered it for a moment, then stepped toward it. It was exquisitely rendered in marble, the figure gripping a long iron sword with rust spots along its blade. The old piece of ironmongery seemed to be set in the hands of the statue. The oddly shaped handguard looked familiar: an eastern Patriarchal cross.

Ethan squinted in the dim light. The face of the statue looked familiar to him.

Ethan's eyes went suddenly wide.

The statue bore a perfect rendering of London cabbie Valja's face.

"A fitting display, don't you think? He said he would join you here if he could. It seems he has."

Ethan turned quickly toward the voice.

He stood near the entrance to the cloisters on the north side of the church. As the figure moved closer, Ethan could see the simple lines of the grey suit, the voided face, the veiled eyes, and the shadowed smirk at the corners of the mouth. He held gloves in one hand, which drew interest away from his face, but the chill that Ethan felt on his approach was unmistakable.

"Mr. Demissie, I presume," Ethan muttered.

"How kind of you to remember me, Mr. Gallows," said the figure.

Benoit, a smile spreading on his face, moved forward, but Collette stepped in front of him, the muzzle of the MP40 in her hands moving up at once, pressing into the flesh under his jaw. Her eyes remained fixed on Benoit as she spoke. "Ethan? What do we do?"

"Yes, an excellent question, Miss Montrose: what shall we do?" The Grey Gentleman stopped, his soulless eyes fixed on Ethan. "You brought your camera, I see. Enjoying the tour? Taking in the sights?"

Ethan licked his lips.

"But that's what you do, isn't it, my good friend," Mr. Demissie continued through his half-smile. "Al-

ways the observer; never the observed. We have a lot
in common, you and me. I cannot help but be overwhelmed with sympathy for you. All those years of
being safe behind that lens of yours, the luxury of
detachment and impartiality. Never having to take
sides. Never having to be involved. And then that Jonas fellow—fool that he is—comes along and takes
your perfectly honest work and destroys you, tears
the veil down, leaves you naked to the wolves. All
those lies that he told about you! Dragging you into
the harsh light of ridicule and censure. Such a pity!
Such a travesty!"

"I can live with it," Ethan said, though his voice
shook a little as he spoke.

"But you don't have to, that is my point." Demissie opened his hands easily in front of him, his partial grin deepening. "I can give it all back to you—
the life you loved. Praise, accomplishment, respect.
They could all be yours again, without all that cum-
bersome nonsense of having to stick your neck out
for someone else's problems or principles."

"No one can give me that," Ethan said, swallowing.

"Oh, but consider the possibilities! What a match
we will make!" Demissie began circling about Ethan
as he spoke. "I'll make the news—and you'll deliver
it. I can give you an exclusive on the dawn of a new
world, Ethan—and the perfect shot every time!"

"And what happens to the old world?" Ethan
asked, trying and failing to look more closely at the
Grey Gentleman as he moved around him.

"What do you care if the world burns—so long as you know where to put the camera?" Demissie said. "It's not your fight, Ethan, and you can't change the tide. The old world is passing away and a new order is coming. You can't change that, Ethan, but you *can* make a profit from it! You can get back everything you've lost and more. I can give it to you."

But Ethan wasn't listening. His cameraman's eye had caught sight of something even in the growing darkness of the terrace. A strand of blackness—a ribbon of taint—that flowed into Demissie from beyond the low wall.

"Everything I've lost?" Ethan asked.

"Yes," said Mr. Demissie with an almost-gentle smile as he stepped closer to Ethan, gesturing down the outer wall of the abbey. "And I've set up your first shot for you."

Ethan moved to the wall and glanced down the sheer face.

The walls plunged downward nearly a hundred feet to the steep granite mountainside below. Even in the dim light of the rapidly receding day, Ethan could see the thick, black tendrils weaving their way out of the sands around the stone, clawing their way upward along the surface, pushing and breaking like dark, sticky waves against the rocks of the mount. It was the embodiment of the taint rising to engulf them. Black beyond black tendrils reached upward from the sands around the mount. They were shattering against the stones, but in their place clung dozens of grey human shapes—men or women, it was impossible to tell—each clawing their way up the sheer face of the stones like spiders emerging from an egg sack.

"Film it, Ethan!" Demissie whispered into his ear. "The slaying of a dragon!"

Ethan looked down at the camera in his hands, fingering the record button.

The wind blew softly across the courtyard, rustling his hair.

Ethan smiled.

He dropped his camera to the ground and turned away, reaching for the hilt of the sword and wresting it from the statue's grip. His eyes flashed with sudden memory.

It took only a moment.

Then Ethan smiled—the blade suddenly aflame before him.

CHAPTER 23
PAST AND PRESENT TENSE

"Don't throw it all away, Ethan," Mr. Demissie said, something like a frown disturbing the calm on his face. "Pick up your camera. This is history... shoot it!"

Ethan glanced down the dizzying height of the exterior wall of the abbey one more time. As he watched, more tendrils of the dreadful, unspeakable black mass smashed against the stones, depositing dozens more of the vile forms across the rocks. They were swarming up the sheer walls of the abbey now, carpeting its surface like enormous roaches.

They were climbing toward the terrace.

Ethan turned back to face Mr. Demissie.

"I tried to help you," the gentleman said slowly, tugging at the pressed cuffs of his shirt which extended beyond his coat sleeves. "Tried to save you, even tried to dissuade you from coming here at all.

But you had to force the issue, Ethan. You insisted on dragging my good friend to this place."

"You don't like it here, do you, Mr. Demissie?" Ethan said, his smile turning grim in the light of the blue flame shining from the blade he held in front of him. "Not your kind of place at all. That taint of yours does not seem to have much of a taste for this place, either. It prefers to send its slaves rather than touch the walls of the mount itself."

"You are a fool if you think this place will protect—"

Ethan took a sudden step toward Mr. Demissie, thrusting the sword toward the Grey Gentleman's chest.

The figure screamed, held form for only a moment, then erupted into a splayed mass of black, shining horror recoiling before the light. The form kept shifting, but the images were burned into Ethan's memory: tentacles with barbed nails, rows of needle-sharp teeth gnashing in a gaping maw, a hundred blood-red eyes staring with fury, and arms with claw-fixed hands whose palms were screaming faces.

Ethan took a step back in shock as the monstrous apparition jumped back, collapsing again into the form of a Grey Gentleman.

Ethan let the shock subside before smiling in resolute understanding. "You don't much care for this light, either, do you?"

Ethan's smile deepened. He began to circle around Mr. Demissie, back toward where Collette and Rudi stood with Dr. Benoit near the doors of the cathedral at the pinnacle of the mount.

Demissie kept a respectful distance as he spoke, his eyes locked on Ethan as he moved toward him. "And just what do you expect to do with that? Have you ever even held a sword?"

"Oh, yes," Ethan replied. "I seem to remember that I've held a sword many times down the ages, and through lives I'm only just beginning to understand. Occasionally I was even thought of as accomplished."

Grey faces were rising up over the walls. Indistinguishable from each other, devoid of any emotion but hatred, they flowed over the stone, the arcing tendrils of the taint reaching high over the walls, dragged to the terrace by the figures which they controlled.

"Then you should be pleased that your long journey has come to an end," said Mr. Demissie, advancing with the horde toward them. "It is time you slept forever."

Ethan shouted over his shoulder as he stepped carefully back from the pack of malevolent predators advancing against them now on three sides. "Back! Back into the church!"

"Hey, the man wants Benoit?" Rudi shouted, holding Benoit at gun point now. "Maybe we should give him to them."

"Ah, the voice of youth," Demissie said, opening his arms in a welcoming gesture. "An excellent suggestion! And what about you, Collette? Is your life worth saving a man who does not want to be saved?

You and I have put off meeting each other for far, far too long."

"No! Don't listen to him! We need Benoit!" Ethan barked. "Collette, the door. Get inside! Now!"

Collette pulled open the heavy door of the church. She shoved Benoit through ahead of her with the muzzle of the MP40 in her hands. "Come on, Doc! You're on the tour!"

Collette and Rudi ran down the center aisle of the thousand-year-old nave, urging Benoit in front of them with the machine guns. They ran beneath the vaulted interior of the church, lit by the eerie light of Ethan's sword behind them.

"Keep going!" Ethan urged, backing away as quickly as he could from the church doors.

Utter blackness covered the tall windows at the back of the chapel. All three sets of doors swung open. The unholy horde poured into the chapel through the doors—there was nothing to be seen beyond them. As Ethan backed up, he could see the windows above the aisles on either side of the nave being covered one by one by the inky blackness of the strands of taint connected to the Grey Gentlemen.

Mr. Demissie stood at the head of the faceless mob. "Lighting a single flaming sword in the darkness, are you? Yours is the only light left, Ethan Gallows. There's a long night coming into the world. Wrap yourself in its comforting darkness. You've nothing to fear there, Ethan. No responsibilities. No questions. No decisions to be made."

Ethan backed across the raised floor of the crossing, the flaming sword wavering in his hands. The transepts stood on either side, but there was only one other door, out the end of the southern transept.

Collette was pulling on it. "It's locked, Ethan!"

"Leave it then," he shouted at her, his face alight in the blue of the flaming sword. "Get back here! Back to the altar!"

"The altar?" Mr. Demissie smiled with genuine humor. "After all this time, do you really think that a prayer will help you? Do you actually plan to appeal to Saint Michael to be your guardian angel, Mr. Gallows? Please do! I have so little real entertainment in my life…"

Ethan backed into the choir, the fluttering blue light reaching up into the vaulted arch of the gothic apse overhead. The towering windows in each of the apsidioles went black one by one until the Lady Chapel at the far end of the cathedral was shrouded, as well.

"There's no way out!" Rudi shouted, standing next to the altar with Benoit and Collette.

Ethan licked his lips again, backing slowly up the steps to the altar, his back to Collette, Benoit, and Rudi.

"There's one way out," Ethan said, drawing the sword back behind him, cocking his arm to swing the blade.

He held it there for just a moment, hesitating.

Benoit, a triumphant grin on his face, reached up suddenly, gripping the long hilt of the sword and pulling backward. The curator's form expanded, his shoulders widening, his chest broadening, tearing open his jacket and shirt. The glasses fell from his face as scales began to emerge on his flesh. The monstrously transformed Benoit pulled back.

Ethan lost his balance and fell backward painfully across the altar. The shock loosened his grip, and Benoit wrested the sword from his hands. The half-dragon man swung the blade, the flames cutting through the air with a ripping sound until its point was over Ethan's chest. With a terrible yell, Benoit gripped the hilt of the inverted sword with both hands and plunged the blade downward.

Ethan shifted, but Benoit was unexpectedly agile. The blade pierced Ethan's chest just below the shoulder, the force of the thrust so great that it drove the blade into the stone of the altar until the cruciform hilt nearly touched Ethan's chest.

Collette's scream was nearly matched by Rudi's.

Ethan cried out in agony.

Benoit grinned in malevolent satisfaction, both his hands still locked on the hilt of the sword as he leaned over it with his face inches from Ethan's own.

His muscles shaking, Ethan opened his eyes, locking them with Benoit's.

Then, through gritted teeth, Ethan smiled.

Benoit's eyes went wide.

Ethan reached up with his right hand, gripping it firmly around the back of Benoit's monstrous neck. Benoit tried to back away, but somehow Ethan held him firm. Benoit could not let go of the sword's hilt.

Rudi stood gaping next to the altar at the opposite end from the stunned Collette.

Ethan reached out with his left hand, grabbed Rudi's hand in a grip that threatened to break his bones, and dragged him also to the altar.

Still staring into Benoit's eyes now a hand's breadth from his own, Ethan said a single word through his pain.

"*REMEMBER!*"

*****

Fafnir flew through the pain, his eyesight failing him.

The battle with the taint-taken dragons had been fierce and their defeat incomplete. Fafnir had known that he was inadequate to the task, but he had hoped that he could purchase time enough for his brothers—time enough for the Seelie to hide their souls among humankind and seed their hope for a dawn beyond the dark millennia to come.

Now the taint-taken were nearly spent, their powers, too, draining from the world. But their own seeds had been sown in him. His own power failing, he had allowed himself to be taken by the taint—succumbed to its temptations—so that he could purchase time for his brothers.

Now, his soul blackened with taint, he flew westward, chasing the failing sun. He was corrupted, but before he passed into the darkness, he wished to know his brothers were safe.

A mountain—Mount Olygeas. It was situated in the midst of a glacial lake high in the lost Arcadian Alps. It was not a mountain in the sense of the great towering pinnacles around it, but it held a specific virtue: Olygeas was a wellspring of karma. Its roots plunged deep into the earth and focused the energies of power and magic through the stone, drawing it up in strength from the depths of the world. If there was any karma remaining in the dying world, it would be here.

So the last of the Seelie had summoned Abraxas and his brothers to this place.

The glacial mound was dim in Fafnir's sight. He barely managed his landing, collapsing on the crest of the stone.

The Seelie were there, their incantations nearly complete. Three human babies—dead at childbirth—lay on the altar, their souls having fled from them. Tsanya—the Seelie priestess—stood at the altar, a bright, flaming sword with the double-guarded hilt typical of a Seelie sword in her hand.

Great Abraxas of Trocea and Apalala both stood in the circle, their heads drawn back in shock and surprise at seeing their fallen brother.

Fafnir raised his head with effort. He cried out, "Brothers! Why are you still here? Go quickly!"

"We waited for you, brother," Abraxas said. Fafnir felt the great dragon grip his shoulder gently with his talons.

"*You must go without me,*" *Fafnir cried out, tears welling up in his sightless eyes.* "*I have made a foul bargain to save you, my brothers. The taint has taken me. The darkness in me must die here. You must go on without me.*"

"*No, brother,*" *Abraxas said, his resonant tones shaking the stones of the island.* "*You have saved us all. You will go ahead into the darkness. We will follow. And in that day when the dawn comes again, we will find you, brother, and bring you into the light once more. You will be free.*"

"*Is this wise, Abraxas?*" *came another voice—Tsanya's, Fafnir realized in the gathering darkness of his mind.*

"*It will be dark, brother,*" *Fafnir said, quaking.* "*Perhaps one day I will see you again.*"

"*You will see us in the light,*" *Abraxas replied.*

"*Yes,*" *Fafnir struggled,* "*the light of home on the shores of the Western Sea. The sun is brighter there...*"

"*The breezes fairer,*" *Abraxas said quietly.*

"*Like fair Atlantis...*"

Tsanya raised her sword, burning with the faerie flame, then spun the blade around its axis, releasing it in the air and reversing her grip, the blade now upside down.

Tsanya's sword plunged into Fafnir's heart.

Light and dark collided.

A baby gasped and cried.

*****

Karma exploded upward through the altar, channeled by the ancient sword, reconnected to its wellspring after time uncounted. It surged through Ethan and Rudi, burning into the soul of Rene Benoit, cutting through the darkness.

"You will see us in the light!" Ethan shouted, still holding onto the back of the curator's neck.

Benoit threw back his head, his screams echoing through the cathedral. Shafts of light exploded from his eyes, cutting the darkness. Ethan let go of both Rudi and Benoit, his hands falling back across the altar.

Benoit rose up, his hands still clinging to the hilt of the sword jammed into the stone altar. His hair stiffened, coalesced, winding into horns. He grew larger and larger in the cathedral hall, his jacket tearing to shreds over growing scales, talons, and wings.

Mr. Demissie took a step back as his minions waited uncertainly.

Great leathery wings unfolded, filling the vaulted ceiling.

Fafnir had shed his human host.

Fafnir had come back to the light.

Fafnir, dragon of the Western Sea, turned to protect his brothers.

He faced the horde and roared.

Chapter 24
Time and Tides

M r. Demissie took several steps back into the throng of the other grey beings. Black tendrils of taint were wriggling into the church through the open doors and broken glass at the back of the nave, their strands weaving among the figures in the hall, caressing them, urging them, and empowering them.

Slowly they lifted Demissie up higher into the vaulted space of the nave. The individual Grey Gentlemen reached with their arms together, their bodies becoming the sinews, muscles, and bones of a single, horrific creature bound together by the writhing strands of the taint. The individual, agonized faces could still be discerned among the members of the beast that grew before them.

Soon the general shape became more evident: massive, powerful back legs, an arched tail like a scorpion, six arms each ending in claws with black talons, and a shifting maw with endless rows of sharp teeth.

The creature struck at Fafnir.

Fafnir shifted slightly in the confined space of the apse, his neck whipping downward and to the left to avoid the thrust of the beast's claws. The monster was swift for its enormous size. Three more claw thrusts struck home, raking the scales along his right ribs and tearing a narrow slit in his right wing.

Fafnir roared again, the terrible sound shaking the dust up from the floor of the cathedral. The dragon drew back on its haunches as if to strike. The Demissie-beast took a step backward, scattering broken pews, as it braced for the expected strike.

Fafnir instead leapt upward, smashing through the roof of the cathedral and into the cloud-laden sky above. Timbers, tiles, and other debris cascaded down on top of the taint creature, which stumbled backward against the rear wall of the nave, causing a second section of the roof to collapse on top of it.

"He just...he just *left* us here," Rudi gaped next to the altar. "The bastard ditched us! Damn! We are so screwed!"

Ethan, his shoulder still pinned to the altar with the sword, struggled to get up, but lay back, crying out in pain.

The taint-fueled Demissie-beast shrugged off the debris at the other end of the cathedral, its long arms pulling it forward across the nave, dragging the tentacles of taint behind it. The maw was working its rows of teeth.

Madly, Ethan's thoughts were of his camera, left on the terrace beyond the beast. He briefly regretted being unable to film his own impending death.

Lightning exploded outside the cathedral, illuminating the clouds as thunder boomed and rolled through the ruined cathedral. Several of the sap-like ribbons of black taint trailing from the beast severed, whipping forward as they vanished. With each separated tendril, the great beast howled, staggering as it struggled to maintain its form.

Suddenly, the creature was dragged backward, away from the altar. The back wall of the cathedral collapsed outward as the beast struck the stone walls, exposing the terrace beyond.

There stood Fafnir, his claws wrapped around the tendrils of taint, heaving on them like black cables and dragging the Demissie-horror toward him with every pull.

Bolts of lightning continued to rain down on the terrace, snapping the tendrils of taint where they struck. The Demissie-beast rolled over in outrage, screeching an unholy scream that echoed off the stones, its easy prey on the altar having been denied to its hunger. Several more of the taint ribbons snapped and recoiled, further weakening the monster, and then the taint creature suddenly dissolved into its component figures.

The Grey Gentlemen swarmed toward Fafnir, flowing through the opening in the collapsed wall like a plague. Demissie stood among them, directing the horde against the dragon whose threat had momentarily left the chapel and its altar abandoned.

"I knew you were lucky," Collette said as she quickly climbed up onto the altar stone. She straddled his chest, gripping the cruciform hilt of the sword with both her hands. "But I didn't know you were crazy."

"Get out of here, Collette," Ethan said, his hands shaking. "Take Rudi, and get as far from here as you can."

"I told you long ago: you need me," Collette said through her clenched teeth. "Now shut up and let me help."

She flexed her legs against the altar as she pulled. The blade of the sword suddenly released from the stone, and Ethan screamed from the sudden pain as the blade slid free from his shoulder.

Through a haze, Ethan watched Collette spin the upside-down blade around its axis, releasing the grip as it whirled in the air and catching it again right side up. She swung the blade with practiced ease, feeling the balance of the blade and hilt. Satisfied, she jumped down off the altar, setting the blade down across the stone and removing her business jacket.

"Let me guess," Ethan said as he spit blood from his mouth. He devoutly hoped it was from biting his own tongue and not from something more serious. "You used to play swords with your brothers in Georgia."

"Easier than trying to get them to play with my

dolls." Collette smiled as she started tearing cloth away from her jacket. She handed strips to Rudi. "Put some pressure on that wound. Let's try to get the bleeding stopped. We'll wrap it as best we can, but we don't have much time."

"Do you think?" Rudi said as he pressed down on Ethan's shoulder with considerable vigor.

Fafnir roared on the terrace. The sound shook dust loose from the rafters overhead and caused several large stones to fall from the shattered wall. The Grey Gentlemen were clawing at the dragon's flanks, the ribbons of taint whirling about him, threatening to engulf him.

"That will have to do," Collette said as she tied off a third wrap across Ethan's shoulder. "Through and through, right Ethan? It was a clean lunge—missed the lung—and there's not a lot of bleeding, so he missed an artery. You are lucky, aren't you? Get him up, Rudi! We've got to go."

"Go?" Rudi chirped incredulously. "Go where? The only way out of here is the way we came in, and in case you've been asleep the last few minutes— there's a war on out there!"

"Yes," Ethan said, dragging himself upright. The pain in his shoulder nearly caused him to black out. He couldn't move his left arm at all. He paused and took in a deep breath before continuing. "And it's our war now. We'll make our way along that right wall. There was a door over there. We'll try to flank them on the terrace on the right side…"

"You want to go out there?" Rudi asked.

"You want to die in here or out there?" Collette asked the youth as she pulled back the bolt on her machine gun.

"Yippee-ki-yay!" Rudi replied, brandishing his MP40.

Collette reached back and retrieved the sword from the altar. She placed it in Ethan's right hand and, with Rudi, helped Ethan to stand.

The three made their way to the crossing of the transept and then around to the right wall. The collapsed roof had fallen largely into the center of the nave and onto the south side, leaving this aisle largely unobstructed. An enormous pile of debris lay where the wall at the end of the nave had collapsed, but the door on the north side wall was there as Ethan had remembered it.

"There!" Ethan exclaimed. "Through that door."

The windows on their left looked out onto the terrace. Ethan could see shapes moving beyond the glass but little else. They moved up to the doorway.

The screams of the dragon split the air. Ethan wheeled at the sound, as did Collette and Rudi, looking up through the shattered roof overhead.

The spire of Mont Saint-Michel stood against the blackened sky. Fafnir, his wings wide, alighted to the side of the spire's steep roof, his wings folding around the tiles as his legs fought for purchase in the stone work. The Demissie-beast rose as well, the empowering appendages of taint arcing up with him.

His form had coalesced once again, the black taint weaving like veins through the monstrous horror that was his visage. He swept up the side of the cathedral, his talons tearing at Fafnir's wings, the hideous barb of his tail slashing to strike at the dragon's heart.

"We have to save him," Ethan shouted, his face fixed toward the spire.

"Do you know how to work that thing?" Collette asked Rudi, nodding toward the machine gun in his hands.

"Sure," Rudi answered. "Point the end with the hole at the bad guys and pull the trigger."

Collette shook her head and snatched the gun out of Rudi's hands. "Pull back the bolt here, like this, to arm it. You release the clip here, like this, and put a new one in here, like this. Aim down and to the right when you start firing—the recoil will push the aim up and to the left with every successive shot. And short bursts! Don't empty a clip all at once. And stay with me—we don't want to be changing clips at the same time."

She pushed the gun back into Rudi's hands.

"Yeah, OK," Rudi said. "I knew that."

Collette turned to Ethan, nodding toward the sword he was gripping in his right hand. "So what do you plan to do with that?"

"I'm going to cut the power," Ethan said.

"What?"

"I'm going to cut those lines of taint," Ethan said. "If I can separate that monster from its source of magic, then I think Fafnir will have a chance of stopping them."

"What do you want us to do?" Rudi asked.

"Keep those slimy grey things off of me while I do it," Ethan said.

"OK," Collette said.

"And one more thing…"

"Yeah?"

"I've got a sword in one hand and my other arm's useless…"

"And?"

"Could you open the door for me?"

"This is some rescue," Rudi grumbled.

Collette pulled on the door. It swung open easily. Sword in hand, Ethan charged out onto the terrace.

It was deserted. Ethan glanced to his right past the low terrace wall. The side of the abbey dropped ninety feet below him to a garden space on the rock of the island. The thick fingers of the taint were rising up out of the sands surrounding the island, arcing upward over the stone like a shifting, gelatinous wave of darkness, never touching the walls of the mount until they arced over onto the terrace above.

A piece of one of his dreams came back to him.

This was his favorite time. The foundation stone of this place was a focal nexus of karma—a wellspring of peace and joy. The sands surrounding it had been touched by the taint and hovered menacingly about it, but when the tide came in around its base, it cut off the darkness, driving the taint back deep into the sands and letting the stone rest.

Beyond the sands spread the waters of the English Channel. There was safety, Ethan knew, within his sight and yet impossibly far away.

The blade of the sword erupted in flame. Ethan yelled incoherently as he charged along the wall, swinging the blade in long, powerful arcs. The blade cut into the taint, severing the strands like stretched elastic, the tendrils snapping away and dissolving with each blow.

He heard the rattle of a machine gun behind him.

"Hurry, Ethan!" Collette shouted. "They're coming!"

Ethan glanced back toward the spire.

Figures were falling like drops of water from the Demissie-beast, clawing across the broken roof and dropping back down onto the terrace. The Grey Gentlemen were coming for them.

"*Wadu!*" Rudi cried, the MP40 jumping in his hands. "*Wadu! Wadu!*"

A line of the Grey Gentlemen fell beneath the hail of bullets, but the flow of the creatures, their dead eyes fixed on the humans on the terrace, seemed endless.

Ethan's sword lashed outward again over the wall. The taint snapped with a sick, sticky sound, another set of tendrils evaporating.

A group of Grey Gentlemen collapsed into dust even as another phalanx stepped forward to take their place.

"Keep cutting!" Collette shouted. "Rudi! I'm out!"

Rudi tossed a magazine to Collette, then released another burst into the horde approaching them. "They're not stopping!"

"Cut faster!" Collette shouted.

The waves of grey figures nearly filled the terrace. The rattle of the machine guns was interminable, but Ethan could see that they were losing ground. The Grey Gentlemen had pressed them into the corner of the terrace near the statue. The taint was shifting out of reach from Ethan's blade.

There was nowhere left to go.

"Collette!" Ethan cried.

She turned to face him.

"I can't save him!" Ethan shouted. "I'm so sorry!"

"No, Ethan," Collette called as her gaze drifted past the outer wall, "you already have. Look!"

Ethan turned and gazed out across the flats.

The sea was coming across the sands.

"Victor Hugo said that the tides around the mount," Collette shouted, "move faster than a horse can gallop. They cut off the island from the world—much as Atlantis was once cut off, Ethan. They shield the blessed island."

Collette turned back to face the horde, her jaw set as she once again began firing into the encroaching monsters. "Of course, it doesn't hurt if they have a little help."

Ethan set his jaw and raised the sword as he stood between Collette and Rudi. The horde was upon them. Ethan's blade cut wildly through the air, keeping the Grey Gentlemen away from Rudi and Collette as their guns emptied into the mob on either side of him.

The waters rushed in a torrent from the channel across the surrounding sands. It was an unnatural tide—as though the waters had been held at bay, then suddenly released. A wall of water was approaching the island at an incredible rate, the foam caps of the leading waves reaching toward the mount.

The first of the waves crashed over the tentacles of the taint. The embodiment of darkness reacted at once to the waters, writhing and melting like a slug in contact with salt. The waves rushed around the rock of the mount, dissolving the tendrils of darkness, robbing the creature above of its powers and support.

Ethan glanced up at the spire. The monstrous taint creature quivered uncertainly, trying to back down the spire. Grey figures began dropping away from its form, exploding into clouds as they fell, their grey dust drifting and disappearing in the wind.

Fafnir struggled to the top of the spire. Ethan could see the weariness and the triumph in the ancient dragon's countenance. It sprang headlong against the taint creature, knocking it free of the spire and outward. The last of the tendrils of taint from the sands about Mont Saint-Michel were cut off by the raging sea in that instant.

The hordes of Grey Gentlemen on the terrace exploded quietly into dust, choking the air around them.

Ethan followed the descent of Fafnir and the creature, running to the low wall of the terrace with Collette and Rudi.

The Demissie-beast raged as they fell, trailing grey clouds of dust in the arc of their descent, clawing at Fafnir, but the dragon clung fast to the creature. Then, drawing in a deep breath, Fafnir breathed into the creature's chest.

The blast erupted just as they were tumbling past the outer wall toward the angry waters below. Fire and grey smoke exploded up the outer wall. Collette, Ethan, and Rudi all leaped back, but when it dawned on them that they were still alive, each peered down the smoke-obscured wall. They could see nothing.

Ethan leaned over the edge: nothing. He strained, listening for any sound that might tell him the fate of the dragon and the demon he had fought—the demons he had been fighting down through the countless millennia.

The crashing of the sea against the shores of the mount were all that he heard.

Ethan sighed, closing his stinging eyes against the smoke.

Wind blew against his face…the sound of the crashing waves sounded nearer.

Ethan opened his eyes.

The smoke parted in a tumbling rush of wind. Soaring straight up the wall was the enormous form of Fafnir. The beating of his wings scattered the thick layer of grey dust from off the terrace. The smoke dispersed in great, rolling waves in the instant gale. Ethan stumbled backward with its force toward the statue at the edge of the courtyard where all this had started, what seemed now to be an eternity before.

There, at the feet of the statue, Ethan found his camera. Drawing in a coughing breath, he bent over and set down the sword, trading it for the camera—shaking the disgusting powder off its case and blowing the lens clean. He looked up, searching the sky, but could not see the dragon against the sudden appearance of the stars.

Ethan's eye was caught by the statue of Saint Michael beside him.

"He was the commander of the army of God."

Ethan turned.

Collette was walking toward him across the terrace. Her blouse was torn at the shoulder and heavily smudged. She picked up the sword with the cruciform guard with a casual ease in her right hand.

"Who?" Ethan asked.

"Michael," Collette replied, coming to stand with him as she looked up at the statue. "An archangel…a protector."

Ethan felt a breeze through his hair. The smoke was clearing from the terrace, blown by an offshore breeze.

A distant roar echoed around them.

Ethan and Collette both looked up into the parting clouds. Moonlight shone down through the break in a glorious soft light.

Fafnir, his wings spread, passed in silhouette across the moon.

"Hey," Collette nudged him, "shouldn't you be filming this?"

Ethan smiled.

"No," he replied. "I want this memory just for myself."

CHAPTER 25
HOMECOMING

That was quite a stunt you pulled in there," Collette said.

"What are you talking about?"

Collette and Ethan watched as the dragon wheeled overhead, dancing around the moon for a time.

"That act with the sword in the cathedral," Collette said. "You knew the sword was a memory icon. I saw it flash across your eyes when you took it from the statue. You staged that whole thing so that Benoit would take the sword from you and connect with the memory. Did you expect him to stab you with it, or was that just a bonus?"

"I thought I might be able to get out of the way," Ethan shrugged.

"You did," Collette smiled. "He would have killed you otherwise. Did you know that *fate* is actually one of the innate talents of some dragons? I suspect it's one of yours. I told you I thought you were lucky."

The dragon took one final turn over the abbey and then turned northwest, flying across the waters of the Bay of Mont Saint-Michel.

"So you fulfilled your promise," Collette said quietly.

"Yes," Ethan nodded. "Where do you think he's going?"

"Jersey Isle, I hope," Collette said with a smile.

"Near Manhattan?" Ethan asked.

"No! It's a set of islands in the English Channel. He needs to recover. But I think he can now manage it without our help."

"Our help?"

"Well, there is the soul of a dragon in you," Collette said with a smile. "And within Rudi...say, where is he?"

"Probably hacking into my bank account by now," Ethan said, looking around the terrace. "But if I'm supposed to be a dragon, and Rudi is supposed to be a dragon, and everyone seems to be something... who does that make you?"

"I thought you knew," she laughed. "I'm Collette."

"Yes, Collette," Ethan replied. "Collette who carries that sword with remarkable familiarity. I've seen you spin a blade like that before...*Tsanya*."

Collette raised her eyebrows.

"My, you are remembering!" Collette smiled.

Ethan leaned back against the low wall surrounding the terrace. "So you're a faerie...from Georgia."

"And who are you to say that the gates of Tír na nÓg can't be outside Atlanta?" Collette asked, fire flashing in her green eyes, her eyebrows raised. "Have you ever actually been to Stone Mountain?"

"No," Ethan laughed. "Can't actually say that I have."

"Magical place, that is," Collette said, then sighed. "But the truth, Ethan, is that we don't know where to find Tír na nÓg any better than you do. The Seelie that were left behind—those few of us—took the same path that we offered the dragons. Now we need you, all of you, to help us find the way back to Tír na nÓg—to open the gates before it is too late. That's why I found you. That's why I arranged to bring you here."

Ethan drew in a deep breath. "This was all *your* doing, then?"

Collette nodded. "I didn't know about Sojourner until it was too late. I thought she might be taint-taken. It wasn't until after she dumped me back at the London Bureau that I figured out whose side she was on. By then I'd lost track of both you and Benoit. I had to use Jonas to find you again."

"Farben," Ethan scoffed. "He led that Demissie creature right back to us."

Collette looked away, frowning. "How was I supposed to know his contacts were with the Grey Gentlemen?"

"Well, that makes two rookie mistakes."

"Don't start with me, Ethan," Collette sighed. "I've had a long day, and I am still heavily armed."

Ethan nodded. He gazed back across the water. The dark figure of the dragon had nearly disappeared from sight.

"What about him?" Ethan asked. "What will happen to Fafnir?"

"I don't know," Collette murmured. "Hopefully he will help us. There's a war being waged, Ethan."

"Someone else said that to me," Ethan said. "Sojourner Lee."

"She's right," Collette nodded.

"She said she would meet us here," Ethan said, looking around the terrace as though hoping to see her suddenly appear. "Is she gone? Did she give her life up for us?"

"I don't think so," Collette replied. "She is one of the most resourceful creatures I have ever met from the Time Before. It doesn't seem to be in her nature to die. I think if the Grim Reaper himself came to call on her, he'd blink first. We know she survived the Dweller in the Chunnel—she contacted Lois, after all. Still, she didn't come, and that's not like her."

The sound of hurried footsteps interrupted them. Ethan and Collette looked back across the terrace.

Rudi was running toward them.

"Can we go now?" Rudi asked. "This place gives me the creeps."

"I think that's a good idea," Ethan replied. "And where did you run off to?"

Rudi pointed at the iPad bag over his shoulder. "Left this by the altar in the church. Thought it might come in handy."

"Maybe," Ethan said with a grimace. "You get any connection on that thing here?"

"This?" Rudi replied. "Hell, yeah. I can connect anywhere, man. It's a talent of mine."

"Then find me a hospital," Ethan said.

"No sweat," Rudi said, pulling out the iPad. Its glow illuminated his smiling face. "Hey, there's about fifty messages on here from Farben wanting his iPad back. He says he's at the hospital in Calais and there's a substantial reward. Do you think we should collect?"

"Later. First, we need to find out all we can about Sojourner Lee," Ethan said, then turned to Collette. "So you think she's alive?"

"Somewhere," Collette said. "Which is why we need to find her."

"We?" Ethan asked, surprised.

"Well, we should probably get that shoulder looked at first," Collette said. "And, no doubt, we'll need to file a report with my assignment editor. Fortunately, you still have your camera—not to mention one very impressive sword—we're going to need that where we're going." Collette paused for a moment, then looked back at Ethan. "You know, a CNN reporter and her permanent cameraman could go a lot of places in the world and do a lot of good."

"Why, Collette," Ethan replied, "I think this could be the beginning of a beautiful friendship.

THE END

APPENDIX: "THE OLD WORLD HAS PASSED AWAY..."

"This is the way the world ends...not with a bang, but with a whisper." — *T.S. Elliot*

QUATERNARIAN COSMOLOGY

The ancients may have had it right after all: the universe is made of four basic elements. That they completely misunderstood these elements is hardly surprising.

The four classical Babylonian elements were Sky, Sea, Wind, and Earth. These were reinterpreted by the Greeks as Fire, Water, Air, and Earth, with a fifth element in the center called Aether. The Hindus, Tibetans, Buddhists, Chinese, and Japanese all added this fifth element in various forms, calling it some form of space. This was the gate through which both karma and taint were drawn out of the world—and also through which the Seelie passed into their own alternate existence.

Implied in the basic structure, we find the following construct as the foundation of the universe of the Fireborn. It is not a true cosmology, but a founding one, on which it is easiest for us to understand the working of the world after the reemergence of karma and the awakening of things best left asleep.

There are four primary domains, which are further defined as per the illustration of the Mythic Age (Figure 1).

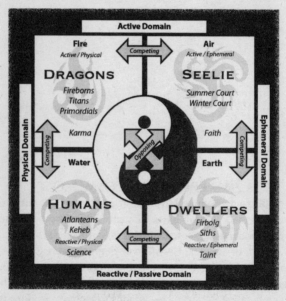

FIGURE 1: MYTHIC AGE

In those times, karma and taint were held in a balance: karma flowed from humans, empowering the dragons, while the power of creation to better the world, wielded by the Seelie Court, flowed from among the Firbolg and

Siths who commanded it. But the Seelie Court's disassociation from the world's cares, as well as the hubris of humanity, caused a wrenching shift in this balance. The Seelie fled through the center of the Taijitu, and the uncontrolled balance collapsed, causing the machinations of humanity to invert and shift magic from a fountain into a bottomless well (Figure 2).

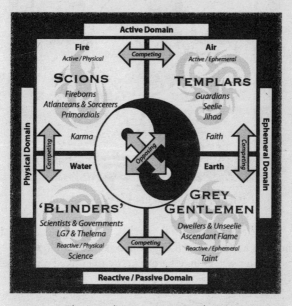

FIGURE 2: AFTER THE FALL

It was only recently, through the chance blundering of mankind, that the situation changed. The polarity of the Taijitu was reversed again, but not the shift in its balance (Figure 3).

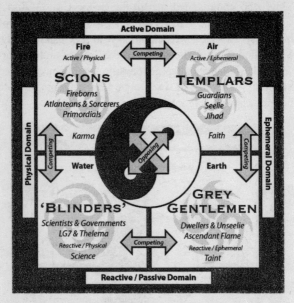

FIGURE 3: MODERN CONFIGURATION

The great purpose of the scions, then, is to shift the balance of karma and taint back into its proper alignment—a mission which they hardly know they have and which they may be too late in discovering.

THE ELEMENTS

These elements are in competing pairs horizontally and vertically with opposing pairs diagonally.

FIRE

Active Physical Power: the domain of karma and the source of the raw power underlying the physical universe and its makeup. It is a force of order. This is the primary domain of the scions, sorcerers, Atlanteans, and primordials.

AIR

Active Ephemeral Power: fundamentally the power of faith—drawing on knowledge beyond the mind of man. It was the drawing of the powers of the spirit and the will that shaped the physical world and gave purpose and form to the karma. Predominant among air aspect incarnations are Templars, Guardians of the Eternal, the Seelie, and the spirit-gifted of different churches, temples, and mosques who are in touch with the Divine Will.

WATER

Reactive or Passive Aspect in the Physical Domain. While physical in nature, it is amorphous, changing and inconstant. It represents the world of man filled with the power of the will of man, but shifting with the limits of humanity's vision and logic. It is science struggling to comprehend the incomprehensible, governments who think they actually can affect global change, and groups like Thelema and LG-7 who stumble blindly in the darkness. It is those individuals of many different religious organizations who are in touch with the taint and the Dark Will behind it.

EARTH

Reactive or Passive Aspect in the Ephemeral Domain. Though it was never expected to find earth aspects in the Ephemeral Domain, this represents the illusion of reality—for its solid appearance is a lie. It represents not the surface, but the deep beneath—the hidden and the dark aspect of the ephemeral, such as the Dwellers and Unseelie.

ABOUT THE AUTHOR

New York Times bestselling fantasy authors Tracy Hickman, with his wife Laura, began their journey across the "Sea of Possibilities" as the creators of *The Dragonlance Chronicles*, and their voyage continues into new areas with the release of Tracy's second novel in his *Drakis* trilogy, this novel, and his current work on *Wayne of Gotham*, a Batman novel for DC Comics. Tracy has over fifty books currently in print in most languages around the world.

Tracy was born in Salt Lake City, Utah and met Laura while they were both attending Provo High School, in Provo, Utah. Tracy left Laura to serve as a missionary in Indonesia, returning two years later, and they have been married ever since. As of this publication, they have four children and three grandchildren.